Also by Susan Bacon

The History Teacher

THE Art COLLECTOR

A NOVEL

SUSAN BACON

Porter Street Press

MEMPHIS / AUSTIN

Jacket design by Taylor Martin
Jacket illustration by Alejandro Milà
Book design by Stewart A. Williams
Portrait by Fran Doggrell

Library of Congress Cataloging-in-Publication Data has been applied for.
Library of Congress Control Number: 2024904507

ISBN: 978-1-7330827-6-1
ISBN: 978-1-7330827-4-7 (eBook)

Porter Street Press
MEMPHIS / AUSTIN

In memory of Elizabeth Zintl
(1951 – 1997)

Part One

CHAPTER 1

She sat, cross-legged on a worn oriental rug. Eyes closed. Palms up, a hand resting on each knee. Deep breath in. Long slow exhale. And another. And again.

Nam myo ho ren ge kyo.

Chanting these words until each melted into the next.

Nam myo horen gekyo. Namyo-horengekyo.

Concentrating, beginning to get in the rhythm of it, to recede into a darkness at the back of her mind when the sound of the buzzer broke through. "Shit," she said, opening her eyes. "Shit."

"Bug man," the guy said when she glared one-eyed through the peephole.

"I didn't order any bugs."

"Very funny," he said, holding up a sheet of paper. "I got an order to spray next door. Super said you have to let me in."

"Have to?" she said. Then, under her breath, "Is that right?" But she unlatched the door and stuck her hand through, under the chain. Looked over the paperwork. She asked him to show her an ID and hold up his bug equipment before emerging half-dressed from her apartment, in a leotard and open kimono, and unlocking her neighbor's door. "I think I'd better wait until you're finished," she said warily, closing the door behind her.

"Suit yourself," he said.

Slapping on a face mask, he turned on her immediately. Lifted the metal drum and shoved the thin, black hose up to her face. He sprayed her eyes first, then her mouth, then her nose. She fell to the floor with a puff of a scream. Then, drifting, envisioned herself falling backward into a black void, a feeling she'd experienced before, as a child lying on the surgeon's table for a tonsillectomy. Ether, she thought, as thinking ceased.

He had time to explore then. To go through everything. Afterward, he opened a south-facing window that overlooked the Hudson River and propped her up, slumped over, her back to the wind, half hanging out over Riverside Drive, her crooked neck bent against the window frame. He left her there, arranged in such a way that she would go flying backward, fifteen stories down, if she began to awaken. If she moved.

CHAPTER 2

"How on earth?" They are standing inside the apartment, three uniformed men. The man who is clearly in charge, the detective, Tomas Brodsky, is examining the window. It is open, but not fully, not enough that the woman could have climbed out or jumped. There are threads, silken threads, at the corner where the sill meets the wall. And there are paint chips from the aging sill and the old molding at the foot of the open window, as if shaken loose. Small, jagged chips, white against the hardwood floor. The forensic pathologist is downstairs, at the foot of the building, where she'll find paint chips on the woman's feet. There are no such chips beneath the other three windows, the ones that are closed. Four tall windows lined up in a row overlooking the Hudson River, one beside the other in an elegant living room with a Persian rug and a grand piano and a wall of books. Also, what seems to be an original lithograph by Toulouse-Lautrec, signed and numbered. The police have already detected the lingering smell of ether. They've noted that nothing else in the apartment seems amiss. Of course, they've already been inside the victim's own apartment next door and found no open windows there.

"How on earth?" the youngest of the uniformed police asks Brodsky again.

"There was obviously a struggle of some sort, if only the woman herself struggling to get free," he says.

"Pushed, you think?" the other officer says.

Then Detective Brodsky finds hair, a few pieces of it, wedged into the window sash. Her hair, the lab tells them later. "Could she have been drugged and wedged into this half-open window?" he says, shaking his head, looking around the room. "Is that even possible?" he speaks into the air. "Jesus."

CHAPTER 3

Emma Quinn charges into the precinct, introducing herself as she approaches the detective's desk and blurting out, "I'm here about Seal Larson," before he even has a chance to look up.

He barely moves, tilting his head up slightly, and seems to have no idea what Emma is talking about. "And she is?"

"My friend. She was my friend," Emma says, extending her hand.

For an instant, she wonders if she's come on too strong, arriving unannounced with that steamroller of an entrance. Perhaps I should have made an appointment, she thinks, but she offers no apology. She's working on that—not apologizing. "It diminishes you," her department head had counseled at some point in the not-too-distant past.

"It was my apartment—the apartment where it happened. She was my neighbor at 370 Riverside," Emma says, trying to clear things up. "Aren't you Detective Brodsky?"

"Yes. Sit," the detective says. But there is no obvious place to sit, so she stands over him as he gets out a reporter's notebook and begins a series of leading statements that turn themselves into questions. "And you now live . . ."

"In Washington DC. Temporarily. I came up as soon as I got the call."

His eye twitches slightly, and he slides his forefinger along the bridge of his nose, adjusting his glasses. "The call from . . ."

"The super. Mr. Javier," she says. And still, he looks confused. "At 370 Riverside."

"Oh. You're the professor." He rises, then, shaking her hand. "Brodsky," he says. "Tomas Brodsky."

"Yes. Professor Quinn. Emma Quinn."

"And you . . ." he stalls for an instant ". . . teach at Columbia."

"Yes. Well, I'm on sabbatical at the moment."

"You teach history. Am I right?" He speaks slowly, as if he's trying to wrap his head around something or trying to recall a detail or maybe just giving himself a little more time.

"Yes. History."

"And you were where on Wednesday?"

Emma is baffled by the question itself. "Working, of course."

"Did anybody . . ."

"Scores of people saw me. I was at a symposium, lecturing. To maybe five hundred people." Then, just for effect, she adds, "In Washington DC."

He pulls up a chair then and signals for her to sit. Asks if she wants a coffee, distractedly, as he searches through a stack of manila folders on his desk. Opening a folder and looking up at Emma again, he clears his throat. "So, we don't know much about this woman," he says, glancing through the file.

"Seal," Emma says.

"Seal? As in Lucille? Her passport says Lucille Anne Lawson."

"Larson," Emma says.

"Lawson," he says firmly, showing her the passport, looking directly at her and asking, "Exactly how long have you known her?"

"Since 1980. So, seven years. I met her when I moved into my apartment." Emma hesitates for a moment, thrown off by the fact that Seal had another name, apparently her legal name, at least according to the passport. *Or was it?* she asks herself, a bit disoriented.

"Can you tell us more?" he says. "Did she have a family?"

"I doubt that you'll find any family in the US. She was quite alone."

"And outside the US?"

"Overseas. Great Britain," Emma says, stopping herself, adding, "I believe." She recalls an evening when the two of them were sharing dinner, eating Chinese dumplings and Peking duck out of take-out boxes in Emma's apartment, Seal remarking that her parents lived in London, and that she and her mother were estranged. "She's not a likable person," Seal had said, confiding that she'd been left some kind of trust fund by her grandparents that her parents couldn't touch, "or they would have taken it from me," she'd said. "They are not nice people. Either of them." But, of course, Emma doesn't tell the detective any of this.

"Well, she's going to end up in a potter's field unless someone claims her, I'm afraid."

"I'll claim her," Emma says.

"It's not that simple, Professor," Brodsky says.

"We'll see about that," she replies.

***

Earlier in the day, on the Metroliner en route to New York to meet Detective Brodsky, Emma had tried to recall the last time she'd seen Seal. They spoke regularly—at least once a month—while Emma was in Washington, and she'd made an effort to contact her friend whenever she was in town. But, when the detective asks, Emma tells him she honestly can't remember the last time they talked, and suddenly it seems as if he's ready to wrap things up, though Emma's not at all ready to go. She has too many questions and can't seem to find any kind of reference point. *Why would Seal have been in my apartment?* she keeps asking herself. *And who would have done such a thing?* She wants some answers. "Maybe tell me a little bit about what happened?" she says.

Her expression strikes him as earnest. It is a look of puzzlement. Her brow is furrowed. He wonders if it tends to stay that way all the time.

"She either fell or jumped or was pushed out of the window of your apartment," he tells her. "No one saw anyone else come or go. And, oddly enough, there were traces of a mix of ether and ketamine in the place."

Emma is silent for a time. Fell. Jumped. Or was pushed. She already has this image in her mind of Seal flying backward out the window, arms flailing, heading for the sidewalk, then broken by the fall. In fact, she can't seem to shake the image. She shuts her eyes for an instant, recalibrating. That was not at all what she had expected from the detective. She'd expected some insight into what exactly happened, more about what he's learned. Feeling fragile, she shifts gears, knowing nothing would diminish her quite like fragility at a time when she's trying to establish herself as someone who can help with the investigation.

"Have you interviewed the couple that lives there? The Loves," she asks.

"You know them?"

"I own the apartment," she says, frustrated now. "They are my tenants, temporary tenants. I've let it furnished."

"Ah, so those are your things in the apartment where she died."

She nods. "And have you talked with them?"

"They were gone—these Loves—out of town, and it looks like your friend Lucille had a key."

"Yes. I'd given her the key in case anything ever came up. Have you tried to reach them?"

"They don't seem to be reachable. They're in the Middle East some-where, according to the university. Living out of tents," he says. "We're still working on that."

She is wondering about this detective. He seems to have made no progress in these first crucial twenty-four hours, or to have any grasp of the fundamental details. "I'd be happy to help in any way I can," she says.

He just stares at her, as if confused.

"Did you see her?" Emma asks then. He is making a note, and looks up, not understanding Emma's question.

"Did you actually see her?" she says.

He shakes his head, and an almost imperceptible look of disquiet crosses his face. He doesn't want to tell Emma that she was unseeable. Couldn't be identified. The super, this Javier, recognized her body. Her clothes, really. But her face . . . "No," he says.

"Well, she had the face of an angel. She was younger than me, by a few years, and she had this innocence about her."

"And was she?"

"Was she what?"

"Innocent."

CHAPTER 4

SEAL

I'd have to say I'm grateful for the anesthesia, whatever it was. It wasn't a bad fall. Almost exhilarating, liberating in some way. The freedom of it and of knowing what my end would be. I had a moment of consciousness there and a sense of, again, being set free. From the bounds of earth, from my strange and rootless life, from obligations and regrets. And worries. Don't forget that.

The experience reminded me of the James Dickey poem about the stewardess who falls from a plane. Only faster. I can't recall much of the poem, but I remember this line: "Her last superhuman act." That's how I like to think of it, as my last superhuman act.

I wonder. Will anyone even care that I'm gone? Probably not. I don't think it was deliberate. I mean, I don't think they were after me. I was just collateral damage. Then again, the whole thing was sudden and confusing. I'm thinking they had to be after something that belonged to the Loves. He's a collector. Antiquities, I think. Something valuable, I imagine. A trinket. A vase. An urn. They've been gone for months, off on some junket in the Middle East. So, a break-in makes sense. Or maybe they were after something of Emma's. She's rich as Croesus. Who knows what she has stashed in that apartment? But what if it was a person and not a thing that they wanted? The Loves—the both of them. Or even Emma herself. On second thought, probably not. They were looking for things. Rare things. Coveted things. Valuable things. Had to be.

CHAPTER 5

It had taken Emma almost two years to find a place on Riverside Drive. She wanted to be in Morningside Heights, near the university and Riverside Park, for her walks. She began her search in the spring of 1978, a few months after her grandmother's death, and found 370, a prewar building at West 109th early on. Somewhat legendary, the building had been home to Hannah Arendt, the historian and philosopher and a hero of Emma's. She was looking for a home, a real home, with a sense of permanence to it. The last of her line, she had family things that needed a place. And she wanted it to be just right. A classic six—living, dining, kitchen, two bedrooms and the smaller room, meant for a maid in the days of old but perfect for an office. At the time, nothing was available at 370, so she put her name on a list. Two years later, in 1980, the building was converted to a co-op, and they called her. A classic six on the fifteenth floor had become available. It was expensive, upwards of $150 a square foot. Emma put in an immediate offer and got it for close to $350,000.

She first met Seal, briefly, in the hall the day she moved in. Her new neighbor was wearing cutoff bib overalls with a little tank top barely visible underneath. That and a baseball cap that concealed her hair. And dark sunglasses. She was lean and fresh-faced, and Emma had mistaken her for a teenager, assuming she lived next door with her parents. She was on her way out at the time. In the months that followed, they'd occasionally run into each other in the hall, but they maintained the customary safe distance common in Manhattan apartment buildings at the time—essential to preserving a sense of privacy, a conscious disconnect. Emma once summed it up this way: "If you live a few feet from someone, you don't want them knocking on your door every five minutes." Over time, it became obvious that Seal lived alone. Her age was hard to guess, perhaps because she seemed to dress in costumes.

When they met in passing, she generally greeted Emma with an expressionless hello. But, one night, long after Emma had moved in, Seal arrived at Emma's door, leaning on the buzzer. "It's me. Your neighbor," she called through the peephole. "Locked out." Emma could see the face of a young woman wearing bright red lipstick, her close-cropped brown hair flecked with white streaks. She had a small tattoo above her right eye. She did not look like a teenager.

"May I?" she asked, stepping into Emma's apartment. This time she was dressed like a punk: a Scottish kilt in a glen plaid, the hemline well above the knee, black fishnet stockings, black leather jacket and thick-soled black boots. Unfortunately, she didn't look quite grungy enough to pull it off. She had an air of wealth about her, cleanliness, order. And an ethereal quality that was distinctly unpunk-like.

Once inside, she demonstrated an appreciation for the finer things, zeroing in on an antique bench in Emma's front hall. Its back was hand-carved, and at its center was the somewhat twisted face of a man who could easily have been the devil. The seat opened to reveal a storage space. It was a distinctive piece, uncommon, valuable.

"What is this wonderful thing?" She leaned over, running her hand along the elaborate wood carvings. Unthinking, she lifted the lid to find it full of Emma's files.

"Pretty cool, isn't it?" Emma said tactfully, closing it back up.

"And this," Seal said, using her finger to trace a strand of wood that wound through the design like a vine. There was this extraordinary calmness to her, a curious counterpart to her outlandish appearance. Her voice, her expression, suggested a lack of interest, but her words and actions suggested enthusiasm. "I've never seen anything quite like it," she said flatly.

"It was on my grandmother's screen porch when I was growing up. It must be from the Pacific Islands or Thailand, maybe. The wood. It's teak."

"How old do you think?"

"No idea." Emma shook her head, as if to say it wasn't important.

"And no idea of the provenance. But I used to sit on it as a child when I didn't want to be inside or outside. Just somewhere in between."

"Ah," Seal said, barely reacting, turning her attention then to the Soviet propaganda posters that hung above the bench. Examining them closely, thoughtfully, as one might examine pictures at a gallery. Moving slowly from one to the next. "I like these. I saw them in the hallway when you first arrived." She pointed to a poster of Lenin dressed in an overcoat, his hands raised in the air against the backdrop of a Soviet flag. "This one's rare, isn't it?"

"Is it? I'm not sure," Emma said to no reply. "It's my passion."

"Poster art?"

"No, no. Radicalism, the Left."

"Ah," Seal said again, and they stood in silence for a moment, as if sizing each other up. "You mean that theoretically, don't you?"

Emma laughed. "Of course. I'm a professor. I teach." They talked in Emma's kitchen for more than an hour, waiting for either Javier or the locksmith to show up. Then they exchanged phone numbers when it became obvious that they were each, fundamentally, alone. No family nearby. No regular boyfriends. In the months that followed, they began to make a habit of checking in with each other. Seal, more often than Emma. "I'm ordering pizza," she'd call and say. "May I bring you some?" Or, "I'm running down to the market, need anything?" Aside from that, they'd remained independent. So much so, Emma realizes now, that during the six years they'd been neighbors she'd never set foot inside Seal's apartment. And although the two had gone out together on occasion to a lecture or an exhibit or an event at Lincoln Center, it was never with any regularity.

In fact, the first time was nearly two years after their initial meeting. Seal had arrived at Emma's door late in the evening, ready to head out but evidently stopping by as an afterthought.

"So, you wanna come downtown with me? To a show?" she said. It was nearly ten o'clock. "I think you'd like it. Art. Music. Crazy people. In the East Village."

"You going by yourself?" Emma asked. Seal nodded. "Seems late for that," Emma said.

"No worries. I'll take a cab."

The East Village was not the safest neighborhood in a city that was, at the time, rather unsafe just about everywhere at that hour.

"We'll take a cab," Emma said.

The taxi dropped them in front of a brownstone on Bleecker Street. The ground floor was home to an unidentified restaurant—no sign, no neon lights, no indication that it was anything other than a private residence. To get in, you had to be someone or know someone and call ahead. "That's a new one," Seal said, nodding her head upward as they headed down the stairs. "One of those secret places for the cognoscenti. Foodies only. Or celebrities. Or Richie Rich." The word cognoscenti—pronounced kanya-shenty—flowed easily off her tongue. Emma was impressed, first, that she knew about this secret restaurant and then, of course, the pronunciation, which somehow didn't feel at all contrived.

When they arrived at the basement unit, Seal knocked, and a slot on the front door slid open. "It's Seal," she said. And they were in.

The club was small, with flashing Christmas lights strewn across the low ceiling and a retro band dressed for the 1940s, playing music with a funky edge to it. Everyone was dancing, many of them in costumes and quite a few wearing almost nothing. One fellow, dressed in what appeared to be a diaper, performed a solo limbo amid the tables. And someone else—a man or woman, Emma wasn't sure—dressed as Wonder Woman in a bustier and bikini bottom, was dancing with a clown. The place was dark, airless, claustrophobic. People didn't seem to be paying attention to one another. They seemed in their own heads. Emma assumed there were drugs involved but wouldn't have known what.

Seal wandered off, leaving Emma to observe the flashing lights, the bizarre outfits, the gender-bending. This was a Manhattan that she didn't know. Hadn't a clue. "Let's get outta here," Seal said when she returned, and they walked a few blocks east to find themselves at the dark edge of the Lower East Side. Oily surface water flowed against the curb beside abandoned buildings and overflowing trash bins. Emma stepped around the empty cans and bottles strewn about and around the street people, the homeless, lying on the sidewalk wrapped in nothing. It felt post-apocalyptic. Twice they were approached. First, a man came close, asking if they were lost. "Bug off," Seal said. The next kept his distance, shouting an unrecognizable word. *Sugar*, Emma thought he said. A drug, she assumed. She was uncomfortable.

When they arrived at an apparent dead end, marked by a sign that read "Shinbone Alley," and found themselves in near-complete darkness, Seal pulled at Emma's elbow, turning her toward a well-lit side street. But Emma was mesmerized by the twinkling lights along the alleyway. They were like fireflies off in the distance, or the sticks of punk that kids used to wave in circles on the Fourth of July, burning like the tips of lit cigarettes. "Look," she said. "Look at that."

"Are you crazy? Those are crack pipes. They're all lighting up. C'mon," Seal said, grabbing Emma by the elbow, pulling her away and adding, "Not so pretty when you know what they are."

When their destination finally appeared, it felt like a beacon, a safe haven, although it was nothing more than an old storefront between a deli and a smoke shop. The name—Anna Lorch Gallery—was painted in blocky black lettering across the front window. They entered a well-lit room where two turntablists in a corner played a low-key mix of jazz and funk. Black-and-white photographs lined the white walls. It was apparently opening night, and the work of two photographers was on exhibit. A small crowd mingled about. A few had multicolored mohawks, but the rest looked like members of the new class of young professional types. Yuppies, Emma thought. They were dressed minimally in black-on-black or jeans. Seal spotted a friend in the crowd, a young man in horn-rimmed glasses and a brown fedora. She walked over to greet him, leaving Emma on her own.

Emma meandered over to explore the first photographer's work. It was abstract, maybe a dozen black-and-white images, eight-by-tens all lined up in a row, and all set in black metal frames with clean, white mats. They seemed to be experiments in contrast, but it wasn't easy to determine what exactly had been photographed. The first few images appeared to be shots of big swirls of black paint or strokes of calligraphy with grayish backgrounds. When she examined them more closely, Emma could see that they were close-ups of graffiti—in one case, X's and O's—painted on white concrete block. She found them appealing in a simple, minimalist sort of way and moved on. Next in line were a few variations on glossy black surfaces with sparkles of light. They looked like stars set in a deep, black sky, but they weren't stars. Emma wondered if they might be clusters of living things, cells or particles, or maybe even jewels floating in space. As she moved in closer, she heard a voice coming at her from behind.

"It's the ocean," someone said. "Shot from above and magnified slightly. Bioluminescence. Sea sparkles." She turned to see a young man in an Oxford cloth shirt and jeans, collegiate, long-haired, well groomed. He could have been one of her Columbia students.

Emma smiled. "That's pretty cool."

"Isn't it?" he said, then he leaned in toward her, almost whispering. "Although it's well done, it's *been* done."

Emma was taken aback; she'd assumed he was the photographer.

"David Lorch," he said, putting out his hand.

"Of Anna fame, I assume."

"My mother." He nodded. "Come. Please. I think you'll like these," he said, drawing her across the room toward three images, large by comparison, maybe two-by-two-foot squares. All three looked like they might have been taken in the 1950s with an old Kodak camera and blown up, with all the splotches and scratches and imperfections that come with age. The first was a classic beach photograph of families playing in the surf but on the grayest of days, foggy and out of focus. Emma was enthralled. It was as if she was looking at a memory, or a shadow of a memory. "Note the scratches and nicks. I love the way she's distressed it," he said. "And see this crooked black border around the edge, so it seems somehow askew." As he spoke, he ran his hand up around the edge of the photograph, getting up on his toes to reach the top, stretching. "See how she created this uneven dark edge and there's no mat. Plus, this black, wooden frame, so it all reads as dark." The second photo in the series was also of a beach. Emma could make out an umbrella planted in the sand and some kids building sandcastles in the blurry mist. The third captured Emma's heart: swimmers on a lake jumping off or hanging onto a wooden raft. It reminded her of a raft at Saranac and the lakefront cabin in the woods where she spent her summers as a child. Dark, cloudy images all of them, testaments to another time. To memories. "I love these," she said.

"Aren't they wonderful? All about time and place," the young man said. "And family. And loss."

"You see what you see," said a voice coming from behind them. The tone was patronizing. Then it softened. "Let her see it for herself, David," she said. The woman was probably in her late forties, and she was obviously his mother, Anna, the dealer.

Seal arrived then. "Ah, looks like you've all met," she said. "Anna. David. This is my friend Emma."

"Ah, so you *know* the artist," the dealer said.

Emma looked confused.

"This is Seal's work," the dealer explained, nudging Seal then, teasing. "Some of her least provocative work, I might add."

"They *are* wonderful," Emma said, utterly surprised, examining them more closely.

"Well, we'll have to get you on our mailing list," Anna Lorch called out as she departed, moving on to her other guests, taking her son along with her.

Seal leaned into Emma. "She wouldn't take the more interesting pieces," Seal whispered.

"But I love these," Emma said. "Really."

Seal seemed unphased by the compliment. "It's not my best work," she said.

CHAPTER 6

The morning after Javier's call, Emma woke up far too early, before dawn, with that leaden feeling, that sense that all is not right with the world that comes with a death or catastrophe. Then she'd remembered the envelope—the one that Seal had delivered unexpectedly a few years earlier, knocking on Emma's door one morning out of the blue. The one that had the words: "For Emma. In case of an emergency" written in slapdash cursive on the front.

"If anything ever happens to me, this is who you need to call," she'd said brusquely, before disappearing down the hall, walking backward and blowing Emma a kiss.

Nothing about it had surprised Emma. In fact, it made perfect sense. Seal was a loner, distanced from whatever family she had. At the time, Emma's only concern was how she would know if there ever was an emergency, for she rarely had any idea where Seal was from one moment to the next. "Good point," Seal had said in her detached way when Emma had raised that very issue later. "Just if it ever comes up," Seal had said. "But don't open it unless you have to. And, for God's sake, don't share it with anyone. It's privileged."

So, on the morning after Seal's death, when Emma remembered

the envelope, she pulled herself out of bed and headed for her office at Georgetown and unlocked her desk drawer, where she found the envelope under a copy of her own will. She held it in her hands for a few minutes, wondering if she was quite ready for whatever surprise might come next. But when she finally opened it, she found a single sheet of paper with two words on it written by hand—Lynley Wright—along with a Manhattan phone number. Emma made the call, and through an unidentified voice on the other end of the line, an assistant of some kind, she set up a meeting.

Now, she is sitting in the outer office of Lynley Wright and Associates, which seems to be some sort of art consulting firm, located at Fifty-Seventh and Fifth in one of the most exclusive buildings in Manhattan. The new Trump Tower is next door, a skyward stretch of sleek black windows that looks like something from *Star Wars* plopped down in the center of Midtown, ominous and dark and futuristic. Emma is leafing through art magazines and old New Yorkers. She has been doing so for more than an hour when a young woman finally emerges to greet her. Dressed for the eighties, she wears a thin, drapey heather jacket that sways across her body as she walks and the inevitable shoulder pads of the new power elite. The matching skirt is straight and slim and stops midcalf, all of which creates a geometric effect—broad shoulders coming to a point at the lower leg, like a triangle of fabric. And she appears to be busy, busy, busy, walking in too-high heels—click, click, click—straight for Emma.

"Ms. Quinn," she says, sharp, professional, adding, "Please come in," with the wave of a hand. Emma detects a Main Line, mid-Atlantic accent, haughty and rich. But when she asks whether Emma wants something to drink and Emma replies, "A shot of bourbon maybe," the woman lets out a surprised laugh before tightening back up.

Beyond the waiting area, everything is all mahogany and mirrors until they reach an inner office, where photographs cover the walls. Not just personal photos and portraits and fashion shots—although there are those—but stunning photographic works of art. Some are signed, others, simply recognizable. Famously so. Emma's eye is drawn to a black-and-white image of a young hockey player on a city street, steam rising around him, gloved, his knees bent and knocked together, his body padded, wearing a ghoulish protective mask. Even Emma knows this is a small masterpiece. It is signed by Diane Arbus. She sees signed photographs by the legendary Gordon Parks, who documented all manner of historic events, and Annie Leibovitz, whose portraits of rock stars and celebrities made her a celebrity. And there's an elegant black-and-white portrait of an older actress, an icon whose name Emma can't recall, obviously a portrait by the famous Richard Avedon. Emma is not terribly familiar with the world of art photography, but she knows full well this is an extraordinary collection. It is also an archive of an era, and as a historian, she has trouble looking away. She dawdles, moving along the wall, examining the images.

"These aren't reproductions, are they?" she asks, finally, looking over her shoulder. She'd assumed the young woman was bringing her to meet Lynley Wright, and that Lynley Wright would be a man.

"No, they're not. My father was a collector," the woman replies, holding out her hand. "Lynley Wright," she says. Then briskly, "So let's talk about Lucille please."

"Oh, okay," Emma says, taken aback by her tone. "I think of her as Seal."

"Yes," Lynley says. "So sudden. So tragic," lowering her eyes to the floor. Emma thinks she is reaching out to steady herself, but she is grabbing a business card, handing it to Emma. "Seal's attorney asks that you get in touch."

"What about her parents? Has anyone contacted them?"

"Parents?"

"I thought her parents lived in England," Emma says. "That her father was an ambassador or something over there. That they were estranged. She and her parents."

"There are no parents," Lynley says. "Her mother died in 1979."

"And her father?"

The woman shakes her head. "No idea." She leads Emma over to a chair and stands opposite, at her desk, framed by a window that over-looks Fifth Avenue.

Lynley Wright takes a deep breath as she prepares to sit, adjusting the flow of her jacket, then settling in. "So," she says, "it seems that we are coexecutors."

"Okay," Emma says, hesitating. "And how does that work?"

"Basically, we—meaning my firm—will oversee the placement of Seal's photographs and the creation of her archive, and possibly other aspects of the estate. You'll just need to get in touch with the estate attorney. Her name is on that business card. She's wonderful. A joy to work with." Wright's tone is becoming increasingly brusque. "She'll explain everything."

Emma looks at the card. "Harriet Freeman." The address puts the attorney in SoHo, a far cry from Fifty-Seventh and Fifth. Emma knows full well that this office is money, and SoHo is not. But she's not yet tuned in to the exact nature of these two distinct art districts and not at all sure about this executor business. Why, she wonders, still staring at the card, would Seal have named me coexecutor of her will? And why didn't she trust this woman, who must be her art dealer or representative, to manage it all by herself? Then she remembers Anna Lorch, who seemed to be Seal's dealer just a few years before.

"Ms. Quinn?"

"I'm sorry," Emma says, corralling her brain. "I think I'm still in shock. I'll set something up with her right away," she says, adding, "Maybe you can be of some assistance with something. I'm trying to help the police."

The woman stands, as if they are done, and walks around to Emma, perching herself on the edge of the desk. "They're looking for her next of kin. Can you tell me about her family?"

"I told you. Her mother's dead."

"Who was she?"

"Honestly, I know very little about Seal's mother. Or anyone else in her family for that matter. And I understand there's some sort of confidentiality agreement. So, it seems I wouldn't be able to tell you much anyway. The attorney," she says, pointing to the business card. "Harriet Freeman. She'll explain everything."

"But the police need—"

"It's been taken care of, thanks to you."

"So, you've talked to them. To Detective Brodsky."

"No. I spoke with the attorney, with Harriet Freeman." As she speaks, she is leading Emma toward the door. "She took care of it."

"Good. Good," Emma says, hesitating for an instant. "So, if I hadn't contacted you, would I be here?"

"If you hadn't contacted me, we would never have known she died."

CHAPTER 7

SEAL

The way I see it, I never really had a family to speak of. My mother was only fifteen when I was born. At the time, she was living with her mother and sister on a two-thousand-acre farm in Tennessee. That's how she described it, always. A two-thousand-acre farm. It wasn't until I was an adult and mentioned it to my friend Simon that I realized a two-thousand-acre farm is a substantial piece of land. He is an investment banker and has a disturbingly keen sense of what he calls the value of things.

We were lying in bed in his old apartment on East Seventy-Seventh Street, which is where he lived before he went broke during what he calls a bad deal and I call his comeuppance. It was late. We were talking about my family because he insisted on it. We had just gotten back from his cousin's wedding out on Long Island, an excessive affair even in good times, where I had met the whole lot of them—not just his mother and father, and brothers and sisters, but cousins, aunts, uncles, second cousins, step-cousins, cousins of cousins and what have you.

If I had ever doubted that Simon had a home, a community of people who knew him and loved him completely and unconditionally, that Simon had whatever it is that makes humans profoundly secure, I would never doubt it again. Of course, it came as no surprise. Simon was Jewish, and I had grown up among Jews. Not to say they are all the same, but it always seemed to me that they know where they come from. They have roots, a sense of belonging. And, in a way, being Jewish defines them, so they don't seem to have to worry so much about the whole identity business.

"It's a very close-knit group," he'd told me on the way to the wedding. He seemed a little uncomfortable or concerned, maybe, that I might be overwhelmed by them, all of them. That was before my mother died, before I went back to school, back in the midseventies, when I was not in such great shape. So, I was more concerned that they'd peg me as inappropriate in some way, as an outsider, as a nothing. I remember Simon telling me to try to spend some time with his Uncle Jack, that he'd make certain to introduce me. Jack had been a tummler, which, as you probably know, was sort of a comedian, an entertainer, in the Catskills back in the fifties. "He's a sketch," Simon said, laughing to himself. "You'll never get to meet anyone like him again." Then he said, "He's practically dead." And then he laughed his ass off.

During the wedding, sometime between the breaking of the glass and the point at which I danced the bunny hop ("Isn't she a good sport?" Simon's mother had said), I met Uncle Jack. He called me a shiksa. "Where did you meet this fine shiksa?" he said in this old croaky voice. I was not amused. Simon pulled me away and apologized, but I felt at once embraced and repelled by the lot of them.

Afterward, it was as if I'd passed some crucial milestone, an initiation of sorts, a test. There was relief to that. But still, I knew I didn't belong. I think they were relieved that I wasn't Black when they met me—because of the restaurant and my name. But the truth is, I really didn't belong anywhere back then. I was so uncomfortable with myself.

Anyway, that night, when I mentioned the farm, the two thousand acres, he grabbed his little black calculator off his dresser and started clicking away. Let's see, he said, hyper-focusing, "That's more than eight hundred city blocks. That's a fifth of Manhattan, Luce." Then he got up and pulled out the real estate section of the Sunday *Times*. After about ten minutes, he spread the newspaper out at the foot of the bed. He had found a property for sale in Tennessee. A private retreat, according to the ad, "745 acres. In Overton County, Tennessee. $300,000." He showed me the classified ad.

When I demonstrated not the least bit of interest, he rolled the page up and whacked me on the head with it. "They're asking three hundred thousand," he said and slapped the paper back down on the bed. I had to strain to see the tiny photograph. It was an aerial view. Trees all around it, pastures, a farmhouse, a barn. Then he put his calculator to it. "Let's do the math," he said. "Two thousand acres. At roughly four hundred an acre. That's eight hundred thousand dollars, Luce. Almost a million dollars."

He was brandishing the calculator.

Here's what I said. I said: "It's not her farm. And it's not my farm." Then I grabbed the calculator from him and shut the thing off and spoke very firmly and enunciated these words very clearly: "It belonged to someone else." That's exactly what my mother told me whenever she talked about it, which she did often when I was growing up. It belonged to someone else.

CHAPTER 8

Emma is staying at a small boutique hotel, an unconventional spot just off Broadway on the Upper West Side that does not advertise or serve the public. With its navy awning and a simple bronze plaque beside the front door that reads "609 110th Street," it looks like an elegant private club. It is, in fact, frequented by members of the British intelligence community, including Angus McLearan, who is Emma's partner, her lover, her friend. They share a mutual friend—a man named Bill Kidman. Emma trusts no one more than the two of them. As soon as she gets to her room, before she even pulls off her jacket or takes off her shoes, Emma dials Bill Kidman's private number.

"Hey," she says.

His voice lifts. "Well, well. To what do I owe this—"

"It's not good news. I have a friend in New York, a young woman. Looks like someone killed her," she says. He can hear her voice quaking as she speaks.

"How can I help?" he says. He is calm, professional.

"Well, I'm not really sure," she says. "But let me give you her name, which I thought was Seal Larson and turns out to be Lucille Lawson."

"I trust you were not close."

"I thought we were. She was my neighbor. She told me her parents were living in England, which I have since learned they are not. And it seems I'm a coexecutor of her will, which I never would have imagined. I haven't met with the estate attorney yet. But my fellow coexecutor—who is an art dealer—tells me she's not at liberty to share any information about the family. Except that her mother died in 1979. When I asked about the father, she just shook her head." Emma's voice seems to accelerate as she becomes increasingly agitated. "The police detective won't let me into her apartment. And there's police tape across my front door. They won't let me in there either. Although they do want me to walk through it with them at some point to determine whether anything's—"

"Whoa. Whoa. Slow down," he says.

"Okay. I can do that," she says, mechanically.

"I'm sorry to hear about your neighbor," he says. Emma considers Bill Kidman a friend, but he is also a high-ranking CIA officer, a member of the intelligence community, a spy.

"So, when did it happen?" he asks.

"It just happened."

"You got your ass up to New York pretty fast."

"Yeah. Well, she was killed in my apartment."

"Okay. Hold on. Could you have been the target?"

"I'm not living there. You know that," Emma says. "Seal had a key. She must have let someone in."

"Or surprised someone who was already there," he says.

Calming down now, Emma stops for an instant, mulling over the question. "There were traces of ketamine and ether, which is strange. As if it was a planned attack."

Kidman is silent for a moment. "What about the people who are subletting your place?"

"They're in Turkey. I sent them a telegram. But, at the moment, I'm just trying to figure out who exactly has been killed here."

"Okay. Fair enough. So, how old was she?"

"I'm thinking seven or eight years younger than me."

"Like . . ."

"Like, I was born in 1949. I'm thirty-eight. I'm guessing she was about thirty."

"Best you can do?"

"I know her birthday. June seventeenth. Better?"

"Yes. Anything else?"

"I don't know." Emma stops for a moment, struggling to get her brain in gear. "I mean, 370 Riverside isn't cheap. She has money. I assume it's family money. She said she had a trust fund, but who knows if that's true. I'm meeting with her lawyer, an estate attorney, tomorrow. I should know more then. She was a photographer, and apparently her photographs are valuable. I'm guessing she didn't trust either the attorney or this art dealer."

"Or both. Smart girl."

"Girl?"

"Sorry," he says, offhandedly. "But she must have trusted you. And there must be some reason for the confidentiality. Did your friend appoint the coexecutor and the attorney? Or did some trustee? Who's paying who? See what you can find out."

"And this detective," she says. "He needs to bring me in on the case somehow."

"I doubt that's going to . . . make him happy," Kidman says, shifting gears. "But I'll see what I can do."

"That sounds a bit noncommittal."

"Just being honest. And listen—I want you to be careful. It could have been someone planting a bug. Or someone looking for some of your records. Or for information about your contacts."

"Meaning you and Angus?"

"Doubtful, but possible. But I don't want to assume . . . did she have a boyfriend or anything?"

"I don't think so. She never seemed to bring anyone around. I never met a boyfriend. I do know she was with a fellow named Simon for a while—before we met. But he's long gone, I believe."

"Doesn't seem like a crime of passion, does it?"

Emma agrees, winding things down. And thinking of Angus then, not knowing where he is, she shifts the conversation. "By the way, any word on our mutual friend?"

"Can't say. But maybe I'll hop up to the city to see you in the next few days."

"Please. I'm at—"

"I know where you are," Kidman says.

CHAPTER 9

SEAL

The thing with this Scottish guy, this Angus—I didn't get it for the longest time. I only saw him like once, but I know they were serious because she was always off meeting him somewhere. He was a good-looking guy, but older by quite a bit I'd guess. Maybe like sixty or something. She said he taught at the University of Edinburgh. That he was a historian, like her, and a professor. She showed me this book he wrote, which she said was a bestseller—*The End of Communism as We Know It*, which actually sounded kind of interesting. But I never read it. Other than that, she didn't say much about him. I thought that was pretty cool—I mean, that she didn't go on and on about him.

One time, when I asked her how they met, she did a real tap dance around it. Something about when her grandmother died, there was some kind of investigation, and he helped her somehow through his research or something. She said that's when she fell for him. Sounds like he's a bit of a rogue. Always traveling, asking her to meet him on the fly, then disappearing for months on end, but she didn't seem to worry about it. She's an independent sort. Admirably so. That said, she doesn't seem to see any other guys, at least as far as I could ever tell.

The only time I ever saw him was late one night a few years ago. I'd been to some party with my friend Reynolds, and we were sharing a cab. When we got to my place, Emma and her guy, this Scotsman, this Angus, walked in front of the cab. They were headed into the building all wrapped around each other, and they must have been some place special, because they were all dressed up. It was cold, maybe around the New Year. She had on a long black coat and black stockings and heels, and this silky red scarf was flying out behind her. And he had on this elegant cashmere coat and a fedora—like something out of a movie in the 1940s. Rennie said something like, "Well, that's a dashing couple." He seemed surprised that it was my neighbor. "The woman, I mean," I explained before I got out.

Then I rode up with two of them in the elevator, and Emma introduced us. "Angus McLearan," she said. "Meet my friend and neighbor." And he said, "Ah, the photographer, the famous Seal," and then did little more than nod, but he had this beautiful Scottish accent and this disarming grin, and when the elevator stopped, he stepped aside, put his arm out and held the door open for both of us while we exited. That's when I understood.

CHAPTER 10

On the other side of the world, winter is coming to an end. The weather is warm off the coast of Haifa and the sea is calm, a mix of deep blues and greens. Angus McLearan is belowdecks on a small fishing boat. He is holding a radio microphone, its cord stretched to the limit, looking up through the hatch at a cloudless sky, closing one eye against the sun.

"We found him," says a voice on the other end of the line.

"Where?"

"Don't know. We went through an intermediary. Seems he's trying to keep a low profile."

"That's a laugh," Angus says. There is silence on the other end of the line. "Just tell him it will be worth his while."

"Can you be more specific?"

"Maybe we can get him off the hook if he'll cooperate."

"Understood."

***

Angus is on a mission for the British government but hoping to steal some time by the sea for a quiet meal, a bottle of wine, a view of the glistening sea before his departure. His plan is to contact Bill Kidman this evening. And Emma. He doesn't want to forget to call Emma. Probably best to try her around midnight IST, he thinks as he emerges from the cabin. He is awaiting word from Mossad on the availability of a Saudi billionaire and arms trader, a highflier who is rumored to have brokered a deal between the United States and the nation of Iran in what has recently been dubbed the Iran-Contra affair. In fact, he's a man with a broad portfolio of information. Angus wants some of it.

CHAPTER 11

The office of Seal's estate attorney is in SoHo, above a small gallery, reached by a freight elevator that opens directly into a loft space that must be a good three thousand square feet. The attorney is not nearly as fashion-forward as Lynley Wright, the coexecutor, with her midi-length suit and photography collection. Harriet Freeman is dressed simply but elegantly in a white blouse and black pants, but she has photographs that make a statement of their own.

Hanging on the wall adjacent to the entrance are three enormous images from the 1960s. The first is a large blowup of "I Am a Man" placards from the Memphis garbage strike, an iconic image by Ernest Withers reproduced on such a massive scale that it must be a silk screen.

The garbage strike, of course, was happening in Memphis when Martin Luther King was assassinated there. The second photograph is a giant reproduction of the last photo taken of Bobby Kennedy, instantly recognizable from all the world's front pages in 1968. He is lying on the floor of the Ambassador Hotel in Los Angeles. The photo is grainy and appears to be touched up with paint. The third photo appears to be from a civil rights march in the 1960s—an image of the police spraying water from a fire hose on demonstrators in suits and ties, and in dresses and heels. They are falling on the sidewalks and in the streets.

"We marched," she says, following Emma's eyes. "My brother and I were there. He took that picture. In 1963. I was a young woman then."

This tryptic is at once stunning and disturbing. Emma is not quite sure how to respond, what to say. She finds it awkward, discussing the civil rights movement with a Black woman who she doesn't know, as if it will be nothing more than a weak attempt to prove they are on the same side, which, by birth, they are not. She says, "I'm sorry you had to go through that," making the situation all the more awkward, and walks quietly behind the attorney to the sitting area at the center of the room. There are documents on the coffee table and bottled waters. Emma wants to tread lightly, to find out more by pushing less.

"So, you're her neighbor," the attorney says, turning to Emma. "You can call me Harriet, by the way. We're not formal here."

"Emma," she reaches out her hand, but Harriet does not take it, instead motioning for her to have a seat, while Harriet remains standing, looking down at her. "I was her neighbor and her friend," Emma says. "I lived in the apartment next to hers, although I'm not living there right now."

"Yes. Well, she's not living there either, is she?" Harriet says. "Any idea why she would have been drawn into your apartment?"

"Maybe because someone wanted something out of hers," Emma answers.

"Or yours," Harriet says.

"Yes. I'm afraid that's also a possibility, isn't it?" Emma says.

Having made her point, Harriet seems to switch gears and loosen up a bit. "Well, I'm grateful she gave you our contact information. I don't know what would have happened if she hadn't. Seems she hasn't been using her real name lately."

"How did you know her? If you don't mind me asking."

"I knew her mother. I met her years ago through the restaurant. We were friends."

"The restaurant?"

"Her mother's restaurant," she says, then looks Emma in the eye. "You're in the dark, aren't you?"

"I am. She told me her parents lived in Great Britain."

Harriet rolls her eyes and shakes her head, but there is affection in her voice. "I love it," she says, laughing under her breath. "I understand she was quite a character. And what did she tell you they were doing over there?"

"Diplomats of some kind," Emma says.

The attorney shakes her head, chuckles, takes a minute to gather herself, stands. "Let me grab the will," she says, rising. Emma is dwarfed by the enormous space. The ceilings must be a good twenty feet above the floor. Three windows on the east-facing wall, each one ten or twelve feet high, complement the three enormous photos at the entrance. Facing the triptych is a dividing wall. The attorney heads for the space beyond.

By now, it's apparent to Emma that neither Seal's attorney nor the coexecutor, seem to be mourning Seal's sudden death—that these were clearly business relationships. And Emma wonders whether the two— Harriet Freeman and Lynley Wright—have a business relationship of their own. When Harriet returns carrying a file, Emma begins to explore some of the questions her coexecutor—Lynley Wright—was unable to answer. Among them: "Can you imagine why Seal would have told me her parents lived in England—and that they were estranged?"

"I have no idea," the attorney says. "I didn't know her well. And I'm afraid I can't tell you anything about her family."

"But you and her mother were friends?"

"Yes, but I was also her lawyer," she says. Then she speaks slowly and looks Emma directly in the eye to make sure she grasps the full weight of what she's about to hear. "And, unfortunately, I'm bound by a confidentiality agreement."

"Why on earth?" Emma asks, at which point Harriet leans forward with her arms folded across her chest and says, with apparent sincerity and a hint of frustration, "Look, I've got no choice in the matter."

Then Harriet Freeman sits back again, making it clear that she's given it a great deal of thought, and she begins again. "What I *can* tell you is this," she goes on, tapping her forefinger on the arm of her chair periodically as she speaks: "Seal's mother, Maggie—Maggie Grace Lawson—died in 1979. And Lucille—or Seal, as you call her—had an inheritance. As I assume you know, she also had established a reputation among certain collectors. Particularly those interested in the downtown scene since the midseventies. She's done quite a bit of chronicling of that era. In addition, as a young girl she was in one of Warhol's four-minute films, with her mother. The later ones, screen tests, he called them. He also did her portrait when she was a young woman, in her twenties. I assume that was before your time. So, we have a public persona to protect and certain assets."

Emma had no idea of the relationship with Warhol or that Seal's work was so well respected. She knew she had traveled in fast circles, art circles, the specifics of which Emma knew little, but this put Seal on a different plane and in a different perspective. Harriet's remarks have quieted her. "And my job as coexecutor?" she asks.

"She must have trusted you a great deal," Harriet says, again with what Emma deems to be sincerity. "As you can see, this is a complicated estate. Lynley Wright, who you met, is in charge of the art assets and protecting her, shall I say, connection with Warhol, or rather, with the Warhol estate. As I'm sure you know, he died a few days before Lucille's fall."

"Fall?"

"Until the investigation is finished, I don't think we can assume anything."

"Oh, there's something else. Are you aware that the detective on the case is talking about burying her in a potter's field?"

"I've spoken to the police. She'll be buried in Tennessee."

"Tennessee?"

"Yes. Next to her mother. In Tennessee. We've claimed her remains."

"Is there any other family? A father? Siblings? Cousins?"

"I can't tell you that. What I can tell you is this: As coexecutor, you're responsible for her personal belongings. So, once the police allow it, you'll have the authority to go through her things. I can't stop you from learning whatever you find to be important, relevant, meaningful or pertinent to an investigation. But, again, I can't tell you anything else about her family."

Emma takes a deep breath. "And I'm one of three executors?"

"Two executors—you and Ms. Wright. I'm acting as the estate attorney. And I'm responsible for the financial piece. There's the inheritance and her apartment. And there's a studio. Ultimately, I'm charged with selling or distributing her assets, as needed. Lynley Wright is dealing solely with Seal Larson's art, her photographs, her reputation as an artist and her relationship with Andy Warhol. Her legacy, if you will. It's her job to manage that, per Seal's will. My job is to manage everything else, per her mother's request."

"Per her mother?" Emma makes no effort to hide her surprise.

"Correct."

"Her mother hired you?"

"Correct."

"And who hired Lynley Wright?"

"Lucille. Or Seal, as you call her."

"And you can't tell me anything else about her family."

"Just a technicality. I promise, it won't take you long to find out more about Lucille's situation if you need to. Her mother was the co-owner of Merna's Place in Harlem. It shouldn't be difficult for you to follow that lead. I am simply bound not to tell you anything beyond what I've told you."

"I understand Seal had a trust fund. Where did that come—"

The attorney shakes her head, interrupting, "That's confidential. If you have any questions at any point about your responsibilities as a coexecutor, I'm here to answer them." Then she begins to read from Seal's will, which gives Emma the authority to go through her apartment—to decide where her things might belong and how to distribute them, and to read her private papers and sort through all her personal effects. Essentially, legally, Seal left all her personal possessions to Emma, everything except her photographs and art, which fall under the aegis of either Harriet Freeman or Lynley Wright. Harriet hands Emma an envelope containing three keys—the key to Seal's apartment, a key to her studio and a smaller key. Each one is labeled. The small key says simply, "File Cabinet."

"One last thing," Emma says before she departs. "Can you imagine why anyone would have wanted to kill her?"

"Yes, I can," she says. "But I have no idea who that person would be."

Emma's head is reeling when she leaves. She carries with her the three keys and a letter from the attorney giving her permission to go through Seal's things. *Of course there's a studio*, she thinks, but she knew nothing of it. There is also this business about Andy Warhol. How did she not notice his obituary? And how could she not know that he had done Seal's portrait? Or that she was in one of his films. The meeting confirms what she's suspected since this began—that she really knew nothing at all about Seal. Not her name or where she came from or who she really was. This bafflement settles, for the moment, on an interest in seeing Andy Warhol's obituary. She wonders how he died and if there might be a connection between the two deaths. She wants to read it, if only to confirm the one piece of information that she can confirm. That, and her mother's association with Merna's Place, the only gateway to her family. *Why all this talk of confidentiality?* she wonders. And if there is a family, that leads to the obvious question of why Emma would be selected to inherit her possessions. *What is that about?*

"Why me?" she'd asked Harriet Freeman.

"I assume because you're smart. And because she trusted you and respected you."

"Are there those among us she didn't trust?"

"I don't think Lucille would have known who to trust," she'd answered.

CHAPTER 12

Merna Jones was born in 1923 in Arkansas on farmland that was within reach of the Mississippi River. And she knew as much as anybody could about letting things go. Her parents were sharecroppers on the old Lindenwood Plantation, and when the Great Flood came in 1927, she was coming up on five years old. That made her old enough to remember the sound of the gigantic seawall of muddy water coming from the east, crackling through the woods, breaking up the trees. But she didn't have to remember, because, for a long time, that's all anybody talked about. It was the biggest flood in the history of the Delta.

It had rained for weeks on end that April, the water seeping into the fields so deep that when Merna and her father walked around the south end of the old plantation, he said he didn't imagine he'd be able to do any planting. "No telling what'll grow now," he told her. When they walked the fields, the water seeped right through the soles of their leather shoes and soaked Merna's stockings up to her knees. Every step wet and cold, it didn't seem like April, more like January. Then, just a few days later, the Mississippi River burst through the levee, one crevasse after another from Marked Tree to Greenville, until seven million acres of land was flooded in Tennessee and Mississippi and Arkansas.

On that day, she and her mother, with the baby in her arms, went clamoring up a ladder to the loft, her father passing food up in a basket, then the dog and a few of the chickens, whatever they could save. The water coming in, rising so high they thought it would touch them, her mother wailing, "Lord Jesus, this is it. This is the end." The baby crying for three full days, all of them running out of food and hope, until the men came in boats to take them to the camps. Muddy camps full of mosquitoes and the smell of people living up under one another, standing in line to get their food. All the coloreds, as they were called back then in polite company, put together in one place, in big tents full of beds, men in one tent, women in the other with the children. But they made it, all of them. And for Merna, it was like a big party after the biggest nightmare she could have dreamed.

In the end, she became an industrious young woman, with a talent for cooking and catering and entertaining large crowds of people, and a mind for business. At the age of twenty, she moved to Oxford, Mississippi, and worked her way up through the town's restaurants to the famous Oxford Grill in the historic square at the center of town. Of course, Oxford is viewed as the intellectual center of the Delta. Home to the University of Mississippi and all manner of cerebral white people, including, famously, William Faulkner. After James Meredith fought his way into being accepted at the University of Mississippi—a.k.a. Ole Miss— and segregationists rose up in protest, and President Kennedy sent the National Guard and federal lawmen down to the town of Oxford, Merna decided it was time to go. She worked at the Grill until 1962. Then, just before Thanksgiving, she said she'd had enough of Mississippi. That winter, she followed her cousin up to New York City, where he had a job in construction, and she had a dream of starting her own restaurant. Merna Jones is a woman with a strong will and a generous spirit.

***

She greets Emma Quinn in dark sunglasses with the words, "Oh Lord. It makes me so sad," embracing her and welcoming her into her home, the brownstone apartment that sits atop Merna's Place, which Emma has discovered is a popular soul food restaurant in Harlem. A brief review in the *New Yorker* summed it up this way:

> Not your typical ham hocks and barbecued ribs, Merna's Place takes soul food uptown. Specialties include fried green tomatoes and a mean fried okra. The crème brûlée and pecan pie are nothing short of exceptional. But it's the entrées that set this place apart: a peppery fried chicken, a spicy gumbo and a blackened catfish that's on fire. Authentic southern cooking in the heart of Harlem, at 125th and Broadway. No reservation required, except for groups of eight or more. Jazz on Fridays. Closed Tuesdays. Hours: 5:00 p.m.–midnight.

Merna's living room is spare and elegant. Modern furniture of black leather and steel. White walls. A series of African masks lined up along one of them. Through the front window, Emma can see the cast-iron arches that support the subway train near 125th and Broadway. And, although the sun is barely risen to the top of the sky, the lights are flashing across the street at a bar called the Harlem Scene.

This is the first person Emma has encountered from Seal's life who is visibly upset. Instead of diving right in, which is Emma's way, she falls in step with Merna. She slows down. She acknowledges their shared grief, asks if they are planning a service and how Merna found out about Seal's death. She tells Merna that she was worried, that the detective had threatened to bury Seal in an unmarked grave. "Well, thank the Lord we got that straightened out," Merna says.

By the time Emma reports, "She told me her parents lived over in England," the two are sitting next to one another companionably on the leather sofa.

"Why would she say a fool thing like that?" Merna says, shaking her head, two dangling tortoiseshell hoops clickety-clacking. "I've seen her change it up. Her name. Her hair. Her voice. I remember when she started talking with a French accent. She was never sure who she was. Think about it. To go from living over top a restaurant in Oxford, Mississippi, to this Walden School on Central Park West." She raises her eyebrows and shakes her head, drawing out the words *Walden School* and *Central Park West* as if they were *Windsor Castle* and *London,*

England, then goes on. "And imagine this: At first, her mama wanted them to live up here in Harlem. I said, bad idea. This pretty little white girl growing up in Harlem. I don't think so. So, they got a place down toward the university, near where she lives . . ." Then she stops herself and tears up again.

"When did you last see her?" Emma asks.

"I hadn't seen her much since her mama died. That was 1979. That was a long time ago. She pretty much disappeared."

"I'm so sorry. And I hate to ask, but how did her mother die?"

"Her mother was sick, very sick . . . for quite a while before it took her," she says. "Lucille—we called her Lucy, mostly, or Lucy-Anne. Until she was grown, anyway. Her mother didn't like Lucille. Seems her grandma picked it. When she went off to college, she took on a Frenchified version—Lucienne, she called herself. And after that, she started up with this Seal business. I don't know if her mama ever called her Seal." She hesitates a moment, as if she's searching her memory. "Maybe in the end. Anyway, after her mama got sick, the two of them went down to Plantersville to stay with her little sister before she died. Back to the farm."

"Plantersville?"

"Plantersville, Tennessee. Where they come from." Merna straightens up a bit.

"Whose little sister? Seal's?"

Merna's brow wrinkles. "What's your name again? Emily?"

"Emma. Emma Quinn."

"Look, Miz Quinn. I don't mean to be rude. But I don't know you from Eve. I've known Miss Lucy since she was a little girl. I just got this news, and I'm still digesting it. So, I'm wondering if maybe you could come back another time with your questions."

"I'm trying to understand who might have done this."

"Well, I say, best leave that to the police."

"I understand," Emma says. "Here's the detective's card. Call him," she says. "He'll vouch for me." Merna's leading Emma to the front door. "Just one more question. Did she ever—"

"No more questions," Merna says firmly, cutting her off.

***

Emma heads for the subway at 125th. She's talking to herself, trying to remember as much as she can. "Plantersville, Tennessee," she says aloud, waiting for the train. "A sister in Plantersville," she says, and "Oxford, Mississippi," trying to imagine what she might find in the library database and wondering what Detective Brodsky must know by now, when a policeman approaches her. "Are you lost, ma'am?" he says.

She realizes she must look like a crazy woman, talking to herself. "Sorry, Officer. I'm just thinking."

"I understand," he says. "I'm just gonna wait here with you while you think until the train gets here, if that's okay with you." She realizes then that she is the only white person around, that she looks like exactly what she is, and that he is protecting her. On Broadway, the gulf between 125th Street, where Merna lives, and 116th Street, where the university is situated, is enormous—the precise reason Emma had chosen to ride the subway instead of walking the nine blocks.

When she arrives, her tiny office at Columbia feels like a haven. It's midmorning and the department is empty, the doors sealed tight. Surrounded by her books, she sits quietly, jotting down a few notes, gathering her thoughts before leaving a message for Bill Kidman, her CIA friend and confidant. "Okay," she says, into the phone. "Her mother's name was Maggie Grace Lawson. She was from Plantersville, Tennessee. Also lived in Oxford, Mississippi. At some point, they moved to the city. This all according to Merna Jones, who runs Merna's Place in Harlem. She and Maggie Grace were partners. Maggie Grace died in 1979. Lucille went to Walden, the private school on the Upper West Side. I'll find out what I can about the restaurant, when it started, when they got here. If you'll look into the other."

As she hangs up the phone, a former grad student pops his head in. "Hey, you!" he says, startling her. And: "What the hell are you doing here?" He's caught her completely off guard. "I heard you were in Washington on sabbatical," he says.

"You heard right," she gathers her things up as she speaks. "What about you? I would have put you on Wall Street by now."

"I'm teaching an economic history class with one of your colleagues.

Just for a kick."

"Is that right?" She is reminded of how much this particular student used to throw her off-balance. His cockiness. His relentlessness. His, well, presumption. Rolley Smythe. The name suited him somehow.

"How long you in town?" he asks, with the same familiarity that always felt inappropriate to her.

"Just a few days, I think."

"Well, let's be sure to get together for a drink." He seems wired, hyped up.

"Sounds good," she says, not meaning it, as he writes his number on a slip of paper. Hands it to her. Clever boy, Rolley, she thinks as the elevator door closes. Always keeping her on her toes. Smart. Too smart for his own good.

CHAPTER 13

SEAL

When my mother died, I stopped sleeping and started dreaming. Dreams of kitchens mostly, full of songs I hadn't recalled until then and all kinds of people I knew when I was little but hadn't remembered in a very long time—women wearing massive white aprons, men slinking around the kitchen picking at the biscuits, the cooks smacking at them and laughing. "Get your cotton-pickin' hands outta there." I dreamed of a slight young man, his head shaved, his clothes too big for his slim frame, washing dishes with giant hands over a steamy sink, singing to himself: "I'm a soul man." Then a couple of others joining in with a soft, low chorus, drowned out by the clap of the silverware and the dishes being slammed about: "Doo-doo-doo-do-doo-do-do-do-do." Then the dishwasher starting up again: "I'm a soul man." And someone coming in with the horns. "Shut up," Merna would call. "You about to run me crazy." My dreams are a parody of the South, that old kitchen at the Oxford Grill coming to life again inside my head in a minstrel show of a memory, the song itself an anachronism.

In another dream, I see my mother as a young woman wrapped in a half apron, one that's folded over at the top and tied in front, loose around her waist, her golden hair pulled up in a ponytail, wiry curls flying about, the sleeves of a faded, cotton shirt rolled up around her elbows, slight and pretty, standing by a stove in a small kitchen, one hand on her hip, a spatula flopping around in the other. "Aren't you hungry, sweet pea?" she says, turning back from the stove. I am sitting on top of a white, tin-top table, watching her. I must be about five, which would make her about twenty. "Don't you want a little fried egg sandwich to help you sleep?" It is dark in my dream, and it is just the two of us.

That would have been in Oxford, where she learned to cook. We lived over top of the restaurant there, in a little apartment that smelled like the smoke from the barbecue pit out back and overlooked the town square out front. We slept in the same bed, her and me. I remember that. And she'd leave me there alone at night and go back to work, down the back stairs that ran outside behind the restaurant. That's how I came to find it hard to sleep. I imagined too many times that someone was coming up those stairs, peeking into our kitchen window or waiting for my mother to leave. Lying in that big bed alone, voices coming up from the street, drunken students from Ole Miss, fancy folks out for a night on the town, and Merna and her crew hanging out back on break or when the kitchen was closing down, laughing and full of hoo-ha. In my dream, I lie there listening with my eyes open, waiting. And later, when she comes home, the light still on, she wakes me and makes me something to eat.

I call these the Oxford dreams. I recognize the people I see in them—good old Merna, Fred the busboy, Raymond, who used to come around to bother Merna in the kitchen. I don't know any of their last names. Except for Merna, of course. I probably couldn't find any of the others now, even if I tried, but I spent my days with them for seven years. Merna was mean back then, before she got up to the city. "You better get that child out from under my kitchen knife," she'd say to no one in particular.

One night, after my mother died, my dreams took me to another place, to a flat, scruffy field, and my mother holding me with one arm. We are at the edge of a pasture, right up next to a blackberry bush growing against an old fence that seems to go on forever. The sky is a creamy blue, with puffy clouds floating around overhead. My mother is picking blackberries and popping them, one at a time, into my mouth. I can see the scene from two perspectives, it being a dream: I can see my mother through my young eyes, from inside the nook formed by our bodies. And I can see the whole scene at a distance, as an observer. From one angle, I am looking into my mother's face, straight on, as she pops a blackberry into my mouth, then licks her fingers. She is smiling, red-faced from the sun, and looking to be a teenager. From another angle, I can see that I am slung across her hip, my legs wrapped around her waist. She is wearing blue jeans and a print shirt with a Peter Pan collar that fits snug around her body. Me, I'm in a puffy little flowered sunsuit. And I can hear her singing, just to me, drawing out the words, long and slow, with her southern accent exaggerated. "Aaaah don't want a pickle . . . Just want to raaad on my motorsickle . . . And Aaaah don't want a tickle." Then she leans back just a little, laughing with her eyes, and starts tickling me on the tummy, and she throws her head back and starts up again, louder this time. "'Cause Aaaah'd rather raaad on my motorsickle. And I don't want to daaaaaaaa."

That's when I wake up. She is so young and beautiful and happy. And I wake up alone, feeling warm and sad at the same time, missing her, clutching my pillow and trying to hold on to the memory, hoping to slink back into sleep and see her again.

I don't want to die, she sang. But I know that couldn't be. Because it's another anachronism. I know I never heard that song until I moved to New York. And I never heard "I'm a Soul Man" until I was almost a teenager. I remember it. But those songs leached into my dreams as part of the romance of them.

CHAPTER 14

Emma is in her own world. In a reading room on the first floor of the main library at Columbia University, going through recent copies of the *New York Times*. She finds Monday's paper, dated February 23, 1987, settles on a spot in a corner at a nearby table and unfurls it to read the Warhol obituary. It surprises her. She knew about the Campbell's Soup cans, the portraits of Marilyn Monroe and Liz Taylor, of his pre-occupation with fame and wealth, and his films featuring a coterie of downtown crazies. The obit references his genius, the range of his work, his experimentation. Credits him with inventing Pop Art. But she is surprised to find that Warhol was born Andrew Warhola, the child of emigrants from a remote village in Eastern Europe. She reimagines him now as an outsider, realizing that English would have been his second language and that he grew up in Pittsburgh, Pennsylvania, a steel town, a working-class town, at a time when his homosexuality would have been, well, a liability. Those two things alone would explain his famous shyness and his cryptic quotes. She reads that he had difficulty making the transition from commercial art, where he was a great success, to breaking into the rarified world of fine art; difficulty finding a dealer who would represent him. His first art show, featuring the famous soup cans, was in L.A., not New York. Now, nearly two decades after being shot by one of his followers, a wound from which he recovered, he dies of a heart attack in his sleep following a routine operation. At the age of fifty-eight. Something tragic about his life.

She knows he also sparked tragedy. Emma remembers being in graduate school at Columbia, living in a parallel universe in the same city, when Edie Sedgwick, perhaps Warhol's most famous It Girl, died of an overdose in the early seventies. And from this obituary, Andy Warhol's obituary, she sees that, most recently, he had been supporting young artists, new wave artists, street artists, graffiti artists—Keith Haring and Jean-Michel Basquiat—but Emma doesn't even know who they are. What she does know now is that her friend Seal had crossed over at some point into Mr. Warhol's universe.

She finishes the obit and makes a copy of the paper, awkwardly centering the story on top of the Xerox machine, using the weight of her hands to flatten it out, half closing the cover. She goes through the same cumbersome process to copy the rest of the obit, which is continued on an inside page. By the time she finishes, her fingers are blackened with newsprint.

Of course, she knows now why she hadn't read Andy Warhol's obituary on the day it appeared, hadn't even noticed it. Because, the upper right quadrant of the front page, above the obituary, is dominated by news of what they're calling the Iran-Contra affair. That Monday, the Tower Commission, a Congressional committee charged with investigating the scandal, was preparing to release its findings. The story not only dominated the front page of the *Times*, but there were more stories on the subject deeper in the paper. It was becoming clear that Reagan's security team had secretly sold weapons to Iran in exchange for Iran's help in freeing American hostages being held in Lebanon—and that the money from the weapons sale had, illegally, been funneled to right-wing Contra rebels in Nicaragua. Based on the news reports, it looked like the CIA—and the president himself—may have been involved.

That's where Emma's attention had fallen on first reading because of her friend Angus McLearan and his work in the Middle East. And now, as she wrestles the newspaper back together, she realizes she wants those news stories. Surreptitiously, she folds the entire paper and stuffs it into her bag because that's where her mind is—on Angus. She has no idea where he is. February is nearly over, and she hasn't heard from him since December, when he had appeared unexpectedly at her lakefront cabin in Saranac, New York. She'd been in the front bedroom when he arrived, and it was late. The book she'd been reading—*Marxism and The French Left* by Tony Judt—lay splayed open and spine-up by her side. Her dog, Seamus, a robust Irish setter, was sleeping at the foot of the bed. At 4:00 a.m., a few days before Christmas, Seamus rose and let loose a howl like a banshee. Half-awake, Emma spun around, threw open the drawer of the little bedside table—the olive green one decorated with a delicate decoupage of roses at each corner—and pulled out a handgun. By the time Angus made it to the bedroom door, she was sitting upright with a gun pointed at him. And Seamus was wagging his tail, rushing toward the Scotsman himself, very nearly knocking him off his feet.

"Sorry to alarm you, darling," Angus had said, sounding like a caricature of James Bond himself.

"You are a cliché, Angus McLearan," she'd responded, stashing the gun back in her bedside table.

And he'd laughed out loud, pointing at the massive book by her side. "And you, my dear? A little light reading?" Although it's only been a few months since then, it feels too long. She wants to see him, talk to him, touch him. Especially now.

CHAPTER 15

When Emma gets back to the little hotel at 110th and Broadway, two telexes await her. The clerk at the front desk, a slim woman of Indian descent dressed in a sari, shoots her a knowing glance, her head cocked slightly to the right. *You are one of us*, the gesture says. Emma has never seen her before.

Angus's message is straightforward: *Sorry to hear your news. All good here. I will call.*

So is Bill Kidman's. *Meet me at the Broadway Deli on 72nd at 10 am tomorrow.* There is also a message from Rolley Smythe, the former grad student. It reads: *Call me. 765-1221. Let's have that drink.* She holds it up to the clerk, looking confused.

"He phoned, maybe an hour ago."

"Did he have my room number?"

"No. No. He called on the main phone line," she responds. Emma crushes the message into a ball and stuffs it in her pocket.

Once upstairs, she barely has time to kick off her shoes and pour herself a bourbon and water before the phone rings. It's Angus calling from across the world. She knows better than to ask where. Probably the Middle East.

"I'm sorry, love," are the first words he says. And her eyes begin to well up.

"Good to hear your voice," she says, surprised by the flood of tears. And hearing it, he is silent for a moment.

"What time is it over there?" she asks.

"Midnight," he says. And, "Tell me about her."

She cannot seem to stop the flow of words. She tells him that they weren't as close as they might have been, and how little she really knows about Seal. That she was independent, self-contained, maybe even secretive. "I didn't even know her real name. And she told me a complete story about her parents," she says, and then, with purpose, "But she was really something. So full of energy and curiosity. And she was so open.

Curiosity. Openness. Good qualities to have in a friend."

"Interesting," he says. "I would think honesty would be right up there."

She hesitates a moment. "Spoken like a true spy," she says. The hotel's phones are secure lines. She feels as if she can speak freely, but the subject that is absorbing her interest has nothing to do with international politics or his work. "The thing is," she says, lying on her back, staring at the ceiling, listening for Angus's breath. "Seal inspired me. She sparked my imagination."

"How so?" he says, inviting her to open up.

"I remember last summer, just before my move to Washington, she came by and insisted we go downtown to a show at the Museum of Modern Art. She said it was a big deal, an international show of living artists. Apparently, that was uncommon for the Modern. I might never have gone. And I'll never forget it. We saw these sculptures that floored me. I'm not sure how to pronounce the artist's name. A-ba-kano-wicz. She was Polish. Magdalena Abakanowicz. She had laid out this field of large, egg-shaped sculptures. They were crafted of fabric, some sort of woven fabric, like burlap, and spread across the floor, like so many sacks of flour. They felt like discarded beings. Abandoned souls. They had a profound effect on me. Her work was stunning. I'm not sure how else to describe it."

"That was pretty good."

"Thanks," she laughs softly. "It's so nice to talk to you," she says, and takes a deep breath. "Anyway, afterward, I went and researched the artist."

"Of course, you did," he says. And Emma can hear the smile in his voice.

"This woman was born in 1930. When I saw she was from Poland, I thought of the war. And the Soviet occupation. And what on earth her experience must have been like. To be a girl during the Nazi occupation and then the Soviet occupation. Her history would have been tragic. They were originally from Russia—her family, aristocrats who left during the revolution. And, after the war when the Soviets moved into Poland, they had to hide their roots." She pauses for an instant, taking a breath. "Apparently she's never spoken about her work, but it must relate to that experience, those experiences." She knows that Angus is listening because that's what he does. And she goes on.

"I felt compelled to find out more so I could understand it. But Seal taught me something. She experienced the work itself. She saw the experimentation with materials. These were sculptures made of cloth. Fiber art, really. She saw them, too, as symbols of human forms, metaphors for alienation, emptiness, our humanity and our inhumanity. But mostly, she drew my attention to the visceral reaction we both had to these pieces, the sadness and darkness we felt. Then how inspired she was by them. Where I saw only darkness, she pointed out the fact that we were both experiencing these seemingly random objects in a profound way. And I realized she was right, the art itself was uplifting. That's the beauty of it. It taps into our humanity. It touches us. We both felt that. The strength of the work. Seal taught me how to look at art in a new way. To see it differently."

"Quite a gift," he says. Then he lightens things up a bit. "You know, art's not really my realm."

She laughs. "I know. It's not mine either. Obviously." She takes a long, deep breath, lying on her bed, looking up at the ceiling. And there is another spell of quiet.

"This is a hard one, isn't it?" Angus says.

"Yeah," she says. Then they are just listening to one another's breath before turning to what feels more like business.

"Kidman tells me she died in your apartment. You'll be involved in the investigation, won't you?" he says.

"I'm trying to nose myself into it. Meeting a little resistance."

"No surprise. Be careful, will you?" His tone is casual. "I'll try to get over there as soon as I can," he says, preparing to sign off. But she's not ready to let him go.

"I assume you know the Tower Commission report is coming out in the next few days," she says. "Want me to hold onto the newspapers for you?"

"You can. But it's old news, Emma."

"You don't have a horse in that race?"

"Well, not technically. Not at this point." He falls silent then.

"Can you at least tell me how you are?" she says, stretching the conversation out.

"My dear, at the moment, talking to you, I'm over the moon."

"Very smooth. Well, come down from there, will you?"

"Can't, I'm afraid," he says, adding, "I have no news."

"Can I tap your brain about this business in New York? Bill says follow the money. What do you think?"

"That and the secrets. Everyone has secrets. Find out what hers were." She nods, as if he's in the room. "And another thing: Don't assume anything. I mean *anything*."

"I think I understand you."

"In all matters," he says. "I'm serious." He pauses. She can hear him breathing. Then he says firmly, "Take care of yourself."

"I will," she says. "And you."

There's one last, long silence, then he signs off. "Bye, love."

CHAPTER 16

SEAL

The soup cans. That's the first thing that pops into your mind when you think of Warhol. Or maybe Marilyn. I think of him as an idea man. Mass production at the factory. Art as business. And as the ultimate experimenter. He once did a series where his protégés pissed on a bunch of paintings. Somebody probably sold them for a fortune. Sometimes it was hard to tell whether he was shy or just saying fuck you to everybody. I saw him talking to a reporter once. The guy asked about his art and what it meant or something, and he said something like, "What do you think?" Or "Whatever you want it to mean." He came off kinda like one of the Beatles. Ironic, playful, but straight-faced. He was obviously a provocateur. I think it was Cy Twombly who believed, basically—and I know I'm misquoting him—art is the process of making it and doing it, not the product itself. Andy said it was all about production, but it sometimes seemed like it was the product itself.

I have to admit, he was a little creepy. He was gentle and sweet. But his eyes had a darkness to them, and his hair and his skin were so white—with that makeup, that wig, he just looked kinda eerie. He did my portrait in the midseventies, after I left Sarah Lawrence. It was around the time I met Simon. I knew he was using me, kinda the same way it felt like Simon was using me at the time. You know, pretty shiksa-girl. Because of what they perceived as my beauty. I don't know how any of Warhol's subjects could escape that recognition—that they were being used, that is. Of course, I paid for the portrait. Everybody did. But they all wanted fame. So, they were using him as well. I didn't care a bit about fame. Except maybe when it came to my own work. But I far prefer to be on the other side of the camera. We didn't do my portrait at the Factory. It was at his new place on Broadway and all that craziness of the Factory days was pretty much over by then.

When we did the film, the short film, I went to the Factory with my mother. Here's what I remember. The place was filled with the strangest characters. Of course, I was just a girl. Maybe eight or nine. I don't know why my mother would have agreed to such a thing, except she was a bit of a free spirit. You know, we looked alike. If you see her picture, you can see for yourself. I was like a mini version of her. I think he was drawn to that angelic quality she possessed. Very fragile, wispy. But it was misleading. She was a strong woman, my mother. And he was kind of wispy himself.

I always assumed he met my mother at the restaurant. According to what my mother told me later, we were visiting New York when he saw us, and he just became enamored with us. He introduced himself, and he looked at her and he looked at me, and he asked if he could film the two of us. What I don't know is where he saw us together or how. But I remember going to the Factory and walking down this long hall filled with stacks of papers and boxes and just stuff. It was a tight space, and kinda dark. Seemed like maybe he was a hoarder or something. And there were a few other people there, some dressed in costumes, as I recall. Others in black leather. I'd never seen people dressed like that before. He asked all of them to go in the other room. Then he was very quiet.

I remember he asked us to sit down together. My mother put her arm around me. And he said he just wanted to film us close to one another. He asked me to kiss her cheek and asked her to wrap her arms around me. We kinda snuggled. I know I giggled because I've seen the film. I saw it at a Lincoln Center retrospective, not too long ago, in fact. It was dear. We were very loving. And it was a close-up, black and white. It was beautifully lit, so you could see the shadows. He shot it from such a wonderful perspective. Zeroed right in on our faces, at an angle, like he was looking over my left shoulder. Very intimate. And we did look like twins. I was my mother, in miniature.

I watched a few of his other early films when I was at the New School. They were amazing, shot in a kind of slow motion, because of the way he adjusted the shutter speed, with the camera set on a tripod. He called them stillies. One was a close-up of a man eating a mushroom, in black and white. It was stunning really. He did an hours-long film of a man sleeping. Again, very intimate. He did those in 1964. And that's when he started what he called screen tests, which were all close-ups like ours. He did hundreds of them. Some were of famous people—Salvador Dali, Lou Reed, Dennis Hopper—which fit right in with his usual theme: art as commodity, people as commodities. Of course, that was before he did his better-known films, his talking films, the ones of those crazy people at the Factory.

Anyway, later, when I was getting started in photography, he was helpful to me. Introduced me to some people. Other photographers. Dealers. I met Lynley through Andy Warhol. Lynley Wright, my rep. Creepy or not, I always liked Andy. Because he was so kind to me. It was upsetting when he got shot. That was no good. Afterward, I think he pretty much steered clear of those people, those crazy people. And he left the Factory. I guess it held dark memories. Right before we split,

Simon called him a homo. I thought that was unnecessary, archaic. Idiotic. He called me a fag hag. He was mad at me because I stayed out all night or something, downtown. I don't know what I was doing. But Simon was a homophobic prick. In fact, I'd say that's one of the things that triggered our split.

Not long after my mother died, I went to see Andy Warhol. I wanted a copy of the film, for posterity, for me. To remember my mother by. He said he'd take care of it. But he never did. He bought one of my pieces, though. And he had some still photos of my mother and me. He gave me one of those. We talked a lot about my mom. He was a regular at the restaurant at some point, back when it was the place to be. And I think she hung out with him. But I don't know any details on that. Wish I did.

CHAPTER 17

Emma loves Bill Kidman. He is eminently reliable. There is nothing about him to suggest that he's career CIA. Tall, lean, shaggy-haired, he looks like he might be a high school English teacher. Approaching sixty, he has been happily married for most of his life and has two grown sons. They all vacation together at his summer place on the Chesapeake Bay in the town of Easton, Maryland, where he keeps a small sloop. His neighbors think he teaches at the War College. He has never lived abroad, except when he fought in the Vietnam War, which makes him something of an anomaly among CIA officers.

When he arrives, he is carrying a folio detailing the background of one Lucille Anne Lawson, born June 17, 1956, in Oxford, Mississippi.

"There appears to have been some hanky-panky," Kidman says, being silly, raising his eyebrows.

Emma, who had just taken a sip of her coffee, spits it out, snorting, sullying the tablecloth, bottling up her laughter as one does when experiencing pain or grief, or when they are unconsciously elated to be with someone who cares for them, accepts them totally. Or, as in this case, both. When she can speak again, she says, "Hanky-panky. Where did you come up with that, Mr. 1950s?"

"Well, that is my generation, isn't it?" he says, muttering, "Smart-ass."

"Okay. Okay."

"So, your friend, Miss Lawson, was born in Oxford in 1956 in a home for wayward mothers called the Well Place."

"Good God," says Emma. "Really?"

"That's what I meant by hanky-panky. Based on the records, her mother Margaret—Maggie, as you know—got pregnant when she was living on a farm near Plantersville, Tennessee. *Her* mother, Seal's grandmother—whose name was Nancy Lawson—lived there until she died in the early seventies. Apparently, Maggie went to public school in Plantersville. She was a pretty girl. And only fifteen when she got pregnant. There's no record of a father."

"Okay, so how did Seal get to New York?"

"You already know the answer to that. She came up here with her mother. Her mother worked at the Oxford Grill in Oxford, Mississippi, with Merna Jones. She opened the restaurant Merna's Place back in 1966. With your Merna."

"My Merna. Ha! She barely spoke to me. When did they move here?"

"1966. So, Seal would have been ten. As you know, they enrolled her in the Walden School. It's a progressive, alternative school on the Upper West Side."

"They?"

"Well, her mother. Not sure how she pulled that off. Suggests that they had some money to begin with. Then your Seal—"

"Will you stop!" Emma says, and Kidman goes on.

"Sorry. Lucille Lawson, a.k.a. Seal Larson, went to college at Sarah Lawrence in the midseventies for a couple of years. Dropped out. No record of where she was from 1976 until 1979. So, from the age of twenty to twenty-three, she was off the grid. There's no record of a residence. The mother had an apartment on West Seventy-Second Street. That lease expired in 1978. Her mother also co-owned the building that houses Merna's Place. And she owned an apartment or something in Chelsea."

"That would have been Seal's studio, I think. Maybe she was living there."

"She resurfaces in 1979 and enrolls in the New School with this new name—Seal Larson. A year later, she bought the apartment next to you on Riverside. Moved in right before you did."

"I found her mother's death notice the other day at the library. It's tiny," she pulls a copy of it out of her bag, reads it aloud, clearing her throat first. "Her colleagues at Merna's Place mourn the passing of Maggie Grace Lawson, restauranteur, mother, friend extraordinaire and lover of art. A private service will be held in Plantersville, Tennessee. She is survived by her daughter, Lucille Anne Lawson, and a sister, Jennifer Lawson Henley." Emma hesitates a second.

"Right," Kidman says. "Nancy Lawson had another daughter, Jennifer Lawson—Seal's aunt. And Seal's aunt is still very much alive and living on said farm."

"So, Jennifer Lawson Henley still lives down there," Emma says, thinking out loud, and then, "So when did Seal enroll in the New School?"

"Mid-August, 1979."

"Good Lord, her mother had just died. How did she die?"

"Cancer." He hesitates a moment, looking down at the table, then back up at Emma, shaking his head as he speaks, "Hospital records suggest that it was a long, unpleasant slog. Started as breast cancer. Spread. She was only thirty-nine years old."

"Oh God. That's awful." They're both quiet for a time. "So, Seal's off the grid for three years, during which her mother was sick," Emma says.

"She may have been taking care of her mother, for all we know," Kidman says.

"I don't know. I had the impression they weren't close." Emma's thinking, mulling it over. "But we know she went back to school right after her mother died."

"She might have inherited some money," Kidman says. And Emma's just nodding as if she's slipping off somewhere in her head. "You okay?" he says, putting his hand over hers. "You with me, Emma?"

"Yup," she says finally, looking up at him. "You're a wizard, Mr. Kidman."

"It's a start," he says. And they sit for a time, without speaking, as if just being in the same room is enough. Kidman gets restless first. "I think I'm going to have to call your detective. Tell him you're affiliated with us. That'll help you with your friend Merna." She shakes her head, casts him an exasperated look. "And enable you to get access to any files he has."

"I can't even get into my own apartment, much less hers," Emma tells him. "Although I do have permission from the estate. I'm going to go see Merna again this afternoon. I'll see what else I can find out about Seal's mother."

"Might be valuable to know how successful that restaurant is and where all this money is coming from. I mean—Walden? 370 Riverside? They were living pretty well."

"Maybe family money? A farm in Tennessee?" Emma shrugs. "And I need to get into her studio, look around."

Kidman nods. "Just let me talk with your detective," he says. Then he's up. Leaning over as if he's kissing her on the forehead, he slides the file onto her lap and whispers, "And I trust you heard from our mutual friend from across the sea." She nods. He raises his eyebrows. "Speaking of hanky-panky."

"You're a dork," she says.

CHAPTER 18

SEAL

I have tried to imagine what it was like for my mother, at the age of eighteen, to pack a single bag—which is one of the few things I know to be a fact—and get on a bus in Plantersville, Tennessee, alone, with her little girl. ("Just you and that one bag," my mother would tell me.) To land at the bus station in downtown Memphis, which I'm guessing was sort of a grubby place. I can see her sitting with me on a mucky Formica chair, feeding me, waiting for the next bus to Oxford, Mississippi, where God only knew what exactly she was going to find. My own recollections of these events are nonexistent, so they come out a muddle of chronological inaccuracies. I have no written record, no photographs, no home movies or videos of these turning points. I always picture my mother in black and white, a poor, sallow-cheeked young woman wearing a clingy hat and a sack of a dress in some kind of washed-out floral print and hose—not pantyhose, but the kind that used to clip onto a girdle—and thick, sensible shoes. And I imagine her getting on that bus with an infant swaddled in her arms, all of which is absurd. For one thing, I was three years old at the time and perfectly capable of walking. And I have to remind myself that it wasn't the Great Depression or the Dust Bowl, that it wasn't 1929 or 1940. It was 1959, almost 1960. Even so, I don't imagine many women were traveling alone across the country with their small children at the time, although I could be wrong. When I think of 1959, I think of Elvis Presley and suburbia and housewives with shiny refrigerators and cars with fins. Of the American Dream, as advertised. And I think of what it was like for people like Merna to live down there, and for my mother to be a single mother, a woman who had a child but had never married, to live in a place called Oxford, Mississippi. That was no American Dream.

CHAPTER 19

"Greed. Or maybe passion," Detective Brodsky tells Emma when she asks if he has any leads, any sense of why her friend Seal fell to her death. Or who would have done it.

"Or surprise," Emma says. "Maybe she surprised someone in my apartment."

"I think we've eliminated that possibility," he says, as he unlocks the door to Seal's apartment. Although Emma has never been inside, she's stood at the threshold many times. She knows it's barely furnished, at least the front room, but only from glimpses.

Emma and Brodsky have had several phone exchanges in the past twenty-four hours. "Information sharing," he called it, after welcoming her grudgingly into the investigation in the wake of Bill Kidman's phone call. Yesterday, they'd discussed the Loves—the couple that's renting Emma's apartment—as the target, and Emma had shared this bit of information: "They're in Turkey. I sent them a telegram. Heard back this morning. They're doing a presentation over there—a place called Hattasu Örenyeri. South of the Black Sea. Nothing remote about it. They're at a tourist site, then moving on to a dig in southeastern Turkey. The mountains, I believe. All above board. He says he left no artifacts, nothing of value at my place, not even any notes. Everything's in his office." When she informs Brodsky that the work he's doing is respectful of the culture, he says, "I don't even know what that means."

"Basically, it means he's not a looter. He's not taking anything out of Turkey. And, in his short career, he has never removed anything from its nation of origin. He's allied with the AIC, and he's following the rules. I just don't think he was a target. Of course, I don't know anything about their personal life. But he gave us permission to go through his office at Columbia yesterday. It was undisturbed."

"Are they friends of yours?"

"No. They answered an ad I posted at the university. And I checked their references. He's a prominent archaeologist from Great Britain."

"Interesting. And what about you? Given your apparent affiliation with the intelligence community, could they have been after something of yours?" This was all said last night, but this morning, on the phone, he was quite clear: "We're pretty sure your friend was the target at this point."

That reason becomes more obvious to her the moment they step through Seal's front door. The detective, of course, has been here before. A multicolored wall hanging, some sort of fabric art or tapestry torn down from the wall in the front hall, lies shredded on the floor. Someone has rifled through the coat closet near the front door and drilled a series of holes in its inner walls. In the living room, the sofa has been torn apart. A large, framed photograph that clearly sat above the sofa—maybe six feet high by four feet wide—has been taken down and removed from its frame, the glass shattered about. The photograph itself is crumpled, obviously cast aside. There are four rooms in the apartment plus a kitchen and bath. Every closet has been torn apart. All three hanging pieces—each one larger than the last—have been mutilated in some way. Either there were no rugs, or they've all been removed. The mattresses have been unstuffed. And holes have been drilled in a couple of walls. Someone obviously spent a good long time exploring this apartment.

"Greed or passion?" Brodsky says when they are through.

"There's a lot of anger going on here," she says. "But given the drilling,

I'm going to go with greed. Someone is looking for something."

"Unless it's some weirdo," he says. "What do you know about her, hmm . . . her relationships? Were there a lot of men in her life?"

"Probably. But I'd wager that they never visited this apartment. We were friends—and I've never even been in here before," she says. He's just staring at her, waiting. "Look, she was an unusual person."

"Meaning . . ."

"She had no need of men. I mean that literally. She didn't need them. Wanted nothing from them, which probably made her all the more attractive."

"That right? So, she was a lesbian."

"No. You misunderstand. It's just that she wasn't looking for a partner. She had money. And she definitely wasn't looking for a husband. I have no idea what her sexual preferences were. I do know that she was drawn to artists and musicians. The former more than the latter. All kinds."

He listens quietly, respectfully, unmoving. Emma suspects that he's just a few years older than her, but it feels as if they're a generation apart. And she has the distinct impression that he hasn't done much work on the case. The file is thin. She finds that troubling, although it's only been a few days.

"Hmm. Meaning . . ." he says.

"Black. White. Gay. Straight. Young. Old. Mostly young, actually."

"Her lovers . . ."

"I didn't say that," she says. He rolls his eyes. "I'd have to say friends, fellow travelers, colleagues," she says. "I imagine I was one of her only female friends, if not her only one. In fact, I know I was. I think she found men to be safer."

"Safer . . . You're not making any sense. Which is it? Was she drawn to men or not?"

"I doubt she had many intimate relationships. I think she was capable of keeping men at a distance. That's all. And I never saw anyone coming or going from her apartment."

"Did you know anyone that she was involved with?" he presses her.

"As I told you, there was this one guy. This Simon. But I never met him. And I think they split a long time ago. Probably before she moved to Riverside."

"What I'm getting at is this," he says. "She hung out downtown. She was unconventional, a protégée of Andy Warhol . . ."

"I don't think she would have gotten involved with a crazy person, if that's what you're thinking." She hesitates. "In fact, I'm not sure where you're going with this."

"I'm not sure where *you're* going. Someone's torn up her apartment, and not in a collegial way."

"Look. I knew her. Forget the weirdo angle. I'm going to go with greed."

"Well it's my job to explore every angle," Brodsky tells her.

Part Two

At some point, early in her relationship with Angus McLearan, when she knew he was working in the Middle East, Emma had taken it upon herself to learn more about the region. She'd befriended another Columbia professor, Farzin Hatani, a member of her department with a specialty in contemporary Middle Eastern history. He was born in Iran, and his family left the country shortly before the 1979 revolution when the shah was overthrown, a time when those who could—academics, members of the ruling class, high-ranking military—had fled. At some point in their many discussions, Professor Hatani had said of the US-backed shah Mohammad Reza Pahlavi—a man who reigned over Iran for many decades—"I feel I must remind you that the shah was no saint. It was the CIA that put him in power and his rule had become increasingly repressive."

On the first of their visits, when Emma had unashamedly admitted her own lack of knowledge, he'd remarked, "I am no longer surprised by how few Westerners know anything about my country." He'd hesitated a moment, adding, "Or about the region in general." He said it with an air of generosity, pointing to a map that covered the wall behind his desk. "That's why this is my wallpaper."

She'd smiled. "We're terribly provincial, aren't we?"

"Americans? Or New Yorkers?"

"Take your pick," she said, and he'd given her a brief history of US diplomacy in the region, ending with: "As you may know, politically, for the twenty-five years that the shah was in power, my country—Iran—was your country's most important ally in the Middle East. And when the revolution came, when the shah was overthrown in 1979, the balance of power in the Middle East shifted. And the US lost its only friend there—aside from Israel, of course."

This first discussion took place back in 1980, when Angus and Emma had only been together a few years. Back then, the governments of both Iran and Iraq had changed leadership, and the war between Iran and Iraq had just begun. That was seven years ago. For all those years, Angus has been slipping in and out of the region; the Iran-Iraq war has been going on; and for all those years, Farzin Hatani and Emma Quinn have been conversing.

Naturally, when the Iran-Contra story broke in November 1986—first in a Lebanese magazine, then in the American press—Emma had turned to Hatani to get his thoughts. "Well," he'd said, "first, tell me what you know." And she'd basically explained that administration officials had made a deal with Iran—Iran would help with negotiations to free American hostages being held in Lebanon and, in exchange, the US would secretly sell them weapons.

"And . . ." he'd said, professorially.

"And the money from the weapons sale was secretly—"

"And illegally . . ." Hatani added.

". . . Funneled to Contra rebels in Nicaragua by US operatives," Emma had said, wrapping it up. And Hatani had leaned back in his chair and swiveled it slightly.

"So," he said, emphatically, tapping his hand on his desk, "I think you might want to check in with someone who studies Central America. It seems to me your president's obsession with supporting the right-wing Contra rebels in Nicaragua—and destabilizing the socialist government there—has more to do with this scandal than a desire to provide weapons to Iran."

"But what am I missing? Why Iran?"

"Well, if you think about it, it makes sense. You recall the TWA hijacking in 1985?"

"Was that the one that flew all over the place—where they picked out the Jewish passengers?" He nodded. There were so many hijackings in the mideighties that it could be difficult to distinguish one from another. "Then perhaps you remember that Iran played a key role in getting the terrorists to release the passengers."

"Ah," she said. "I'm with you."

"Well, the Iran-Contra deal seems to have been a rather clever game of statesmanship. It seems your president had two goals: to free the Americans being held hostage in Lebanon and to support the Contras in Nicaragua. It is illegal for Reagan to provide arms to the Contras. So, instead, he secretly sold arms to Iran to get money for the Contras in exchange for Iran's help in freeing the American hostages. What you might call a win-win."

"I see," she answered. "But surely Reagan views Iran as our enemy. Why would we willingly give them arms?"

"Not give. Sell."

"But still," she protested, shaking her head.

"You're being naïve, my friend. With all the weapons that are flowing into the Middle East to keep that war going, I imagine the US is selling weapons to both Iran and Iraq. And who knows what other kinds of support your government is providing." Her brow had furrowed, a look Hatani knew well, and he'd gone on to explain. "Look, your government has every reason to want that war to continue. It's smart policy—the war creates mayhem in the region, keeps both countries occupied, and depletes both sides."

"That's a bit cynical, don't you think?"

"It seems realistic to me—particularly in light of this Iran-Contra deal. Of course, your president has yet to be implicated."

"Now, who's being naïve?" she said. And he smiled.

Not long afterward, during Emma's Christmas break, Angus had shown up at the cabin out of nowhere, and they had stayed for nearly a week, uninterrupted. At the time, the Iran-Contra story was still unfolding, and Emma had asked him, outright, what he knew. "We'll go on a hike tomorrow," he'd said. A hike. She knew exactly what that meant. It meant he was willing to answer her question, willing to talk in a safe space. The next day, when they were even farther from civilization than the cabin itself, they sat down on a big, gray rock for a drink—part whisky, part water from a canteen—and for a smoke. It was cold, in the low thirties.

He took a long pull on his cigarette, then held it out in front of him, between two fingers, examining it. They made a pact years ago to indulge in tobacco only when they were together. "I miss these things," he said, smiling, looking up at the sky.

"Perhaps we should spend more time with one another," she said. And he laughed, choking slightly on the exhale.

"Then we'll be forced to give it up altogether, I'm afraid," he said, passing the cigarette to her.

"We'll be old by then." She took a deep inhale, obviously enjoying it. "So, what about this Iran-Contra business? Shall we talk about it?"

"I guess. Although I hate to ruin this beautiful afternoon."

"Are you kidding me? It's freezing."

"Okay. Okay. I know about as much about it as you do," he said, sharing the canteen with her and the cigarette. "This might be interesting to you." She perked up, and he leaned in. "We knew something was going on, but we didn't know exactly what." He shook his head as if he couldn't believe what he was about to say. "Around the time they were trying to make the deal—and based on these news reports that are coming out, it took them a while—we had noticed that Shia terrorist activities were slowing down, and we didn't know why until this thing surfaced."

"What's the connection?" she asked.

"Well, think about it. If the US is in secret negotiations with Iran, the last thing Iran wants is Shia extremists getting in the way. They wanted the weapons. That's a powerful incentive for them to keep things quieter elsewhere in the region."

"So, you suspected something," she said, obviously disappointed. "That's it?"

"That's it."

Emma nodded. "So, you're telling me, one of the outcomes of this imbroglio was a reduction in terrorism."

"Shia terrorism. In the Middle East. But not everywhere." He passed her the canteen and went on a bit about the rise in terrorism in Europe.

"Do you think Bill Kidman was involved?"

"What?" He looked confused.

"With the Iran-Contra transaction."

"I have no way of knowing that. I imagine not directly, but he's got to be looking the other way at this point. It seems pretty obvious that CIA was involved somehow."

"Interesting. You know what else is interesting?" she said, raising her eyebrows. "The news reports say, in the end, only one of the hostages was actually released."

He cocked his head, pensively. "I did *not* know that," he said, obviously impressed, adding—after a slight hesitation: "I guess it just confirms the fact that the primary objective of the operation was to move money to the Contras. Which in turn tells us that someone at the highest level was behind the whole mission."

"You mean the president," Emma said.

"Probably," he said. "Based on my personal experience, nothing of such consequence happens in the intelligence services without orders from the top."

"So, is this something you were . . ." As soon as she started to probe, he leaned forward and took his forefinger and pressed it against her lips, shaking his head slowly. He never spoke about anything he was involved in, not directly anyway.

And on that day, which turned out to be their last day, he actually told her very little. The next morning, in a manner as surreptitious as his arrival, he kissed her on the forehead with a brisk "I'm off," and she hasn't seen him since.

CHAPTER 21

SEAL

About an hour east of Memphis, we exit the interstate onto Route 64 to Plantersville. I am anxious, eager to see the place where I came from, the place my mother escaped. I am twenty-one years old, and I have only met my Aunt Jenny once, although I've spoken to her a dozen times, maybe. On holidays mostly, on the phone and at a great distance. And she is expecting us for dinner.

Simon is driving and listening to the radio, and I'm just watching out the window, ravenous for insights into this peculiar part of the country where I was born.

The landscape is unexpected. It is not green, not in the least, except the trees, huddled together at the edge of the fields, and off in the distance beyond that, tract homes, roof upon roof, and strip malls that line the highway. It is less picturesque than I had imagined it would be. Everything we pass looks brand spanking new, the stores in the strip malls lined up together in neat rows, black prefab roofs, signs in Helvetica caps hanging from them, minimal in a sea of excess, as if to advertise the arrival of retail in McNeely County.

"Recession must have hit them hard. Looks like they had some kind of building boom," Simon says. "And then it just stopped." There are For Sale signs everywhere on big, empty tracts of land on both sides of the highway. "FOR SALE. 100 acres. Zoned commercial." And then another line of stores appears, set on a patch of land, surrounded by an empty parking lot. Simon is doing all the talking. "How many hairdressers and nail salons and martial arts studios do you think this town can really support? I mean, if you can call it a town." And then, "Hey, check that one out. A Mexican restaurant. Too funny." And, finally, "Fuck, it's ugly out here."

After a time, he says, "Now what do you think that is, Luce?" He's pointing to a field that stretches a good distance on the far side of the highway. No silo. No farmhouse. No barn. Nothing so bucolic as that. Just a freestanding field. "That's gotta be a cotton field," he says. It's full of black stalks, which look as if they've been chopped down one by one willy-nilly, then sprinkled with a light dusting of what look like snow-drops. Along its edge is a stand of trees with long, black tendrils that stretch into a white sky with a few gray clouds rolling in. It's desolate.

I don't know what possesses me. I insist that he turn around, go back the other way, so I can get out and see the field, walk it, touch the little puffs of cotton. "Listen," he says, "the market is going to close in thirty minutes. I gotta get to a phone." He tells me I'm crazy. Okay, I get that. He's driven me across the country, and we're almost there. He's made himself available to take me anywhere I want to go for the sake of my mother. And he's in no mood to humor me. But I've never seen a cotton field, never seen the plant itself. "If not now, when?" I say. I'm pulling my boots up from the back seat, and he's pulling up to the field, putting on the breaks hard, waving me out of the car. He's pissed off.

Then there I am standing on the edge of the highway, walking into this field of cotton, hollow black sticks crackling under my feet, my hands in my pockets. There's no sun in sight. It's cold. I reach down and pick up a piece of the cotton, roll it in my frozen fingers. It's dirty and wet, like the stuffing from an old pillow left to mold in the yard. "You're trying too hard, Luce," he yells. "Get in the car."

CHAPTER 22

Seal's studio is something else altogether. It is a massive space, with four substantial worktables, designed so that the natural light comes in through a series of east-facing windows, but it's a cloudy day. The space feels dark and already looks as if it's been abandoned. There are photographs strewn about and sketches of some kind on a worktable. A few of the closets are open. And the floor has been torn up at one end of the loft, as well as a wall, as if it were undergoing a renovation. The place has that musty smell you'd associate with age or abandon.

"Do you think she did this?" Bill Kidman says, pointing to the flooring that's been dislodged.

"It's impossible to know," Emma says.

"Impossible?" he asks. "Who would have been here before? Who would know?"

"Maybe Merna."

"What about this Lynley Wright? That was her dealer, right?"

"Not exactly. But I can check with her. And with the Lorches."

"Lorches?" his brow furrows.

"Anna Lorch represented Seal at some point. I met her and her son quite a few years ago, maybe 1982 or 1983. Anna Lorch had a gallery in the East Village, and Seal had a show there. I imagine Anna Lorch might have come by the studio to see her work."

There's a sleeping area at the opposite end of the loft that seems undisturbed. A sliver of morning light has broken through the clouds and is coming through the east-facing windows. They are covered in a gauzy fabric that casts a weblike shadow across the room, where the ray of light picks up two highball glasses on a coffee table.

"You'll want to get our friend Brodsky over here. Get those glasses to the lab," Kidman says. "What the . . . ?" he says, startled by a massive gorilla mask hanging on a coatrack by the closet door.

"Omigosh, she was a Guerrilla Girl," Emma says, smiling, grabbing the mask. "Of course she was."

"A gorilla girl?"

She is holding up the mask by its hair. "You know, guerrilla. Like a guerrilla movement, not a gorilla in Africa. Like an urban guerrilla. Guerrilla Girls. It's a feminist group. Well known. Protesters. Feminists with a sense of humor."

"I didn't know such a thing existed."

"Very funny," she says, sarcastically. But still, she's smiling broadly, examining the mask. It's made of rubber, designed to go over the head. "I love this," she says. Then, turning to Kidman: "They've been around a couple of years now. Protesting the fact that women aren't sufficiently represented in or respected by the art world."

He shoots her a confused look, and she explains: "Meaning, for example, their work isn't featured as often in museums and major exhibits."

He shakes his head. "Well, I've never heard of them."

"Why does that not surprise me? They did this poster—'Do women have to be naked to get into the Met?'—something like that. With an image of a nude female, a statue. I don't remember exactly. But it was smart, funny."

Kidman shrugs as if he doesn't get it, and she knows he's teasing her. He turns his attention to the closet. It's stocked with all kinds of clothes—jeans, boots, furs and costumes, some of which are pictured in Cindy Sherman-esque self-portraits that Seal had been experimenting with; those photos fill her darkroom and cover one of the worktables. There is a shelf full of wigs, most of them gray- or white-haired, a few are platinum blonde. Later, in the darkroom, she finds a few negatives of men wearing these wigs, young men mostly, shot against a light background. One of them looks uncannily like Rolley Smythe, her former grad student, the one who wants to meet for a drink. But it's a negative and he's wearing a wig, and Emma says to herself, "Impossible. That's impossible." And shakes it off.

CHAPTER 23

SEAL

Feels like Simon and I are getting closer to town. Every now and then we pass a small, nondescript square box of a house on a little hill up from the highway, made of brick or wood with no distinctive architectural details, no charm, a few trees in the yard. Maybe dating back to the 1930s or '40s. There are no signs of people anywhere. Just traffic passing through. I try to imagine what kind of people live in these houses. People who chop their own wood, I think; and mow their lawns with tractors; and have nasty-looking dogs and go to church on Sunday and watch TV at night because there is nothing else to do, the light from the cathode ray tubes shining from their windows. I'm thinking they go to Bob's Big Boy for dinner, although there are no Bob's Big Boys in sight. I am a snob. That is clear to me. And maybe my mother was a snob. And I wonder how she became one. Maybe just by living in this godforsaken place and feeling like an outsider. Maybe that's the truth I'm going to find. I imagine an uncomfortable evening with the sister she left behind.

We can see an old cemetery rising up on a hill, surrounded by barbed wire. Beyond that is a gated community—"Magnolia Heights" written in a lavish script at the entry. No trees. Just big postmodern houses with arched windows that seem out of place, and two- and three-car garages. "Starting at $45,000," the sign says. Looks as if people just sold off their property to anyone who would buy it and let them put up anything they wanted.

Obviously, it wasn't like this when my mother lived here. She told me how, growing up, she would walk across the road, which is now Highway 64, to Deaver's Store to get supplies and how there was nothing else within miles. And, how, after what she calls "the apocryphal incident," she couldn't even go there. It occurs to me, traveling now on Highway 64, probably within shooting distance of the old place, that she has told me a thousand times in a thousand different ways why she left.

Of all the stories she ever told me, it's the one I'll never forget. "Let me tell you what it was like on that farm," she'd say. "Let me tell you about Mr. Deaver. One day, oh, I must have been a teenager, and I walked across to Deaver's to get a Coca-Cola or something. And I was standing in line at the cash register behind an older man, a Black man who lived around there. Mr. Deaver was white. I was in line behind this old man, and Mr. Deaver looked right past that man to me and said, 'How can I help you, young lady?' I knew full well that was wrong, but I didn't know what to do. I didn't say anything or do anything. I just went ahead and paid for my stuff and left. Imagine that. It was the 1950s, for God's sake, and Mr. Deaver treating that grown man like he wasn't even there. I told your Nanaw about it, and she said she was never going back to Deaver's place, even though it was right across the street. She told me I couldn't go back either. I knew in my soul I should've said something to Mr. Deaver like, 'I believe there's someone ahead of me.' Or I could have just walked out, I guess. Everybody at the counter was watching me and probably expecting me to do something like that because they knew my mother. But I didn't want to make a big deal about it. And, let me tell you, I regret it to this day."

The way my mother described it, that man in front of her in the store lived in one of those run-down shacks off the road, one room with a space heater in it, and holes between the timbers in the walls. Places I thought weren't real, but they are. She described it to me many times. "That's another reason I had to get you out of there," she'd say, whatever story she was telling. There was a whole list of reasons why my mother had to get me out of McNeely County, but I think the real reason was she had to get herself out of McNeely County. "It's the kind of place that makes you feel ashamed," she said. And she said it more than once.

At this point, Simon and I are maybe thirty minutes off the interstate. The landscape turns back into country again. Simon is looking for the sign that says "Holder Farm," the one I wrote down in the directions. It's supposed to be posted at the edge of a field not far from the last town. At this point, there are nothing but trees and fields and hills; and the highway running like a river through it. Not a house in sight. Simon steps on the gas then, and a few seconds later a police car pulls up behind us, lights flashing. "Shit," Simon says. He's probably doing forty-five in a forty zone. It's almost dark, and Simon has missed the market close, and he's not happy.

"We're lost," he tells the policeman.

"Where you trying to get to?"

"The Holder Farm."

"Well, that's exactly where you are," the cop says, sweeping his hand across the west side of the highway, which is just a row of trees and brush. "Where you from?" he asks Simon. But I decide to answer. "Sir. My name is Lucille Lawson. And my mother grew up on this farm."

"Lawson," he says. "You married to him?"

"No."

"What's her Christian name? Your mother's."

"Maggie. Maggie Lawson."

"Maggie Grace? Maggie Grace was your mother?" he says, shining the flashlight in my face. "You favor her," he says, then pointing the flashlight at Simon, he asks, "And what's your name, son?"

"Simon. Simon Golding."

The policeman grunts, slips the flashlight back onto his belt and throws his arm off to the left. "Well, you're looking at it. The farm, that is. You done passed Miss Jenny's place. They moved her a few years ago."

"Moved her?"

"Yeah. The house. They picked it up and moved the whole damn thing. It's back that way."

"And who is they?" Simon asks.

"They?"

"Who moved her?" says Simon.

"The Holders, of course. When the county started talking about making the highway bigger, they moved the old farmhouse down Thomason Road, back past them new houses. They were gonna move that little house, too, but the damn thing fell apart."

I didn't know anything about it, so I ask the cop why, and he shrugs and says, "Wanted some privacy, I guess. They were right up on the traffic. You know, they got two thousand acres back there."

"Yeah. We heard that," says Simon.

"Just do a U-turn up ahead and come back to Thomason, opposite that old cemetery and take a right. She stays about a mile down that road, past all the new houses. Can't miss it. Pretty old place." Then he turns and starts to walk away. "And mind the speed limit, Mr. Golding. We keep an eye on it around here. You're gonna get stopped again with those New York plates."

CHAPTER 24

"Follow the money." That's what Kidman had advised. But he's gone now. Back to Washington. Emma and Detective Brodsky are following separate tracks. She hasn't seen him in days. Relying on Kidman's instincts, Emma had contacted Lynley Wright—her fellow executor—and Harriet Freeman—the estate attorney.

They met, the three of them, at Lynley's office on Fifth Avenue, in the shadow of the new Trump Tower. It was clear from the start that the two did not know each another well. Harriet seemed stiff, uncomfortable, and they were patronizing to each other in equal measure. Emma began with a few questions about the estate itself—the extent of Seal's wealth and the source of the trust fund. They were not helpful. Or rather, Harriet was not helpful. Lynley Wright just shook her head. "Not my bailiwick," she said, deferring to Harriet. And again, Harriet maintained that she was bound by a confidentiality agreement. "As I've told you, I can't share that information," she said.

"Where is Andy Warhol's portrait of Seal?" Emma asked Lynley at one point. "It's not among her things."

"No. It's in a vault. I have it stored with some of my more valuable pieces."

"More valuable pieces?"

"She owns a few gems—a painted photograph by Gerhard Richter, a William Christenberry."

Emma didn't recognize the names and plowed ahead. "The portrait," she said. "I would think that with Warhol's death, it would have increased in value."

"I'm not sure that's going to be the case," Lynley said, in a tone that always seemed to verge on patronizing. "Apparently, he had an abundance of unsold work, and, at the moment, his prices are going down. In fact, I'm advising clients to buy now. But there's not been a lot of interest."

"Do you think this could have been about her work?" Emma asked. "Doesn't an artist's work typically increase in value after they die?"

"Seal's work wouldn't fall into that category. She's not big enough." She put a stress on the word big, her jaw protruding slightly.

"So why was she working with you then?" Emma asked, interested in determining whether Lynley's answer might be different from the explanation Harriet had given when they first met—which was, essentially, because of Ms. Wright's connection to the Warhol estate.

"I'm not a dealer," Lynley explained. "I'm an advisor. My clients are banks, businesses, corporations. I work for the collectors, not the artists. I help them find art. Some of my clients prefer photography to an abstract painting or maybe they'd rather hang a reasonably priced piece on their office walls than one that's part of their investment portfolio.

Of course, some of them just like the look of black-and-white photos. It's minimal, sophisticated."

"So, it's not about the work itself."

"Well, they're not hanging Diane Arbus on their walls for decoration. I'm talking about architects and design firms. People who, well, again, are going for a certain look. I have a few architect clients that bought Seal's photographs and a few investors who see some potential in her work. She was doing well, making a name for herself," Lynley said. "Some of her photos appeared in *Rolling Stone* last year. That spurred some interest. Her work wasn't expensive, but her prices were going up."

"Everyone's prices have been going up," Harriet said.

"Except Warhol's?" Emma interjected.

"I'm sure his prices will as well," Lynley said. "There's no question of that. As I'm sure you're aware, we are in the midst of a revolution where art has truly become a commodity."

"And that doesn't bother you," Harriet said. It was a statement, not a question.

"Of course not," Lynley said, chipper, light. "It's how I make my living."

"Yes," Harriet said. She made no effort to hide her disdain. "I'm well aware."

Lynley just shook it off. "Anyway, most of my clients are looking for well-established artists. Or emerging artists with a high profile. The instantly famous are obviously the most appealing. A Jean-Michel Basquiat. Or a Keith Haring."

Harriet rolled her eyes. "The *It Boys*," she said.

But Lynley ignored her and went on: "I work closely with Citibank's people, to help them find art for investment portfolios. That's how I built my relationship with Mr. Warhol. He connected me with Seal. Or rather, he sent Seal to me so I could introduce her work to my clients."

"Why did she choose you to be an executor?"

"A lot of reasons. One, because I have physical control over some of her pieces, including the Warhol portrait. A lot of her work is stored in our vaults. And, once you've gone through her things, I will store whatever we recover from her studio. Two, I'm in a position to sell whatever Harriet and I agree needs to be sold, and to make informed decisions in that regard. Three, I have the contacts to facilitate the sale and distribution of Seal's work through any number of dealers. We've planned a show with Anna Lorch, just out of respect for that relation-ship. But I have the authority to look elsewhere."

"Are you working on commission?" Emma asked Lynley.

"Flat fee. Anna Lorch is working on commission," said Lynley. "But, for the record, these pieces won't bring anyone a windfall."

Harriet, who had been listening intently to this entire exchange, jumped in again at this point. "If you're suggesting that any of us stands to profit from her death, I think you're on the wrong track."

"I'm not suggesting anything. I'm just trying to understand the pro-cess here," Emma said. Harriet nodded, and Lynley leaned back in her chair, and Emma began to feel as if this was going nowhere. "Just one more question," she said. "Where will the money go when you sell her work? And where will anything go that doesn't sell? She has no heirs, am I right? Or is her aunt an heir?"

"Seal wants—sorry, wanted—to use her money to establish a scholarship at the New School. Her sales will contribute to that fund, and anything that doesn't sell will go to an archive at the New School," Harriet said. "And, just for the record, I don't imagine her death has anything to do with her art." She hesitated for a moment, looking directly at Emma. "Anything to do with its value, anyway."

"Meaning?"

"Well, who knows what kinds of people she met through her art? That's what I mean."

***

Emma left the meeting frustrated, with no greater insight into what may have led to Seal's death—aside from the implication that she may have drawn unsavory characters into her life. She felt as if she'd asked all the wrong questions, wasting her time and theirs. En route to the police station, she feels ill-prepared to sit down with Tomas Brodsky, incapable of bringing anything new or substantive to the table. When she arrives, she finds that he's pinned up images on his boards of just about everyone he knows was associated with Lucille Lawson, down to the super at the building and Emma herself. There are also photos of

Merna, Harriet, Lynley, the Lorches and Simon Golding on his wall. That's who he wants to talk about now.

"So, what do you know about this fellow," he asks Emma, pointing at Simon's image. It's the first time Emma has seen Simon's face. He was not a classically handsome man, but Emma can see that he had a certain animal magnetism. The dark eyes, the dark curly hair, the intensity.

"Where is he now?" Emma asks.

"California. Married. Has a kid," Brodsky says. "Any idea how close they were?"

"Not really. Like I said, they split up before I met her. I can't imagine she would have stayed in touch with him. She said he was a bully."

"That's it?"

"I know he was involved in finance, somehow. And—I don't quite know how to put this—but I think she said he was, and I quote, a bit of an asshole."

"Ahh," he said in his characteristic way. "Well, this asshole works for Salomon Brothers and, according to her phone records, she'd been getting a lot of calls from their offices of late."

CHAPTER 25

SEAL

This is what I remember about my first visit with Aunt Jenny: Simon and I are sitting at her kitchen table, drinking beer. She's put out a bowl of pretzels for us. Her husband is gone, left early in the morning, and she's feeding the dogs, which seems to be a fairly elaborate ritual. There are four of them, all brown, but different sizes, like they all might have come from the same mother and different fathers. Which according to Aunt Jenny is exactly what happened. "We had one brown dog," she says. "And she had four litters. We kept one pup from every litter. Quite a brood. Probably best that she died young." She says it with laughing eyes, the way my mother might, spinning something dark into something light. And she looks just like my mother when she says it.

She makes good work of it, talking to the dogs while she organizes everything. "It's comin'. It's comin'," she tells them. They are sitting in a row, watching every move she makes. Panting. She's washing each of the dog bowls at the sink and wiping them clean, scooping the dog food out from a big barrel. Then she takes a big lump of peanut butter, puts it on a spoon and stirs it around in each of their dinners. When Simon asks, she explains, "Makes 'em eat faster, so they stick to their own bowl. Your grandmother taught me that little trick," she says, looking at me. "She was a genius with animals."

I am keenly aware that this was my mother's place growing up, the kitchen where she first learned to cook. "You're the reason I'm such a good cook," my mother once told me. "I was home so much when you were a baby and wasn't much else to do."

I ask Aunt Jennifer if this was the way the house looked when they were little. "Well, pretty much. Big difference is the directions all changed around when we moved it, and that changes everything. Used to be, we faced due south. Now we face due east, so the sun comes in through the main bedroom in the morning. And, at night, we can watch it set from the screen porch here. Kitchen doesn't get much light in the morning anymore. That's the downside. We used to eat breakfast on this porch here in the mornings, but that's not so nice anymore. And we got the gardens in a different place. But, otherwise, the inside's about the same." Simon and I are going to be staying in the bedroom where my mother and I had slept when I was a baby. The other bedroom, where my Aunt Jenny and her husband sleep, what she calls the main bedroom, is the one Jenny had shared with their mother after I was born. She explains all that. I don't sleep very well for soaking up the feeling of it.

The whole house has a dusty quality. The front door opens right into the living room, a long, thin room with a brick fireplace on the outer wall and a worn, old, braided rug at its center. The TV is in the fireplace.

What must be some sort of reclining chair sits in one corner, covered with a sheet. And the sofa and the oval coffee table look like something you might see in a Salvation Army store. It takes me a minute to figure out why the room looks so bleak. It's not the sorry-looking furniture or the odd placement of the television; it's the fact that there is no art. There are no photographs. There's not even a knickknack or a magazine or a book. It feels bleak because it is bleak. It feels temporary, like no one really lives here. And it smells of dogs and dust.

We can see the living room from the table in the kitchen. I can, anyway. Simon is facing the screen porch, where the dogs have now been dispatched to eat their dinner. "Don't get up," my aunt says, when Simon starts to help her out. "It'll just confuse 'em," she says.

"I'm not the cook your mama was," she says, taking out a few cooking pots, a bag of potatoes, a pack of spinach from the freezer. She pulls a can of black-eyed peas off the shelf and starts to open it, her back toward us.

"We're going to Memphis tomorrow to go see the Holders," I tell her, looking at Simon. He rolls his eyes and turns his head up, as if, for God's sake, why bring it up? And I give him a look and a shrug that's meant to say, "What's the problem?" My aunt doesn't even turn around, doesn't say anything, pours the peas into a pot and flicks on the gas.

"They were very hospitable when I called," I tell her.

"Oh, they're hospitable all right," she says. "They're experts at hospitality. They're professionally polite." She still hasn't turned around. She's looking down, stirring the black-eyed peas.

Then she reaches for the trash can and sets it beside my seat, turns back and pulls a paring knife out of a drawer. She slams it shut and drops the sack of potatoes in front of me on the table and tosses the kitchen knife down beside my beer. "How would you like to peel these potatoes for me, missy?" she says.

If she weren't my aunt, I might not have seen it. But I can see the anger welling up in her in the same way it used to well up in my mother. She is trying to control it. I can see that. But it's there, just the same. She turns away from us again, starts on the cornbread. She's moving deliberately, concentrating, measuring out the cornmeal, pouring in the boiling water, whisking, moving around us, without speaking, without looking up. Reminding me of my mother.

Simon's sipping on his beer. "Sometimes, Luce doesn't know when to leave well enough alone," he says.

"Well, she comes by that honest," Aunt Jenny says. She puts the cornbread in the oven and turns to us then. It's clear that she wants to let it go. She slaps her hands on her apron, and her voice gets all breezy-like. "Now, tonight we're going to have a home-cooked southern meal. Not a restaurant-style one. If you can peel those potatoes, honey, I'll mash 'em up. And we'll have a good old-fashioned vegetable plate with some cornbread right out of the oven. How about you grab me one of those beers, Mr. Simon."

"Will do," Simon says, breezy himself.

But I won't let it go. "I'm glad we're going. I want to meet them."

"Why on earth?" Aunt Jenny says, sipping her beer. "I've never even been in their house myself."

"I'm doing it for my mother," I say, proudly, foolishly. "So, they'll see how she raised me. I want them to see that we're respectable people."

"Well, thank you, Miss New York. I've been doing that my whole life. And let me tell you something. They're not thinking about you. And, what's more, we don't need to be thinking about them."

She turns back to the stove, agitated, pushing the black-eyed peas around in the pot with jerky motions. Then she wheels around again, waving a spoon at me in precisely the same way my mother would have. The resemblance startles me, the way her eyes narrow and her face reddens, the glare, the spoon waving in my direction. "And let me tell you something else," she says, setting the spoon down on the counter and wiping her hands again on the towel tucked in at her waist. "This may be a hard lesson for you, little missy, but nothing you do or say is going to change what they think. Because they don't think. They're not like you and me. They got their minds made up about everything before it even starts. They're not interested in facts," she says. "Now give me those potatoes."

CHAPTER 26

"Her beauty was magnetic," Merna says of Maggie Grace, pouring boiling water into a stoneware pot. "Come," she says, setting the pot down. "This can wait." She leads Emma toward the back of her living room to an elevator that takes them down a level and opens into a long hallway on the ground floor. Emma can hear the clatter of dishes and chitter-chatter of voices beyond. The sounds of the kitchen coming to life. The wall is covered with photographs of people eating and drinking and smoking, like something out of the 1940s, when photographers would table-hop at the city's clubs and restaurants, and everyone was dressed for the moment. Some of the subjects are luminaries. Musicians and actors. Politicians. Intellectuals. Emma recognizes quite a few of them. Louis Armstrong. Charlie Mingus. Ossie Davis and Ruby Dee. There's a photo of Mayor Lindsay, young and all smiles, obviously taken during his tenure. Even seated, he towered over everyone else. And there are others—Susan Sontag, Tom Wolfe, James Baldwin. Merna hovers over the Baldwin photograph, brushes it with her fingertips. "What a great man. You recognize him, don't you?" she says. Emma nods, and she goes on. "He used to come in whenever he was in town. Smart man. Gentleman. Haven't seen him in a long time." She takes a deep breath. Moves on.

"As you can see, we were mighty popular back in the day," Merna says. By "back in the day," she means in the sixties and seventies. They arrive at a wall of rock and pop stars, all performing on the same outdoor venue. Stevie Wonder. Sly and the Family Stone. Mavis Staples. "The Harlem festival in 1969," she says, unmoving. "Looky here." Emma draws closer. "Nina Simone," Merna says. "Whooooo. That woman was on fire."

"This way," she says, drawing Emma toward the entrance to the restaurant itself. "Here she is. And here they are together." The photos are set in simple black frames. Emma is struck by the ethereal quality of Seal's mother, Maggie Grace. She is slight, fine-boned with dark eyebrows and a mane of light hair. Seal and her mother are twins, except that Maggie's smile exudes a warmth that she's never noticed in Seal's. There's a larger photo of the three of them—Merna, Maggie and Seal. "That's the day we opened. Saturday, October 15, 1966." Maggie looks to be in her twenties; Seal is a young girl, maybe nine or ten. Merna's hair is graying.

Nearby is an image of Maggie Grace sitting at a table with an elegant older man, probably in his sixties. Seal stands behind the man with an arm wrapped over one of his shoulders and her head resting on the other. "Who's this?" Emma asks.

"Oh, that's Leo Castelli," says Merna. "He was a regular customer for a long time. Brought the art crowd in."

"He's an artist?"

"Where have you been living? He's about the most famous art dealer in Manhattan. And here he is with Marian Goodman. She started a gallery on the Upper West Side and produced wonderful things—art books, three-dimensional sculptures, lithographs—things that people could actually afford to buy. Maggie Grace admired her so. It's those kinds of people that introduced her to art—and to artists."

"You mean to Andy Warhol?"

"Oh no. No. No. No. Andy Warhol introduced himself. He saw the two of them—Maggie Grace and Lucille—on the street near Penn Station before they even moved here and invited them up to the Factory. That's how the story goes, as I recall it anyway. Just visiting and they meet Andy Warhol." She starts back down the hall. "Come on," she says, leading Emma toward the elevator. "I'll tell you all about it."

CHAPTER 27

SEAL

My mother was one of Marian Goodman's many admirers. I don't know if I'd call them friends. But they did know each other, and Marian Goodman definitely had a profound influence on my mother. That's about all I can tell you about their relationship.

I imagine they met through the school, but I was just a kid at the time. Her kids also went to Walden. As I got older, I'd see her there. She was a tiny woman, but she's become a real powerhouse in the art world. In the beginning, she had this co-op in her apartment on the Upper West Side. Then, she opened this store called Multiples—she sold just what the name says: multiples. Lithographs and prints, some were limited editions. I think she published art books as well. When we first set up our place, my mother covered the walls with prints from Multiples. I'd bet the first piece of original art she ever acquired was something she found through Marian Goodman.

Goodman's been recognized for changing the market, because she made contemporary art affordable, available to more people. Plus, she had a talent for identifying talent—emerging artists who would become big names. And European artists. She's the one who introduced my mother to the work of Gerhard Richter. Plus, I mean, how many galleries were owned by women? Not many, I'd guess. She was a real pioneer. I remember, around the time my mother got sick, Marian Goodman was opening a gallery on East Fifty-Seventh. That was a big deal. And I think she actually represented Gerhard Richter. Anyway, she's credited with bringing his work to America. That was a big deal too. And I think she represented Nan Goldin. You know—the iconoclastic photographer. But I'm not sure. I adore her work. These are people who were doing something new, something daring and original—and accessible. Good stuff. Not like some of the Pop trash we're seeing now. That stuff is kind of a joke. Patronizing even.

My mother adored Gerhard Richter. He's extraordinary. The range of his work alone is mind-boggling—painted photographs, photographic realism, collage, experiments with glass, painting with squeegees and these ethereal drawings. He has that perfect balance—a gift for experimentation and playfulness, but a level of training and craftsmanship that's obvious in everything he does.

Around like 1982 or 1983, he did these amazing photorealistic paintings of skulls and of candles. I read somewhere that they "hover brilliantly between the precise and the vague." I've never forgotten that description. "Hovering between the precise and the vague." That's perfect. I can see those paintings even now in my imagination. They were perfectly real and perfectly ghostly at the same time. God only knows what Gerhard Richter is doing now. Just an amazing artist. And Marian Goodman is an amazing dealer. That's a killer pair.

CHAPTER 28

"It started when Maggie Grace first arrived. That summer before Lucille went to school, she'd take her over to the Metropolitan Museum and the Museum of Natural History on Fifth Avenue. To keep the child entertained, you know." Merna is looking off into the distance as she speaks. "Course, they didn't know a soul. Just us. Then one day, they went to the Museum of Modern Art. She couldn't get enough of it. And pretty soon, it wasn't for Lucy anymore. It was for Maggie Grace. Course, the benefits went to Lucy too—to Seal. She has the spirit of an artist." Merna takes a deep breath and looks up at the ceiling. They are back in her apartment and, for the first time, Emma notices that there's a mobile in the corner of the room. Why she hadn't seen it before, she doesn't know. Either it's a terrific knockoff of an Alexander Calder, she thinks, or it's an original. It consists of black and red kidney-shaped disks and smaller oval ones, suspended from wires and black rods of curved metal, like hypothetical birds flying beneath the ceiling. Merna turns her eyes back to Emma before she speaks.

"I remember," Merna says. "Late one afternoon I went into our kitchen, downstairs. We were working on dinner, and she pulled me away. She could be very insistent. She said she saw Picasso's masterpiece and that she cried real tears standing there in the museum. She told me I had to see it."

"Which masterpiece?"

"The painting of the war in Spain, with the giant bull in it. The one that's like a scream on canvas. The *Gwer*. . ." she stumbles over the pronunciation. "*Guernica*. I may not be saying it right, but I know you've heard of it." Emma nods. "Well, she dragged me down kicking and screaming—*the next morning*—to look at it." Merna shakes her head. Makes a kind of a "humph" of a sound under her breath. "Damned if I didn't cry like a baby myself. Good Lord, how could you not?" Merna has a firmness about her, a directness that says, *Don't mess with me.* But at the same time, she doesn't hide her humanity. Emma is trying to compare her to Annie Daniels, the woman who half raised her, the woman who managed her grandparents' household. In order to do her job, Emma thinks, Annie had taken on white mannerisms, white ways, whether consciously or unconsciously. It seems to Emma that Merna Jones has found a way to succeed in a white world on her own terms.

"That was the beginning of it. That Picasso," Merna goes on. "Then she fell in love. And I mean, in love, with this artist."

Emma tilts her head slightly.

"A German, no less," Merna says. "This Gerhard Richter."

"How did they meet?"

"Oh no. I don't mean in love with the man. I mean in love with his work, his art, his painting. You know, she was political, Maggie Grace was. I think it went back to living on that farm and what she saw in that town and in that little house on that farm. And remember, we lived in Mississippi." She reaches for a platter of cookies. "Here. Have another," she says. But Emma waves her off with a thank-you and a nod. "I didn't move up here until 1965," Merna continues. "Maggie Grace and Lucy came up in 1966. So, we were down there when the civil rights pot was boiling over. We'd already been through the integration of Ole Miss, and all the anger bubbling up around us. Then Medgar got shot in Jackson, and those two white boys from Chicago got killed. Of course, I guess that's when the world started paying attention. None of that surprised us. You can't live in Mississippi without choosing sides. Anyway, she was political. And she loved the Kennedys." She draws out the word "loved" like it was a snake. "When he was killed, the president . . ." She just shakes her head, lets the words hang there. She's still for a moment, then plows ahead.

"Anyways, Maggie Grace sent Seal to that school, that Walden School, and like I said, she made friends there who were all about art." Merna pauses for an instant, then goes on, "That's when she fell in love with Richter. He did this picture of Jackie Kennedy and Lyndon Johnson together. It was from a photograph that appeared in the paper, when Johnson took the oath of office on the airplane and Jackie was by his side. You remember that? After the assassination. It was famous."

"Actually, I do. She was wearing that pink suit that was splattered with blood."

"It was an iconic photograph. Andy Warhol did his *Thirty-Five Jackies* based on that image. Well, this photograph was taken at the same time. Not during the oath exactly. But Lyndon Johnson's standing beside her, as if he's comforting her. It was published in a German magazine after the assassination. Gerhard Richter did some sort of a drawing or painting from it, and Maggie Grace got a print of that piece. I only know all this because she was obsessed with it." As Merna stops for a moment to take a breath, Emma realizes that Merna is finding the conversation comforting, as if by releasing this history, this knowledge, she's holding on to it, holding on to Maggie Grace. "I guess that was the beginning.

Then Maggie Grace and the ladies who owned that store where they sold the prints, they got close," she goes on. "And Maggie Grace began meeting people and sending them to the restaurant. She started going to art shows downtown. And to openings and parties. That's where she met Mr. Castelli. He introduced her to the up-and-coming artists. And when she started buying art, he helped her with that. I thought it was foolishness, until I realized that it wasn't."

"So, Seal's mother was a collector?" And it clicks, the note in her obituary—art lover, Seal's love of art and understanding of it, her interest in photography. Maggie Grace was a collector.

"Of course," Merna says, and just keeps talking. "One advantage was that Lucy—or Seal, as you say—grew up with the most beautiful art all around her. I think that's what made her a photographer. And it's what changed Maggie Grace's life. Also, there were several artists, men, who became her . . . her friends. Of course, nothing ever came of that. But the collection was something else. And, you probably know what a good piece goes for these days. Tens of thousands of dollars or hundreds of thousands even. Her collection would be worth a fortune."

"Well, what happened to it?"

"What do you mean?"

"Where is it?"

"Last time I saw it, it was hanging on the walls in their apartment on Seventy-Second Street."

"That would be when?"

"Well, it'd be before they moved out. That winter—1978 or 1979. That winter before she died."

CHAPTER 29

Robert Love—the man who is subletting Emma's apartment—is in Turkey at a crossroads not far from the Syrian border. There's a small building there, an abandoned outpost. The terrain is flat with brown-green grasses and mountains in the far distance. The scene has a feel of an American western—the dry landscape, a lone man sitting on a simple wooden bench on the porch of a wood-frame building. Love is dressed in khaki and a broad-rimmed, olive green fedora fashioned of oilcloth—outfitted, in other words, rather like an Indiana Jones. But, bespectacled and reed thin, he is no swashbuckler. His white hair is hidden under the hat, but the skin on his face—splotchy, pink, almost sheer—betrays his age. The look serves him well. No one would figure him for a foreign agent. His temporary ID from Columbia University identifies him as a guest of the archaeology department, a visiting professor.

The building where he waits, listening for the sound of a motorcycle and sipping water from a canteen, is probably an old checkpoint along the border. Nearby is the Turkish city of Nusaybin in the province of Mardin. Beyond it are fertile fields that surround the town of Tepeüstü, and beyond that, the mountains. To the south, Syria—Iran's sole Middle Eastern ally in the war against Iraq, a war that has been going on for nearly seven years now—is relatively quiet at the moment.

Robert Love is waiting for a fellow professor from the University of Edinburgh, the illustrious Angus McLearan, author of *The End of Communism as We Know It*, friend of Emma Quinn and fellow MI6 agent.

Angus peels in at a little after noon, Turkish time, kicking up dust. He pulls off his helmet and a kerchief that covers his mouth and takes a deep swallow from a metal cannister.

"Robby," he calls out. He is tanned from his time on the Mediterranean Sea. That and his untamed beard make him look like a local.

Love rises, smiling. "Welcome to the cradle of civilization, you bastard," he says. He tosses Angus a small backpack as he approaches the motorcycle. "Three rolls. In one metal tin," he says.

"Good. Do we know who took them? And where?"

"One of yours, where the shipment arrived. In Jordan. Should be clear proof."

"Jordan."

"Everything moves through Jordan," Love says.

"From where?"

"This flight was originally from Britain via Germany."

"Good. And what the hell are you doing over here?"

"A dig in the mountains. About ready to go back."

"Yeah. Well, we need to talk," Angus says, his voice tinged with anger.

"I know. I had a telegram from New York." Love is eyeing the landscape, avoiding Angus's gaze.

"Did you have anything in her apartment? Anything at all?" Angus says.

"No."

"You told me you weren't doing any work for the bureau over there."

"That's correct. Research. Purely academic. There are Turkish antiquities at the Met, and in Boston and Philadelphia. That, and Columbia is funding this dig, which puts me right where I want to be. Two birds. One stone."

The sun is burning a hole in the sky. And they're standing out in the open in a remote spot. Still, they are both on high alert and eager to wrap this up quickly, to move on. "Could someone have been looking for you?" Angus asks, the edge still in his voice.

Love pulls his sunglasses out of his breast pocket and slips them on casually. "Not likely," he says. "You know I'm inactive. I'm seventy-two years old, for Christ's sake."

"What about this transaction?"

"This is about it. For the year. Just a courier. Nothing more. And only because it made sense. Here we both are." He shrugs, making light of it, and Angus grabs him by the collar. Gently, but as a clear warning.

"If I find out otherwise . . . If I find out that you put her at risk or endangered her friend. And if I find out you're lying . . ."

"You won't. I assure you," Love says, brushing his hand against Angus's as if he were swatting a fly, and then pulling away.

"I've known you a long time, Robby." Angus shoots him a skeptical look. "I'm going to try and trust you," he says, then squats down to examine the contents of the bag.

"You'll find everything's in order, Mac." Love shifts gears easily, smoothly, collegially. "You have time to run into Tepeüstü for a drink?" he says. But the answer is a no, delivered as a shake of the head.

"I have to get back. Headed for Belgium in the morning." Angus nods toward the empty building, adding, "Any facilities in there?"

"See for yourself," Love says, turning away. And he's inside his Jeep before Angus even reaches the porch.

CHAPTER 30

Emma is alone in Seal's studio, in the small kitchenette built into the west wall between the workspace and the sleeping area, near where the floor has been torn up. She is rifling through the refrigerator—tossing an old carton of half-and-half, a container of Chinese food, a hunk of Parmesan cheese. The smell is not pretty. She wonders when Seal was last here and how often she would have stayed here, slept here, met people here. In the freezer, she finds a plastic container that holds a half dozen cannisters of film, color film, undeveloped. She checks the cabinets and the kitchen drawers. The deepest is half filled with boxes of unused film and a handful of cannisters containing undeveloped black-and-white images. She finds a cannister that contains what seems to be cocaine.

She wants to go through the old sheet-metal file cabinet in the back closet near the bed, the one that's locked, see if she can find any financial records. So far, they've not located a computer. Heading toward the closet, something seems off. During her last visit, she and Bill Kidman had toyed with the gorilla mask. They'd removed the highball glasses for the prints, nosed through the closet and unlocked the file cabinet just to get a sense of what was inside. Emma would return, they'd agreed, to go through everything carefully. She's certain they'd hung the gorilla mask back up on the hat rack, but it's lying on the floor beside the bed. And, when she opens the closet, there are piles of manila envelopes strewn around the floor. She goes back to the front of the studio and checks the worktables. They are exactly as they'd left them, with photographs tossed willy-nilly all over the tabletops. She realizes then that someone had been in the studio before she and Kidman. And someone has come back, looking for something. She calls Brodsky, leaves word.

The file cabinet is rusty and stained from years of use. One drawer is full of old checkbooks and stubs, another stuffed with bills. They are not Seal's records. They are her mother's, Maggie Grace's, going back to the midsixties. In the third drawer, Emma finds hanging files. They contain images clipped from magazines or newspapers, exhibit catalogs and printed invitations for shows at private galleries going back two decades. They are neatly organized. She finds a file folder labeled "Financial" and another labeled "Portfolio," containing images of paintings, serious paintings that look as if they could be hanging in a museum, each image numbered and dated. She wants Brodsky to see them, and maybe Lynley Wright and Harriet Freeman.

The last drawer, the bottom drawer, is empty and clearly where all the envelopes that are now strewn about were originally stored. The envelopes have dates written on them in magic marker. Some are empty, most are untouched, just laid out on the floor. It's clear that someone was trying to locate a specific photograph or set of photographs. And they must have found it because they stopped.

CHAPTER 31

PHOTOGRAPHER, WARHOL SUBJECT DIES IN A FALL

Lucille Anne Lawson, the photographer known as Seal Larson, died on February 25, following a catastrophic fall. Born on June 17, 1956, in Oxford, Mississippi, she was thirty years old. She is perhaps best known for appearing in one of Andy Warhol's short films, known as screen tests. Mr. Warhol, who died on February 22, also painted her portrait in 1976. Seal Larson's most recent work, praised for its sensitivity, includes black-and-white studies of struggling families living in lower Manhattan and the Bronx. Her more experimental, less well-known work includes a series of self-portraits in various costumes that is reminiscent of the work of Cindy Sherman. A recognizable member of the downtown art scene, she will be missed not only for her talent, but for her kindness and respect for all she knew. Ms. Lawson, who moved to New York in 1966, graduated from the Walden School in Manhattan in 1974 and received her master's in photography at the New School, where she graduated with high honors in 1983. She was predeceased by her mother, the late Maggie Grace Lawson, who was co-owner of Merna's Place, a popular Harlem soul food restaurant. She is survived by an aunt and uncle, Jennifer and Roy Henley, of Plantersville, Tennessee. Remembrances may be sent to the Harmony Funeral Home at 2271 Frederick Douglass Blvd. For those interested in her photographs, please contact Anna Lorch at the Anna Lorch Gallery in Greenwich, Connecticut, formerly located on the Lower East Side of Manhattan.

—*The New York Times*, March 3, 1987

Tomas Brodsky is at his desk eating a lobster roll when Emma arrives at the precinct. "Want one?" he asks.

"Where the hell did you get a lobster roll in Harlem?"

"Ah, I have my ways," he says, smiling. "I got you one too."

"Any good?" she asks.

"Of course it's good. What are you? Some kind of food snob?"

"You found me out," she says, dropping a file folder and a handful of undeveloped film cannisters on his desk. "I have a ton of suspects for you."

"Hmm," he says, rubbing his hands together. "Suspects," his eyes smiling as he turns and wraps his jaw around the humongous sandwich.

"Can you get these developed?" she asks. He nods, and she sets the rest of the film on a corner of his desk. "And these?" He's chewing, nodding, his eyes rolling back in his head comically. She's unwrapping her own lobster roll. "By the way, I'm not a food snob. I'm just your regular, garden-variety *people* snob, I'm afraid."

"What's the fun in that?" he says, smartly. They are warming to each other, which she finds reassuring.

He nudges the obituary toward her with his elbow. Emma looks confused. "Harriet Freeman," he says, his mouth half-full. "And Lynley Wright." She nods. He finishes chewing while she eyes the obit. "I encouraged them," he says. "They wanted to draw people to Anna Lorch's to buy your friend's art. I wanted to bring people out of the woodwork, spread the word. Surely someone knows something." He points to the top of the page, the date. "Ran in Tuesday's *Times*."

"That's a nice picture," Emma says, then reads the first line out loud. "Lucille Anne Lawson, the photographer known as Seal Larson, died on February 25, following a catastrophic fall." She stops. "Catastrophic fall," she says, her head cocked slightly, her brow set in its perennial wrinkle. "Interesting choice of words." He lets her read the entire piece, absorb it, watches her tear up and, finally, ultimately, turn her gaze to his.

"Okay. So, someone broke into her studio again?" he says, no longer wrestling with his sandwich.

"I imagine whoever it was came back," she says, and between bites, asks him about the fingerprints on the highball glasses. "Any luck?"

"Oh, we got prints all right. Lots of them. Was easy to identify the victim's." Emma is uncomfortable with the word victim. She visualizes the coroner checking Seal's lifeless fingers for prints, and experiences it like a punch in the gut, but she doesn't say so and he doesn't notice. "We haven't found a match for the others," he says. "Although, judging from the size of them, it's a man." He looks up at her. "If you give me that key, I'll get a copy made, send someone over to get prints in the closet, and we'll secure the place."

She seems ravenous, as if this enormous hoagie of a sandwich might somehow take away the confusion, the grief, the pit in her stomach.

"Comfort food," he says, giving them a breather, letting her concentrate on the sandwich as he randomly shuffles through some papers on his desk.

When she finally sets the remainder of her sandwich aside and wraps everything up and tosses it in his wastebasket, relentlessly wiping her face and hands with a near-shredded napkin and straightening herself up, he smiles, kicking back in. "So, what about all these new suspects?"

"The file cabinet in her studio is a gold mine—all her mother's financial records, legal documents, you name it. If it doesn't lead to something or someone, I'd be surprised. You probably want to get your people to bring the entire contents here and go through everything," she says. Then, reaching into her bag, "But I found this folder of what could be images of her mother's collection." He kicks back his chair, rising, looking over her shoulder at the images.

"Would you agree that this could be about the art?" Emma says.

"Of course," he says. "Come on."

"Are you just going to leave that?" She points to the remainder of his sandwich.

"It'll wait," he says, his brow wrinkling.

"But you can get food poison—" He cuts her off before she can finish the word.

"Gimme a break," he says, in a friendly way, rolling his eyes, grabbing the folder and leading her to a conference room, where he lays the pages down on the table. There are thirty sheets. Each includes a color photograph of a work of art and the artist's name. The related information—value, date acquired, even the name of the pieces—is sketchy and inconsistent, but it's clearly an impressive body of works.

Together, as they examine them each one by one, Emma is surprised by her inability to recognize many of the artists and by just how much Tomas Brodsky knows. "Wow," he says, perusing them. "Okay. Wow. This is a Jasper Johns. And that's a Mark Rothko." Then, "I don't know what this is, but I suspect it's something . . . Oooooh," he says, leaning over, reading the text. "This is a painting by Willem de Kooning."

"It's her mother's collection, isn't it?" Emma says.

"Bingo," he says.

"And these are extremely valuable, aren't they? Look, she bought this one for eighteen thousand in 1967. That's got to be worth something in the high six figures now."

"Or more," he says. "I gotta tell ya. I mean, this isn't an art collection. It's an investment portfolio."

"Do you think this is what got Seal killed?"

"I don't want to assume—but, if anything could get you killed, this would be it. These are valuable paintings. Where the hell are they?"

"They definitely weren't hidden away. Merna said the last time she saw them, they were hanging on the walls in their Seventy-Second Street apartment, but she doesn't know anything about what happened to any of them."

"Her mother was sick for how long?" he asks.

"Several years."

"And when did they leave the place? 1979?" Emma nods in assent as he goes on. "So, either she sold the paintings, or they're stored somewhere."

"Or they *were* stored somewhere," Emma says.

Emma is walking around the table, looking at the images again. There are names she doesn't recognize—Lyonel Feininger, Ruth Asawa, Alan Shields. But she knows that doesn't mean anything. They all give the impression of being masterpieces.

Brodsky blows out a deep breath, shaking his head. "We need to explore the subject with the ladies who are handling the estate, Ms. Wright and Ms. Freeman, don't you think?"

"Surely, they know about it."

"We'll find out, won't we?" he says, lost in thought for a moment. "Are you familiar with the Rothko case?"

She shakes her head no and her brow wrinkles, which Brodsky now recognizes as her trademark.

"Well, when Mark Rothko died, his dealer was shortchanging the heirs, his two children," he says.

"How do you know that?"

"It's my job," he says. "Plus, we studied it in cop school. The case was settled in 1975. That was my year."

"So, how did they do it?" she asks.

"Complicated," Brodsky says, gathering up the paperwork, and explaining as he leads her out of the conference room and back toward his desk. "There are all kinds of possible scams. A lot of art sales go on behind closed doors. On the secondary market. It's like an unregulated industry. But essentially, the executors—who also represented Rothko's gallery—were selling his paintings at below market prices to their own gallery, and then the gallery was selling them to collectors overseas for a higher price. The executors were making a profit, and the family was getting shortchanged."

"Interesting," she says. "So, what are you thinking?"

He shrugs. "We'll pursue it if it makes sense," he says, lingering beside his desk. "I'm going up to Connecticut this afternoon to meet with the art dealer, this Anna Lorch. We haven't even scratched the surface with her." He hesitates a moment, the two of them still beside the desk. "Wanna join me?" he adds.

"That's very generous," she says, appreciating the power of Bill Kidman's intervention on her behalf. "But I can't. Too much on my plate—and I've got to get back to DC for a conference at Georgetown, although I hate to leave in the middle of this." She's grown fond of Brodsky in these few long days, and it feels like an awkward goodbye.

"Of course," he says, turning the remnants of his lunch into a ball of trash and tossing it into the garbage can across the room. "I'll keep you posted."

CHAPTER 32

SEAL

Here's one of the greatest lines I ever heard: "I hope to paint something that will ruin the appetite of every son of a bitch who ever eats in that room." Which is apparently what Mark Rothko said like thirty years ago after Philip Johnson commissioned him to do some paintings for the Four Seasons restaurant in the Seagram Building.

Maybe it was impossible to turn down a request like that from a famous architect who had just designed this amazing building. Or maybe Rothko just wanted to do a group of paintings that would all live together in one space. Or maybe he was just flattered by the invitation. I can see that. But Mark Rothko was a notorious lefty, and, as we all know, the Four Seasons is not exactly a hangout for the workers of the world.

Anyway, interesting story: He created a stunning—albeit dark—series of paintings in his signature multiform, abstract style. Then he took his wife out to dinner at the restaurant, and during the meal he famously told her—and I'm paraphrasing here—*Anyone who'll eat this kind of food at these prices will never look at a painting of mine.* Then he pulled out of the deal. Later, he donated some of those paintings to the Tate Gallery in London. I imagine that's where they are now.

But there's more to the story. Rothko was not what you'd call a lighthearted soul. He was a heavy drinker and I'm guessing he was clinically depressed. The day those paintings arrived at the Tate was the day his body was found in his studio. He had committed suicide. Tragically, his wife died shortly afterward. So, his daughter, who was a couple of years older than me, and her much younger brother, were suddenly orphaned. What's interesting at the moment is that the two kids ended up suing the executors of the estate. Turned out they were ripping off the kids. And, in the end, the Marlborough Gallery—a.k.a. the executors—paid $9.2 million to settle the suit. Happy ending to a ridiculously sad story. So, now that I think about it, you can't help but wonder about executors in the art business.

CHAPTER 33

Set on Old Greenwich Avenue with its shoppes and apothecaries and all manner of charming places where residents can spend their old money and their new money, Anna Lorch's gallery is closed. "Omigosh," she says, responding to the bell, unlocking the front door. "You must be Detective Brodsky." And, without skipping a beat, adds: "That obituary was ingenious." While not exactly bubbly, given that her style leans toward the jaded, the ironic, the sophisticated, and given the circumstances under which they are meeting, Anna Lorch is in curiously good spirits. Addressing him as if he's a business partner, she explains, "I've had seven calls. And a woman came yesterday and bought nine portraits. She's paying eighty-five hundred for the lot of them. And some were almost identical."

"Interesting," he says, less enthusiastically. "My phone has failed to ring."

"I had no idea Seal had such followers," she says.

"Tell me about the portraits."

"They weren't her best. But they were all images of the same person. A young man."

"Any idea who?"

"No idea. But most of them were part of this new . . . well, let's see." She invites him in. The gallery walls are filled with paintings of what you might call high-end beach art—clean, simple acrylics in bright primary colors—a string of red-and-white-striped deck chairs, a rooftop set against a sunny blue sky, a lone beach umbrella on a stretch of sand. Decorative images for the discerning buyer. Matisse meets Nantucket might be the theme. They are large canvases and expensive for their time. Upwards of $15,000 apiece. She leads him to a back room where Seal Larson's photographs are lined up on a large worktable.

"I went in to see her several times over the past year," the gallerist says. "She was experimenting with a couple of things. One was a series of self-portraits, where she was often in costume. These were not so interesting to me. It's been done—although I did ask for some prints of the ones where this young man appears. He has a quality about him that seems to transcend gender. A yin/yang, masculine/feminine thing going on. Those were in color. There was another series of portraits where she used paint over black-and-white photos. It's not a new idea. Gerhard Richter did it years ago, quite successfully. But hers were original and compelling. Again, she seemed to be playing with gender and gender norms, with the use of a pastel palette. I'm planning on showing those here." As she talks, Anna Lorch is walking Brodsky through the images, circling the worktable, picking one up and then another.

"Here you can see that she was doing some, let's say . . . more jour-nalistic work. Pieces that chronicled the times. Black-and-white images of people in the downtown scene, on the Lower East Side, graffiti artists, hip-hop dancers, musicians, punks, clubs, that sort of thing. I need to take them into Manhattan, I think. Not things that would show well here. I'll check with Lynley."

Brodsky is paying attention, examining some of the photographs closely, occasionally lifting an image off the table. "What about these portraits you sold? Was this man in any of those photos? How about this guy?"

"No. She bought them all."

"And who was she?"

"I don't know. She said she'd prefer to remain anonymous. I'm waiting for the wire. It should be here any minute."

"So, you still have the images."

"In fact, I do. They're wrapped up in the back. She said someone would be coming by for them by end of day. A messenger service of some kind. They should be here soon," she says, checking her watch.

She escorts him to a small closet in a storage area behind the workroom. A shadow passes across her face the minute she flips on the closet light. "Oh dear," she says. "They're gone. The portraits. They're gone." There's a rear door to the alley in the back, and it's clear that someone broke in during the night. When Brodsky grills her about the man, the images, the woman who bought them, she describes the woman as "tall, in her forties or fifties, rather chic. Olive complexion. Maybe Hispanic? And I think she was wearing a wig, in a kind of pixie cut. Auburn. And a Chanel suit or knockoff. You know, they're everywhere. Oh, and she never took her sunglasses off."

"Sounds like a disguise."

"Oh dear, you may be right. I didn't think of that."

He asks about the young man, the subject of these portraits. The gallerist describes him as "very attractive," leaning in on the word *very*. "He was young. He had these intense brown eyes with an elfish sort of twinkle to them and these high cheekbones." She pushes her fingertips against her own cheekbones as she speaks, then adds: "Surely, he was a professional model."

"Was it anyone you would have known? Did you know her boyfriend Simon?"

"No. And I never met Simon."

"Any of her other boyfriends?"

"I don't think she had any boyfriends other than Simon. At one point, my son was interested in her, and she was quite aloof. Seal was an independent spirit. Anyway, I didn't recognize him. And I would have remembered. As I said, he looked like a model."

"Were you planning to let these photographs go before I arrived?" he says, almost in reproach.

"I'm sorry. I didn't think it would be important." Her enthusiasm is muffled now, and she seems embarrassed by her own cluelessness.

"Everything is important, Ms. Lorch," he says before calling the local police.

CHAPTER 34

Angus McLearan is on the island of Cyprus in the Mediterranean, off the coast of Turkey. He's sending a numerically coded communication via a British radio transmission that will be picked up by a CIA operative in Israel. That information will, in turn, be passed to Bill Kidman in Washington DC. The message, when uncoded, reads:

I have documentation. Shipped from Bayonne via Nederlander. ID 32198 AX25700. Arrived in Baghdad via military transport 2.27.87. Images, paperwork coming via Mr. Singer.

Later, he will call Bill Kidman from his room at the hotel.

"Got your message," Kidman says. "Sorry I couldn't get back to you."

"How's Emma doing?" Angus asks, if only to make it clear that it's not a secure line. The two are close. They've known each other for more than twenty years. They know how to communicate without communicating.

"Emma? As well as can be expected, I guess," Kidman replies, cautiously, awaiting a signal that something may be wrong. "You?"

"I'm good. Looking forward to taking a vacation," Angus says. "Wanna join me?"

"What do you have in mind?" Kidman says. He's read Angus's telex. Knows that Angus has information on a shipment to Iraq from an American company, via a German one. But he doesn't know exactly what it is and hesitates to commit himself.

Angus gets the message. "Maybe a little fishing off the coast," he says.

"I'm swamped," he says. "Doubt that I can get away. But send me a postcard, will you?"

"Will do," Angus says, disappointed, knowing Kidman's not keen to get involved, knowing he wants more information. "Give my best to Emma" is Angus's standard sign-off. No secrets hidden there. He takes a sip of red wine before he picks up the phone to ring her but is immediately distracted by noise in the outer hall, the sound of heavy footfalls. He grabs his backpack before the crash comes, the unmistakable sound of someone breaking down a door nearby. Then the frantic cries for help in Greek, a man's voice and a woman's, followed by threats in Arabic, a language that is relatively uncommon in Cyprus. By then, Angus is already out the window, running across a low, flat rooftop on the edge of Nicosia. He finds a trellis on the south side of the building, tests its strength, shimmies down to the street, landing badly on a craggy sidewalk with a twist to his ankle. "Fok," he says, drawn out in a loud whisper. He's in the tourist district of the island's capital. It's not peak season, but there are still plenty of taxis around. He waves his arms, limps over and seats himself up front, heading for Lanarca Airport.

CHAPTER 35

Once the 10:30 Metroliner kicks into gear and emerges from the tunnel that leads out of Penn Station and into the light, there is the landscape of northern Jersey—the wetlands, the smokestacks, the underbelly of the city—and the mulling kicks in, Emma's brain rattling. She wonders who she can trust. Would Lynley Wright or Harriet Freeman—Seal's own people—rip off the estate? Or conspire to do so? Why not? Emma thinks. No one loses, and they have everything to gain. And what about Merna? Could she be lying? When Emma had asked her about the Calder mobile hanging in her modest apartment, she'd said that it was a gift from Maggie Grace.

Emma had been surprised. "Really?" she said. "That's very generous."

Merna grinned. "It's not an original, for goodness sake," she said. "This particular piece is in the permanent collection at the Museum of Modern Art. She knew I loved it. She gave it to me for my birthday." Merna paused, her head cocked to one side, her eyes laughing. "You didn't actually think it was real, did you?"

"Well, I knew she was a collector," Emma said.

"I gotta tell you, Miss Quinn. What she gave me was worth more than anything any artist—I don't care who—could have dreamed up. I met her when she was just eighteen. She was my friend for twenty years, my business partner for almost fifteen of those." Merna stopped then, putting a tissue to her eye, looking straight at Emma. "I loved her like one of my own." Emma couldn't imagine those words being untrue.

Somewhere between Trenton and Philadelphia, Emma's mind settles on Seal herself. She was a curious soul. She had a stillness about her—if not a contentment, something like a containment. Oh, there was plenty of drama in the way she danced and the way she dressed, the costumes she wore and the places where she wore them—and there was drama to her friends, her scene, her work. There may well have been drama in her past. But she was never dramatic herself, never effusive or overwrought. And, unlike Emma, she never apologized for anything. In fact, Seal rarely showed any sign of emotion. Occasionally she would laugh or smile, but otherwise, she gave neither visual nor verbal clues to what she was feeling or thinking. She was affectless, controlled, something Emma admired. At times, it threw her off. Having grown up in a home with the high drama of a grandmother who was either diagnostically crazy or just insanely moody, she had never known when an emotional storm would hit. She learned to be watchful, mindful, sensitive to the moods of others, accommodating.

That may be why Emma had trouble reading her friend Seal. There were no moods to adapt to. It seemed to Emma, on reflection, that their closeness—if it was a closeness—came from shared experience. Both were women with ample funds, living alone, disconnected from the mainstream. They shared a curiosity about the world beyond, she thought. And they treated each other with respect, which is always a gift. That, and proximity, Emma decides, enabled the friendship. But she recognizes that they were both emotionally self-sufficient—and that they had both been damaged in some way. She just doesn't know enough about Seal to know where that damage came from. She is trying to imagine who might be relevant to the case, beyond the people they have interviewed. Who were the people in Seal's life? Whose fingerprints are on the highball glasses? Who broke into her studio and what were they looking for? Now, Emma considers some of Lynley Wright's comments about Seal's art becoming more political, about poverty and inequality, including gender-bending imagery and portraits from the AIDS crisis. Who might she have met during those photo shoots? The scope of her new relationships would have been broad, if not deep.

Again, she recalls her trip with Seal to the international exhibit at MoMA. Before they left that day, Seal had insisted on visiting an upper gallery, where the work of three photographers was on exhibit. It was a new space, part of the renovation of the museum. Emma had left her there that afternoon, in that space, surrounded by the photographs that were a wholly different kind of art. They were social commentaries, really. One photographer was documenting the lives of the rich and the poor, with black-and-white images of people in settings you might not expect to see in a museum. A man smoking at a nondescript kitchen table while eating a plate of spaghetti. Or a ragged-looking family huddled on a sofa in front of the TV in what could have been a one-room apartment. The photographer had invited the subjects themselves into the process, shown them their pictures and asked for their comments. They'd written—handwritten—their own narratives about their own lives. Emma found the idea of it brilliant, albeit disturbing. She thinks the photographer's name was Goldberg. The photographs were original and accessible. Seal had been captivated by them.

And Emma remembers that before she left, they ran into some people Seal knew. A group of men and women. They were punky looking—backpacks, carabiners, black clothes, torn jeans, funky hair. Dark mascara on the women and two real skinny guys. They were all over her. Like fans. Admirers. Emma was surprised by it. She hadn't known that Seal had a following. Recollecting it reconfirms to Emma how little she really knew about Seal, and the range of acquaintances who may have sought her out.

CHAPTER 36

SEAL

I'll never forget that day at MoMA. It was the summer of 1984. I had just turned twenty-eight. I'd only been out of school for a year or two, but

I'd been taking pictures for what felt like a long time. Since before my mother died, anyway. I hadn't produced anything of real value. Someone had told me to go see that show—the one of the second floor. So, Emma and I went up there. Whoever told me to see it was right. Jim Goldberg blew me away, with these intimate portraits of real people living, well, on the fringe. People with nothing. Here he was, only thirty-one years old—just a few years older than me—and he was doing these beautiful photographs that explored a world that no one would otherwise see, except the people trapped in it. I was really touched by his work. It was a genuinely empathetic portrayal of men and women, families, children, teenagers, the elderly—poor, troubled, ill, drug-addicted, derelict. The disenfranchised, you might call them. People living in the most difficult circumstances, in run-down buildings, in their cars, on the streets. His take was at once human and cerebral. But mostly what struck me was this: it was respectful.

I kept an eye on him. In 1985 he published the book *Rich and Poor*, where he documents the lives of ordinary people in San Francisco. Some of the photographs from the MoMA show were in there. The cool thing he did was, he invited his subjects to write something in their own hands that described who they are or what's happening in their lives or, sometimes it seems like just whatever they want to say. So, just as an example, a young man sits on an unmade bed in a crappy-looking room, leaning against the backdrop of floral wallpaper. His jagged handwriting tells us: "It's kind of stinky living in a hotel. I don't have nothing. Only $10."

Goldberg's work made me want to be more thoughtful in my own work. Years from now, in 1995, he will publish *Raised by Wolves*, documenting the lives of marginalized youths. Therein, beside a photograph of a young man in a jean jacket with a T-shirt rolled up to his chest exposing his scarred belly, these handwritten words will appear: "I'm Dave who the Fuck are you. You need me 2 feel superior. I need you 2 laugh at." Somebody once said that his "in-depth collaborations investigate the nature of American myths about class, power and happiness." I think the man's a fucking genius. Seeing his work made me want to be better. It challenged me. But I didn't have the guts to do anything like that—confronting people head-on with the truth, exposing the cracks in our system, exposing the cracks in people's lives. Inviting myself into their lives and imposing on them in that way. That takes real chutzpah. I was way too much of a chicken to do anything like that.

CHAPTER 37

Sitting now on the train, Emma opens Tuesday's *New York Times* and reads Seal's obituary again. More than anything, she wants to talk to Angus. She has so much she wants to tell him—about the art collection, about the possibility of a theft, that the executors may be conspiring somehow, and that there is a family in Tennessee. She thinks Merna may know more than she admits, and Emma wants to get his input. Sometimes, when she can't reach him, which is often, she feels that half her brain is missing. She remembers his words: "Everyone has secrets." She feels as if she needs to go to Plantersville, to meet the aunt, to find out more about this art collection and to research the trust fund. That's the big secret, she thinks as the train pulls into Penn Station in Philadelphia.

A few minutes later, she looks up to see Rolley Smythe, the former graduate student whose phone message she never answered. She gazes out the window in the hope that he won't see her, that he will pass her by. But there he is, staring down at her, smiling: "Well, well, fancy meeting you here," he says. He is clean-shaven, dressed in black with a brown leather jacket, his long, dark hair pushed behind his ears. Surely, she is thinking, he will see the sadness in my eyes or sense my reticence. She tries to think of a way to repel him that will not make either of them uncomfortable, but she's unable to think fast enough. Before she can even speak, he is setting his duffel on the rack above her seat, settling in. Only then does he see the weariness in her eyes, the gray in her countenance, her grief. He glances down at the paper, notices the obituaries folded across her lap.

"Oh dear," he says, crisply. "Have you lost someone?" She looks up at him without answering.

"Family?" he asks. When she replies, "My neighbor," he seems relieved. But then she adds, "We were quite close."

"Someone from the university?"

"A friend. A photographer. I think of her as an artist," she says, handing him the obituary if only to silence him. "There," she says, "Lucille Lawson," pointing it out, looking away, leaving him to it.

They are sitting so close to one another that their shoulders touch, and she can hear him breathing heavily as he reads. She feels herself tensing up as he sets the paper back down on his lap, folding it, holding it out to her without even looking up.

"I'm so sorry," he says, with uncharacteristic grace, rising as he speaks. "I'll leave you then." Jostled slightly by the motion of the train, he drags his duffel on through to the next car. She has the feeling that he is, if not following her, pursuing her. But she lets it pass unconsidered, unexplored.

CHAPTER 38

It is Friday, March 6, 1987. Around the time Emma's train is arriving at Union Station in downtown Washington, the MS *Herald of Free Enterprise* is flipping over in the North Sea off the coast of Belgium. The evening ferry transporting passengers from mainland Europe to Great Britain capsizes minutes after its departure from the Belgian port of Zeebrugge. Among the 459 passengers on board are day-trippers and day laborers, tourists and soldiers, couples and families heading to the

British Isles, most going home. That, and eighty crew members making their way at day's end from Belgium across the English Channel to Dover. By the time Emma arrives at her office at Georgetown University that afternoon, scores of people will have died—struck by flying debris in the initial jolt and flip of the eight-deck ship or trapped in its belly or cast overboard and drowned in the frozen waters. Thankfully, the ferry lands upside down on a sand bar in the English Channel, or the extensive rescue efforts, which will go on through the night, would have been impossible. It is a horrific disaster of which Emma is completely unaware.

Her Washington apartment is in the Woodley Park neighborhood near the National Zoo on upper Connecticut Avenue. Edging up to Rock Creek Park and not far from Embassy Row, it's a mix of ethnic restaurants, elegant townhouses and historic apartment buildings. Hers overlooks Connecticut, a main artery that connects Dupont Circle downtown to Chevy Chase Circle, where the city melds into Maryland. The apartment itself is small, but serviceable, and has the charm that comes with age—large windows, elaborate crown moldings, hardwood floors. It's an easy walk to the new Metro station and a quick drive down Reno Road toward Georgetown and the university. Convenient. She's relatively isolated in Washington and has made few friends aside from a handful of Georgetown professors, more aptly called acquaintances, and a dog sitter. That and a guy who tends bar at the Italian restaurant around the corner, a place that has become something of a refuge. She is glad to be back.

Her setter meets her at the door, cringing with happiness. "Oh, my sweet boy," she says. "Sweet Seamus." She's been gone for more than a week. On Friday evening, she virtually collapses from the exhaustion. On Saturday morning, she awakens at ten, throws on a pair of sweatpants and a heavy down jacket and takes a walk toward Rock Creek Park with Seamus. They follow her usual path, down Connecticut to a bridge over Rock Creek, then wind their way into the park. It's early yet, sunny but brisk in this first week of March. She feels as if she's approaching an acceptance of Seal's death, but in fact she is preoccupied, distracted. Unaware that Tomas Brodsky is trying to reach her, she is already deep in a kind of grief.

Since his trip to Connecticut, Brodsky has put two people on the case of the missing photographs—a Greenwich officer and one of his own men. They're checking the crime scene, pulling prints and examining video cam footage at gas stations in and around Greenwich. He sent a police artist up to Lorch's gallery to get a sketch of what he's now calling Portrait-Man—the young man in the stolen photographs. Some of the film from Seal's studio has been developed, and he's faxed some of those images up to Anna Lorch for identification; she's identified the man who appeared in the portrait series. But they still don't know who it is. Brodsky wants Emma to have a look, see if she recognizes him. He's called and left two messages on her machine this morning.

But Emma is out walking.

As she walks, her mind rambles. She's thinking that this is about Maggie Grace's art collection, that surely Harriet Freeman will know something. Or Lynley Wright. She imagines that whoever pulled down the wall hangings and drilled holes in Seal's apartment and tore up the flooring in her studio, was looking for art. It just makes sense, she thinks. An art collection that substantial, that valuable, doesn't just disappear. She has every intention of calling Brodsky when she gets home—to see if he's made any progress.

On her way back, she grabs a copy of the *New York Times* from the lobby, snatches a glimpse of the front page. In the upper right corner, above the fold, is the headline: "Ferry with over 500 People Capsizes near Belgian Port; 350 Are Safe, Many Trapped; 48 Dead." Another smaller headline reads: "Terror Aboard the Stricken Ferry: Flying Glass and Rushing Water." There are photographs. At her door, she struggles with the dog and the key and the newspaper. Once inside, she sits, reads, transfixed. The first paragraph tells her that the ferry left the port of Zeebrugge on Friday evening, that more than two hundred people are missing. And that, of course, it would have been headed across the channel to Dover, to Britain.

She's frozen. She knows that Angus was heading home. She's familiar with the port of Zeebrugge, knows that he often passes through Belgium, that he sometimes stays in the old city, in Brugge, and that he often takes the ferry back to the British Isles. Terrified, that's what she's thinking when the phone rings, set inches away on the long wooden table behind her sofa. She fairly jumps, and reaching out quickly, awkwardly, knocks the receiver across the table, hoping for good news, for Angus's voice, fearing the worst.

"There's a guy," Tomas Brodsky says when she finally picks it up, grabbing it by the cord, setting herself right. Of course, Brodsky doesn't know about the ferry that's suspended on a sandbar in the English Channel. Or perhaps he does, since it's on the front page of the *Times*, but he doesn't know what it might mean to Emma.

"What?" she says. "Who is this?"

"It's Tomas. It's Detective Brodsky," he says. They'd last spoken before she'd left New York, in the wake of his visit to Anna Lorch's gallery. She knows about the break-in, and she knows his people have pored through Seal's studio. When they last spoke, she had been intrigued. Today, she greets him with silence. "You okay?" he asks. His New York accent sounds exaggerated coming over the line.

"Oh yeah. Yeah," she says.

"You sound like a train wreck."

"Actually, I think a friend may have been in an accident," she says. "Unexpected."

"Apologies," he says. His tone is genuine, crisp. "I'll call you later."

"No. No," she says. "This is good. This is fine. What is it?"

"We got some of that film developed, from Seal's studio," he says. "And we have a photo. Anna Lorch has identified him as the guy in the stolen portraits. The one I was telling you about. Portrait-Man."

"Who is it?"

"We don't know who it is. We just have a photo. I'm sending it around. It may be Simon, her former beau." For some reason, his use of the word *beau* amuses her, or maybe it's just a release of the tension, but she laughs, which strikes him as odd, slows him down. "You sure you're okay?" he says.

"Fine," she says brusquely, knowing she's not. "Fine."

"Okay. So, I'm going to send it to Merna and the coexecutors. I want to fax it to you as well."

"Oh Lord," she says. "Not my office." She hesitates. *Kidman,* she thinks. He can send it to Bill Kidman at CIA headquarters.

"And something else," he tells her when she gets back on the line with Kidman's fax number. "You know the fingerprints we have from Lucille's studio? Well, we found an identical print on a desk drawer in Anna Lorch's gallery. We're going to check it against the fingerprints from the victim's apartment. We may be onto something here."

After he hangs up, Emma can't move. She listens for a moment to the dial tone before setting the receiver down. Then lays her head on the pillow and can't move, feels in a fog, weighed down, groggy. She's expected at a weekend planning committee meeting for this confer-ence at the university, but she doesn't even bother to call them. *It's not important,* she tells herself. She has barely mourned Seal. In fact, she hasn't mourned her at all. She's poured all her energy into trying to solve the crime, as if it were some sort of mission, as if it would make everything all right. But she's spent no time on absorbing the loss. And now this. Angus.

Seamus is at her feet, wagging his long Irish setter tail. Looking at her with his deep, sad Irish setter eyes, and she can't even respond. It's as if there is a magnet drawing her deeper into the comfort of her sofa, embracing her, suffocating her as she sinks into a kind of half sleep.

Two hours have passed when Bill Kidman calls. She rolls over, her mouth dry. Her hello guttural, slurred, sloppy.

"I just got a call," he says.

"Was he on it?" she says to his silence, her voice rising. "Just tell me. Was he on it?"

"Sounds like you're on something this afternoon, my friend," he says.

"The ferry. Was he on the ferry?"

"Oh shit. Shit," Kidman says. "It never occurred to me."

"For real?" she's angry, and he can hear it in her voice. She's snapped to attention, suddenly alert.

"Wasn't on my radar. Honestly. I'll look into it. But I'm sure . . ." Sheepish, he doesn't know how to make it right.

"Why are you calling me then?"

"Your guy in New York, Brodsky, he sent me a couple of photographs. I assume they're for you."

"Oh," she says. "That can wait." She turns toward the back of the sofa, lays the phone gently in its cradle and turns over on her side, looking up at the sunbeam shooting across the room, a stream of light flecked with tiny particles of dust, all spinning about. Then she closes her eyes again. Later, toward the end of the day, she's barely moved when he calls back.

"He had a ticket," Kidman tells her. "He was on the passenger list. Of course, that doesn't necessarily mean anything. Believe me." But she doesn't hear it.

CHAPTER 39

Over the weekend, the ferry disaster at Zeebrugge is all over the news. It is inescapable. They are calling the search and rescue mission "speedy" and "a tremendous success," involving divers and helicopters and multiple vessels searching the ferryboat that had capsized Friday evening in the North Sea. And they are scouring the surrounding waters. The search goes on until well into Saturday night. But by then, the tides were rising, and the mission was becoming impossible. According to the early news reports, 135 are dead or missing. There are 408 survivors. Of those, only 10 were severely injured. There are adults who survived but lost their children. And children who lost their parents. "I lost my girlfriend," a man tells a reporter. Meaning, when the ferry tipped over, she literally was gone in an instant. Another survivor reports seeing a man who was trying to keep a baby afloat "by holding its clothing in his teeth." On Sunday morning, the *New York Times* reports: "Fifty-one bodies have been found, and 84 people are missing and presumed dead." And reports from Britain are making it very clear: there is little hope of finding anyone else alive.

By Monday, Emma begins to absorb the shock of it, the possibility that Angus was aboard and has not survived. They're reporting that the bow doors were not closed, defying protocol, which would have caused the ferry to fill with water, creating a tragic imbalance, flipping it within minutes of departure. She reasons that it could have been sabotage, and, not thinking clearly, that Angus could have been the target. She responds by sleeping on the sofa for hours on end, walking the dog in a daze, subsisting on next to nothing. Finally, when she begins to entertain the possibility of his death, she has lost two days. And she is furious. She doesn't hesitate to go to Bill Kidman's office at Langley. She knows exactly where it is. At this point, she has given someone her name and is standing outside the metal detector at the public entrance when she sees him approaching. He doesn't look like himself, moving toward her, beyond the metal detector, like a man coming down a jetway, breezy, efficient, unconcerned. He has a cordial, plastic expression on his face, as if he's a senator or congressman greeting a constituent outside his offices at the US Capitol.

"I want to know exactly what he was up to," she calls out as he approaches. She is hotheaded, on the edge of rage. "I need to know what he was doing." She appears somehow threatening, but inside she knows she has no power over him, save their friendship. The security guards are approaching her. Kidman raises a hand, and they freeze in place. Then he takes her gently by the elbow, leads her out of the building.

"Come," he says. Outside, it's cold and clear. She is wearing a coat. He is not. He guides her by the elbow to a pavilion on the grounds, draws her into the shadow of it, whispers, "What are you doing?"

"I want to know what he was doing. I want to know what happened and why it happened. What was he working on?" She looks and sounds a bit like a madwoman, her voice rising, her eyes puffy and glazed over from lack of sleep.

"I wasn't involved. I don't know what he was working on." His voice is flat, controlled.

She's crossed a line she shouldn't have crossed. The expression on his face convinces her of that, but she persists. "You know it's about weapons. And you know why he was in the Middle East."

"Actually, I don't know. He spoke to me once about the project. It's not something that we could collaborate on. We're not on the same team on this one."

"But you knew." She is pacing. He is standing still.

"I know exactly what you know. That it's about weapons and he's been in the Middle East. Nothing more."

"Did it have anything to with this Iran-Contra business?"

He looks confused. "That makes no sense."

"Don't you remember telling me once, that when someone says, 'You're not making any sense,' that it usually means you're on the right track."

"Look at me," he says, holding her by the shoulders, facing her head-on. "How long have you known me? Coming up on ten years. And you trust me, am I right? Now listen carefully. What was the last thing Angus said to you?"

They're surrounded by what may well be the most sterile garden on the planet. A handful of trees and spare concrete columns forming a kind of pergola, the grass that surrounds it, impeccably trimmed. Defeated, she sits down on the edge of an uninviting concrete bench, looking small and bereft in her down jacket and her blue jeans, her hair uncombed. She thinks back to her last conversation with Angus. When had it been, she asks herself. She has no idea. He'd called her at the hotel, she's sure of that. They had talked about what, in her own mind, she now calls "the case," Seal's death, and where to go from here. "He said to follow the secrets."

"That was the last thing he said, 'Follow the secrets'?" Kidman looks skeptical and a bit disappointed. That would not be helpful. But she thinks further. She looks up at him, straight into his eyes.

"No, it wasn't the last thing," she says, her voice lifting ever so slightly. "Aside from an amorous goodbye, the last thing he said was very clear and direct." She's already feeling mildly reassured. "He said, 'Don't assume anything.' Then he said, 'In all matters.'"

Kidman nods. "Okay?"

"Okay."

"Now, come in and I'll show you the fax from your friend Brodsky." He says, wrapping his arm over her shoulder and telling her she needs to comb her hair.

Part Three

"At the turn of the twentieth century, two remarkable women were plotting to change the world. One here, one across the Atlantic," the professor said, a slide projected above her, her body shrouded in darkness. "There's no evidence that the two ever met. But they shared a certain charisma, a radical will and a degree of celebrity."

Emma first met Rolley Smythe back in 1984 when she was teaching a course at Columbia on radicalism and the Industrial Revolution. On the day they met, she had paused for a moment, at this point in this lecture, as she always did, saying, "The first of these women would be . . ."

"Rosa," a student had called out.

Then another, "Luxemburg. Rosa Luxemburg." The name echoing through the room. Most of these students would have learned of the Polish revolutionary, a feminist icon and Marxist superhero, during an earlier semester, in the precursor to this class.

"Of course," she would always grin in assent, then project the black-and-white image onto the screen—Rosa Luxemburg in a loose-fitting cotton dress and a broad-brimmed hat, her features at once sharp and feminine, looking like the slight creature she was.

"And the other woman, the one who lived in our hemisphere?" Professor Quinn would then ask to a wall of silence. On that day, a hand went up in the far back of the auditorium. She pointed in that direction, shielding her eyes so she could see better, and a dark-haired man in a plaid flannel shirt, with a lanky look about him, stood at the top of the stairs, cupping his hands around his mouth. "Goldman. Emma Goldman," he called out. He seemed older than the others, but still young enough to be in the audience.

"Right," she said. She clicked on the slide projector and the face of the stout, bespectacled anarchist, with her grandma hair and Victorian collar, filled the screen.

The professor cleared her throat. "Okay," she told the class. "For the midterm you're going to compare and contrast the two. What they stood for. How they lived. How they died. And why they failed, if indeed they did."

Professor Quinn liked to use words like *indeed*. After more than ten years of teaching, she still felt a need to distance herself from her students, to seem older, to retain an air of formality. "Papers are due before spring break. You have the syllabus, and I'll be giving four lectures in the next four weeks on the American anarchists and Ms. Goldman."

As the students filed out and Emma gathered up her paperwork and turned off the slide projector and threw on her coat, the young man made his way down the stairs of the amphitheater toward her. "Professor," he called.

"Nice job," she said, only just glancing up.

"Yeah," he said, approaching her. "But to be perfectly honest, it wasn't fair. I'm a grad student. Auditing the class."

"In European history? And we haven't met?" she said. She remembers it clearly. She remembers putting his age at twenty-five or twenty-six. She remembers how tall he seemed, maybe six foot four, and how confident he seemed. Compelling, she thought at the time. Maybe a bit cocky.

"Economics," he said. "And, no, we haven't," he added with a self-deprecating laugh. "One foot in the B School."

"Okay. Well, welcome to the class," she'd said. Although he had only audited that one class, he seemed to stay around, to pop in periodically at her office, to run into her at the library. He had been friendly, a bit too friendly perhaps. At first it felt like an innocent flirtation. He would engage her intellectually, challenge her thinking. And it was always out of the blue. She hadn't thought much about it, but toward the end of the school year, she realized that he was one of a new wave of students—grad students and undergraduates. She called them Reagan babies. They all wanted to go into finance, work on Wall Street, be rich, or, in some cases, richer. They seemed to be arrogant, narcissistic, patronizing.

At one point, she remembered telling Angus, "My students seem to have lost their souls. The boys, anyway. And everyone else in New York seems to have lost their minds." That realization seemed to have begun the day she met Rolley Smythe, although she's not sure. Perhaps it's because he made such an indelible impression on her. She was surprised to run into him at her office at the university. And then, there he was again, surprising her on the train. Now she is staring at a stack of images, sent via FedEx to her apartment, retrieved this afternoon from the office downstairs. And there he is, all six feet of him in all manner of costumes and poses.

Just yesterday, in Bill Kidman's office, when she'd expected to have her first look at Seal's ex-boyfriend, Simon Golding, the image that came through from Detective Tomas Brodsky in New York to the fax machine at Langley had been a bit grainy, a bit unclear, but familiar. She knew then who it was, but she hadn't said so. They'd called Brodsky, told him the image wasn't clear enough. He reported that he'd already sent multiple images from the undeveloped film to Emma via Federal Express. And now she is certain.

Rolley Smythe appears in more than a dozen photographs that are now in her possession, including a handful of headshots where he's sporting a beard. He has the same cocky expression on his face that Emma recognizes from his days as a graduate student. He is staring intently at the lens. There are a series of posed shots as well. In one, he is naked from his low-waisted jeans up, except for the snake that is wrapped around his neck. There are several snake shots. In another photograph, he's dressed like a man—in a black suit, a white shirt and a skinny tie—but he's wearing costume wigs, wigs that are obviously meant for a woman. There is one wig image after another, a Warhol-esque repetitive series. And there's another series featuring Seal and Rolley together in various awkward poses and costumes, including one in which she's wearing a Guerrilla Girl mask and he's wearing a dress. Emma looks for some indication of when these photographs would have been taken. She knows they can't be too old. After all, Seal hadn't developed them. Surely, based on Seal's appearance, and his, it could have been in the past year. But Seal is a shapeshifter, a costume-wearer, a player of games. They could have been taken anytime. She wonders if they could have been taken before Emma even knew Rolley.

She is baffled. *How could Seal have known Rolley without my knowing it? How could that be? And what were they to each other?* Ultimately, Rolley's relentless pursuit of her made Emma uncomfortable, and she'd begun to deliberately avoid him the following academic year. But she recalls, early on, sparring with him—in the library or at her office, never outside the boundaries of the university. She used to call him out for overusing terminology, classifications like deconstruction or postmodern. For applying the -isms that seemed to enrapture intellec-tuals at the time—and still did. It felt like a contrivance to her, a pose. He was capable of drawing her down a rabbit hole of her own making until they both emerged spouting nonsense.

"I just tell it like it is," he'd say.

"That's bullshit," she recalls a typical conversation. He would look at her as if she was crazy. She can hear herself lecturing him. "They're intellectual frameworks. They're valid things to teach, but not a valid way to teach. They're designed to obfuscate. They're just not relevant in my classroom." She would have gone on her typical toot, she's sure of that: "Structuralism, contextualism, postmodernism. They're not the lenses through which to view history. They are part of intellectual history. They are theoretical frameworks. Just as Marxism became a theoretical framework. I choose not to interpret history through those prisms. I think they cloud the facts."

She remembers Rolley laughing at her. "Calm yourself," he'd say, baiting her again. "But then you are interpreting history from your own bourgeois perspective," he would have said. "Or maybe your capitalist perspective." He would have prodded and teased. Twisted and turned things until they made no sense. On such occasions, Emma's earnestness always worked against her.

"What I'm doing is not cluttering the minds of my undergraduates," she'd say. "Why would I encourage them to view history through a lens that makes it more difficult to understand?"

"Everything is open to interpretation. So, you'd be wise to make your perspective clear." He flustered her. Good looks can do that. Recalling it now, she knows how foolish she was. Why wouldn't she have said, *Of course everything is open to interpretation*? But she knows why she hadn't. He had a way of turning her brain off. She's fairly certain she'd said something sophomoric, something reactionary. And this would have been how it went:

"Okay. I'm viewing history through the lens of a white American, one-quarter Jewish, East-Coast-born-and-bred, upper-class, feminist student of history in the late twentieth century. Satisfied?"

"You forgot the Ivy League piece."

"Ha ha," she'd have replied. Coy. From the beginning, their discussions were flirtations. They both knew it. Foreplay that went nowhere. And she knew that she cared more than he did. After all, she was the tenured professor. And, as far as she knew, he was a doctoral candidate.

"And you. How do you define your perspective?" Emma said once.

"I am a child of postmodernism," he responded.

"Jesus, what does that even mean?"

"I think it means I'm about ten years younger than you."

Obviously, if he hadn't been so attractive, she would have thought him foolish and would not have made such a fool of herself. But he was, and she did. She feels shame—and anger—now that she's staring at these prints and wondering if Rolley Smythe could have killed Seal Larson. Why? And how would he even have been capable of such a thing?

Before she talks to anyone else, she calls the bursar's office at the university. She lies, says she needs to review his transcript, that he's applied to help her with a research project. She needs to see his transcript, his records from the B School and the name of the professor he's currently working with. For a reference. That they're co-teaching an economics seminar. "I'm at Georgetown at the moment on sabbatical," she says, spelling out his name, confirming her own identity. "Yes. You can fax them to me at my office at Georgetown."

CHAPTER 41

SEAL

Rolley. Ole Rolley. I'd almost forgotten the name. He was a very confused boy. But he never struck me as evil. I can't imagine him dressing up like that, drugging me up, setting me on that windowsill. So twisted. Then maybe I can. But it's more like him to break into my studio or something stupid to get the damn photographs. I never even developed most of them. Of course, he didn't know that. Anna Lorch was rather drawn to those images, especially that first series, when we were experimenting with costumes. And the snakes. "Very vogue," she'd said, meaning *Vogue* with a capital *V*. Rolley seemed to like wearing women's clothing, and I think he liked the fact that I didn't care if he put them on. One evening we both stood in front of the mirror and applied way too much makeup. First, to our faces and then, just for effect, to our upper torsos. We painted graffiti on ourselves, essentially. Then we agreed that the act of doing it was the art itself—laughing, "The Process," we agreed, and that we were "Changing the Narrative." We laughed our asses off.

It was entertaining as all get out, and we wished we'd had someone there to videotape the whole thing. A parody of the whole art scene. But, in the end, it was grotesque, so much so that we didn't shoot any photographs. Too damning. We took a shower together, washed it all off. Rolley was a certified goofball. There was certainly nothing between us. Nothing. He never told me that he knew Emma, if he did know her at the time.

I'd say we maybe hung out for a few months, a year max, in the early eighties, after my mother was gone. Then he kinda disappeared for a while. I started up with him again when I saw him downtown at a show. Blondie. He was with another man. The other one was older, a graying-at-the-temples sort. Rolley was into cocaine, that I remember. I think he was frightened of AIDS. I think it hit the headlines right around the time he was coming out. It didn't deter him entirely, but it may have discouraged him. Stifled his enthusiasm anyway. He grew cautious. Too many sick people. So, he was repressed and then repressed again. A very unhappy guy trying very hard to be happy. I don't think I helped him much. When he came back into my life, he was trying to get his shit together, including a portfolio so he could get some work. That's when I took the pictures. After that, we'd see each other occasionally.

I guess he's always been a little nervous that someone would find those photos. Probably just got freaked out when he heard that I died. Thought someone might find them. He has a job, after all. Anyway, that seems the most likely thing to me. Emma's a smart woman. I can't imagine why she would have had anything to do with him. Except for his looks. They were enticing. And he seemed to prey on drawing people to him, then pushing them away, maybe betraying them in some way. Complicated dude.

CHAPTER 42

For days now, Emma has talked to no one except to check in with Bill Kidman, daily, to see if there is any news from Angus. She's barely gone out except to walk Seamus, religiously, three times a day around the neighborhood and in Rock Creek Park. When she returns, she checks her voice messages obsessively. Sleeping is not easy. You read about a tragedy in the newspaper, and it can sadden you or stun you. You may speak of it later, but you can escape it in an instant, turn away from it, go about your day. For Emma, this, of course, is different. It gnaws at her through the night. The possibility of Angus's violent death. When she finally dozes off, she dreams of water spilling into her apartment, washing over her and over Seamus, tossing them about, air bubbles all around. In another dream, the two of them—Emma and Angus—are wrapped around one another, the feeling of his body against hers almost real until she begins to awaken and remembers. She rises, gets a glass of water, folds herself into the living room sofa with a throw wrapped around her shoulders, her bare feet trembling from the cold. When she awakens, Seamus at her feet, she's weighted again by that feeling that something is terribly wrong, the dread. Then she remembers what it is.

They have been together for nearly ten years, although rarely actually together. They had, the two of them, something of an agreement, an implicit one, never fully defined. He would keep his flat in London and visit when he could, often unannounced. Every year, in the spring, they would meet, sometimes in Paris or Rome, or in a spectacularly exotic location. A hut on stilts in Thailand. A small cabin in Nova Scotia. Once, they rented a little house in Finland with a sauna and swam in the frozen waters. Things that Emma would never have considered doing, even in her dreams, but he had made her more of an adventuress.

The relationship gave her the independence she craved to pursue her work, along with the benefits of intimacy. He would appear in her world suddenly, with little notice but some regularity depending on his assignment. Sometimes he'd show up at her apartment in New York, but they both preferred the place on Saranac Lake, in Slatterly, her family's cabin in the Adirondacks. It was quiet, remote, inaccessible and had the veneer of safety, although they both knew full well that he could be traced there. It had happened before.

Nonetheless, Slatterly became a haven for them, at least during the offseason when they could avoid the others—the owners, the boisterous children on vacation, the tedious cocktail hours where the Manhattanites would endeavor to out-New-York one other, and the older residents, the ones whose families had been at the camp for generations, were engaged in looking down their noses at everyone else. At first, for Emma and Angus, their assignations in Slatterly were just that, like a celebration of one another's presence, more about lovemaking than anything else. But, over time, as the relationship matured, they found a balance, a comfortable mix of passion and friendship, an expansiveness and an ease. They had grown to be true friends.

During their last visit, back in December, he had seemed conflicted. Emma tries to recall the conversation, as if it will provide some clue to the frustrations he faced. And the dangers. Some clue into what may have led to this tragedy. And who is responsible. She remembers him talking about Iran-Contra. About terrorism in the Middle East and in Europe. And about himself.

"Sometimes I think I've lost my moral center," he'd said one afternoon when they were sipping bourbon, the fire crackling at the edge of their conversation, and smoking cigarettes. It was late afternoon, early to be drinking. She remembers being confused, not clear on exactly what he meant by what he said. And she can picture him. Angus had set his drink down and was leaning back on the sofa, rubbing his forehead, thinking before he went on. "I'm less sure of myself," he said. "That means I'm more likely to make a mistake."

She'd moved closer to him then and put her hand up to his cheek. "It's gotten nasty out there, Em," he'd said, pressing his own hand against hers. "This war has been going on too long. The Western powers are encouraging the conflict. The weapons are changing." She recalls the deep sadness in his eyes, the expression of hopelessness in his voice. "So many people are dying. I've seen things I wish I hadn't. And I know things I wish I didn't know."

"Surely this isn't what's on your plate?"

"No," he'd answered. But there was a weariness to his voice, a distance. "If it were on my plate, we wouldn't be having this discussion."

Then he'd hesitated a moment, as if he wanted to say more, as if he was struggling with something. "But it's in my line of vision," he'd said. And then not another word about it. Afterward, she'd talked with Professor Hatani, just to get some context, maybe deepen her understanding.

"Oh yes," he said. "I would say hundreds of thousands of people have died, not just military, but civilians."

"Can you help me understand what role the United States is playing? And the NATO allies?"

"Technically, no role. Your government says it's not taking sides."

"The Iran-Contra scandal suggests otherwise," she said. "I mean, they sold weapons to Iran, didn't they?"

"I would wager that they're selling weapons to Iraq as well. In fact, more so. And who knows what other services they're providing. This Iran-Contra business of President Reagan, this arms deal, it represents just a tiny fraction of the weapons at play over there. And who do you think is making all these weapons, if not the Western powers and Russia?"

"Is it a proxy war?"

"I'm not sure I would call it that. I think the West seems to benefit from keeping the conflict going. Certainly, your country does not want Iran to win this war. It seems that if two Middle Eastern countries are fighting each other, they're distracted—from creating havoc elsewhere in the region, from terrorist activities, not to mention the fact that they're being crippled by war. What smarter way to destroy your enemies than to have them destroy each other?"

"And give them the weapons to do it," Emma said.

"You have to understand that Iran and Iraq have both undergone a major change in leadership. We'd had an uneasy truce for many years. Now all hell has broken loose. And I mean hell."

They had talked for more than an hour. It may have given her more insight into the situation, even into Angus's experience. But now, running through it in her head, Emma knows she's just spinning in circles, avoiding the inevitable, and she has no interest in doing anything else. She's in possession of photographs from Tomas Brodsky that she's barely looked at, and even though she recognizes the man's face, she's told no one. Given Angus's disappearance, she hasn't the stomach for it or the energy.

CHAPTER 43

Emma does not have a happy relationship with things. Everything in her apartment reminds her of someone she's lost. When it was time to give up her grandparents' home, which had become her grandmother's home, she was not torn. She did not struggle with it. She selected only the most cherished and practical possessions. She surprised herself with which objects she chose and by how much she cherished each of them. The case clock that had forever disrupted her sleep as a child. A single black velvet riding helmet that had been her mother's. Her grandmother's silver lighter, monogrammed with the initials MRQ. A few throw rugs that wouldn't have fetched much at auction but had decorated her small bedroom, the one toward the back, the room where she slept as a young girl. And, for some unknown reason, she kept the oil painting from above the mantel in the sitting room, a painting of a sailing ship tossed in the roiling sea, all black and gray and purple. All darkness. Later, she discovered that Angus loved the painting and she'd hung it in her apartment in Washington. When she got the news about Zeebrugge, about the ferry, and when she felt certain Angus had died, she took the painting to the basement of her apartment building and set it up against the concrete wall. She wanted to burn it but didn't know quite how to pull that off in the middle of the city, without burning down the building, so she just left it there.

There's a small shop nearby that offers gourmet meals to go. In the last few days, Emma's gone down in the late afternoon to pick up dinner, trudged really, only half interested in what they have to offer. The chicken piccata, the pasta salad, the grilled salmon. Beyond that, she's subsisting on boxed cereal, crackers and whatever she can dig up in the refrigerator—a half carton of eggs, some cheese, an apple. She has never been prone to depression but feels certain that this is what it feels like—a difficulty raising one's head, the feeling of being enveloped in a kind of vapor, of coming down with something flu-like, a lack of interest in anything. On Thursday night, round about 9:00 p.m., when she runs out of bourbon, she slips down to the bar at Focaccia's. The restaurant is very nearly empty, and there is no one else at the bar. The bartender doesn't ask any questions, welcomes her with a Wild Turkey and water. He leaves her pretty much alone until she asks for a third. Then he nudges her with a soft, "You okay?"

"Not really," she says, twisting a lock of hair between her fingers, then looking up at him. "I keep losing people."

"Like?"

"Well, first my parents. When I was six," she says, pausing. "Then my grandfather, who raised me." She speaks matter-of-factly, as if dictating a list. "My grandmother. Although we weren't close. That was ten years ago. Then we lost Annie in 1985."

"Annie?"

"Our housekeeper. She helped raise me," Emma says, knowing full well that she's sounding like a drama queen with this poor-little-rich-girl thing going. But she doesn't care. She just spills it.

"And now?"

"And now my friend. My neighbor. Sweet, crazy girl. Seal. She would never have harmed a soul." She hesitates for a moment, looking up at him. *Enough*, she thinks. She doesn't tell him about Angus and the ferry accident or why her heart is really aching. Can't seem to say it out loud.

"Is there anybody you're close to? Anyone who can help you right now?" This is the first time she's tapped into his skills as a therapist/bartender. It calms her, in a way. Brings her back.

She sits for a time, quiet, picking her own brain and puts her right hand over the glass to stop him from pouring another. Then she reaches into her pocket for a twenty and sets it on the counter. "Yes," she says, looking up at him. "Yes. Thank you for that." As she leaves, she turns back to him. "And that whole housekeeper thing. Forget about it."

The air in DC has been sharp and clear all week, almost cleansing, and now, in the darkness, it's turned cold, and at this hour there's little foot traffic on this stretch of Connecticut Avenue. Wrapping a throw close around her as she makes her way, she senses someone nearby, to her left, behind her in the dark. Almost at the awning, the entrance to her building, she fumbles in the pocket of her jeans for the keys. She has had a lot to drink, but she maneuvers past the entrance, then turns back suddenly and sees him at the edge of her line of vision, then reflected in the front door, in the glass. At that precise moment, a cab rolls up to the curb and Emma watches as he falls away, disappears. Later, as she packs a small bag for herself and one for Seamus, she will be certain that it was Rolley Smythe.

CHAPTER 44

Brodsky's people have reviewed the contents of the file cabinet. They send their findings in a memo to Tomas Brodsky and, as a courtesy, fax a copy to Emma Quinn.

THE MEMO

The file cabinet recovered from the late Lucille Lawson's studio on March 4, 1987 contained more than forty separate files. These files include tax returns (1969–1978), bank statements (1975–1979), legal documents, receipts for the sale and purchase of art; a folder labeled "Portfolio" containing a description of 28 pieces of art (believed to be her personal collection); the lease to an apartment on 72nd Street that expired on July 1, 1979; news clippings and various magazine articles, invitations to events and exhibits, and catalogs from exhibits at private galleries and museums. It also included a box containing checkbooks and canceled checks, along with credit card and other receipts.

The art collection documented in the file labeled "Portfolio," recovered in Lucille Lawson's studio on March 4, 1987, consists of 28 pieces. As yet, none of these pieces have been recovered. We don't have accurate valuations of these pieces. They include the work of the following artists, in alphabetical order:

Ruth Asawa (drawing, circa 1960)

Alexander Calder (mobile, limited edition reproduction)

Mary Cassatt (drawing, circa 1878)

William Christenberry (2 photographs, 1970s)

Francesco Clemente (gouache and pencil on paper, 1978)

Carroll Cloar (2 paintings)

Elaine de Kooning (2 paintings, 1954 and 1970)

Willem de Kooning (painting)

William Eggleston (2 photographs, 1972)

Lyonel Feininger (drawing, 1953)

Adolph Gottlieb (painting, 1969)

Jasper Johns (flag painting, 1963)

Ellsworth Kelly (white and dark gray panels, 1977)

Lee Krasner (painting, 1969)

Louise Nevelson (1969–1974)

Robert Rauschenberg (oil on canvas, untitled, 1963)

Gerhard Richter (4 pieces/drawing, painted photograph and 2 paintings)

Mark Rothko (2 paintings)

Alan Shields (work on paper, 1975)

Neal Slavin (photograph, untitled, 1974)

Summary of financial information, as follows:

TRUST FUND: Maggie Grace Lawson was custodian of a trust fund. Based on the statements, it is an irrevocable trust. The value of the trust fund, at the time of Maggie Grace's death, was $2.4 million, with monthly payments of $8,000 going to her daughter, Lucille Lawson.

CONFIDENTIALITY AGREEMENT: There is a legal document containing a pledge of confidentiality around the trust fund. It is signed by the victim's grandmother, Nancy Lawson, and by another party that is blacked out with what appears to be a magic marker. In addition, the file contains a pledge of confidentiality related to the trust signed by one John L. Simpson, attorney-at-law, and Seal's grandmother, Nancy Lawson. It was signed on June 18, 1956.

TOTAL ASSETS: In 1977, Maggie Grace's own assets in cash and securities were roughly $150,000. She also owned a loft in Chelsea. That, and the art collection, which is not expressly appraised in these documents but contains the work of major artists and photographers.

WILL: The file contains a copy of Maggie Grace's will. The contents of her bank and investment accounts passed on to her sister, Jennifer Lawson Henley, upon her death. Her partnership in Merna's Place passed on to Merna Jones, who became 100% owner; and her personal possessions as well as the loft in Chelsea, which she owned, she passed on to her daughter, Lucille Anne Lawson. There is no mention of a trust fund. The will is dated May 27, 1979, and the attorney of record is Janice P. Willingham of the law firm Willingham and Willingham in Plantersville, Tennessee. The witness to this last will and testament is her sister, Jennifer Lawson Henley.

Tomas Brodsky chuckles when he first reads the documents. "Written like true accountants," he tells his staff, but he expresses gratitude for their "precision and care," and he asks the legal department at police headquarters for a way to get around this confidentiality agreement.

"They are all dead. Where did the trust fund go? That certainly could be relevant to the case," he says, adding, "possibly registered in Tennessee or Mississippi."

He takes the memo along with him to two meetings—one with the art consultant and coexecutor, Lynley Wright, and the other with Harriet Freeman, the estate attorney. "Where is the art collection?" he asks them. Lynley Wright says only that she was storing Warhol's portrait and a handful of Seal's pieces—"all locked up in a vault," she says, adding that she'd never worked with Maggie Grace. "If there's a collection," she says, "it's not in my shop." She tells him that, in addition to Andy Warhol's portrait of Lucille Lawson, she has four pieces in her vault. He requests the specifics in writing.

Harriet Freeman is more forthcoming. She looks carefully at the list of pieces, the collection, shaking her head in amazement or reading an artist's name aloud reverentially, almost breathlessly—"Mary Cassatt" or "the de Koonings" or "two Rothkos."

"This is remarkable, truly remarkable," she says, finally lifting her head. "I'd have to see the pieces, but I'm guessing the value would have grown from the thousands to the millions. There are quite a few by abstract expressionists that would be worth a fortune." She reviews the list again. "I had no idea," she tells him. "Maggie Grace Lawson was right up there with the Vogels. Or Hester and Harold Diamond."

Brodsky looks confused.

"Regular people, people who aren't rich or in the business, who are just in love with art—good art, real art—and they become collectors by buying what they love—however they can manage it. Financially, that is."

"But Maggie Grace Lawson was not exactly a regular person. She had access to this trust fund, didn't she?"

"Based on my understanding, she would have received income from the trust fund—but I doubt she would have been able to make withdrawals to buy art. I'm thinking she used her own money. After all, the restaurant was a big success. Besides, I was talking more about the choices she made. The art she bought. The Vogels are legendary—Dorothy and Herbert. A postal clerk and a librarian who are masters at identifying emerging artists. I understand they have an amazing collection of minimalist and contemporary art—much of it bought directly from the artists. And Hester Diamond and her husband, Harold, both grew up in the Bronx in working-class families. They built a collection that includes the likes of Picasso, Mondrian, Fernand Léger."

Brodsky is just nodding, waiting patiently for her to tell him something he doesn't already know. "So, it's possible that Seal Lawson's mother acquired these pieces on her own," he says.

"Of course. But she also apparently had an eye," Harriet says. Then, hesitating for an instant, "Or someone who helped her."

"So, where is it? Where is this collection?"

"Good question," she says. Brodsky just waits, giving her an opportunity to think, and she goes on: "It wasn't part of her daughter's estate. And I didn't handle her mother's estate. Maybe she sold it before she died. Or maybe Lucille sold it. Interesting. I don't know."

They talk briefly about how to track it, who might know more, and she recommends searching for individual pieces, talking to some of the bigger dealers, searching the database at the public library. But he decides to explore just exactly how Harriet Freeman got this job.

"So, Maggie Grace Lawson hired you?" he says. "Correct?"

"For her daughter. Yes."

It's like pulling teeth, he thinks. "And how did she happen to find you?"

"Someone recommended me to her."

He bows his head slightly, setting one elbow on the arm of his chair and pushing his glasses up on his nose, frustrated. "And who was that?"

Harriet just shakes her head. To keep it going, Brodsky says sarcastically, in the nicest, most deferential voice, "And who might have handled the sale of a collection such as this, may I ask? Unless, of course, that would be confidential."

Harriet Freeman is not amused. "She probably would have worked with Citibank," she says. "They have an art advisory division. They're the leader. I can't think of who else could have handled it."

Later, when he contacts Citibank to request the information, he is advised that it will take ten days.

"This is a murder inquiry," he says. "I can get a court order for that information."

"Then please do," the bank responds.

CHAPTER 45

SEAL

Obviously, I never found my voice as a photographer. That's my greatest regret. That, and the fact that I never really fell in love. I'm not sure I ever would have. I think I might have been missing a piece. I don't know whether it's physical or emotional, but the longest relationship I had was with Simon and, even then, I never felt either comfortable with him or enthralled with him. It seems to me someone who is in love feels one or the other. As for my work, it was always important to me, and I felt this compulsion to do it. But I don't know how to explain my shortcomings except to say that I was too self-aware, too self-conscious. I knew that I wasn't gifted. And I was living among pioneers. Cindy Sherman. Bill Eggleston. Jim Goldberg. Nan Goldin. How do you compare yourself to photographers like that? They were breaking all kinds of new ground. I suspect I would have been a better photographer if I'd grown up in the Midwest or something, far away from glare. Look at Andy. I mean, Pittsburgh.

Plus, when I was just starting out, everything was changing so fast in a big way. Street art and street music and what you might call the scene, the downtown scene, was changing everything. Art. Music. Dance.

Everything. When I graduated from the New School in '82, I felt like I was late to the party. Plus, I was intimidated, although you wouldn't know it to look at me. I had an attitude. I could dress the part, but I was way too distracted by what everyone else was doing.

I know one thing. You can't play in that arena unless you're fearless—or a genius. And I am neither. Plus, I had nothing to drive me. I mean, aside from her skill, Nan Goldin had her tragic family, her disenfranchisement, her crazy friends. Her lifestyle fed her art. Haring has street cred and his gayness, and he's a smart dude, well trained, not some punk who decided to paint his name on a subway car but someone capable of understanding the beauty of public art. Thoughtful, conscious of the work he was doing, socially aware, deliberate, savvy. Basquiat, now he's definitely a genius, but I don't think he's going to be around for too long. Seems like he's self-destructive.

Some people think art is all about angst. Or hunger. Maybe being angry at my mother didn't give me enough to chew on. Ha! And Lord knows I was never hungry. I feel like my work has always been too tame. Technically fine, but somehow there was no heart to it. And I didn't have any big ideas. When you're creating something, no matter what the medium is, it has to have an idea behind it. Something to hang on to, a backbone, a concept. Meaning. Even if the audience never knows what it is. I grew up surrounded by truly great art. I knew what it was. And I knew I wasn't making it. And I was in a really dark place. I mean, technical skill is one thing. Brilliance is another.

So, I don't know, maybe like six months ago, I started meditating. I thought it would help me tap into something bigger, even it was just something bigger inside me. I used a Buddhist chant—only because I had a roommate at Sarah Lawrence who meditated using this chant: *Nam myo ho ren ge kyo*. I just did it, every day. Chanted it out loud. Then, after a few months, I joined a discussion group. Started reading about it—about Buddhism. It was interesting. It wasn't like a revelation or anything. More like an exploration. And my work started to improve, probably because I wasn't thinking so much about what every other photographer was doing. But that was only a piece of it. My life felt better. I don't know quite how to explain it, but I felt quieted somehow and as if I didn't have to struggle so much, think so much about everything. Happier. I met some new people. Nice, thoughtful sorts, all of which was calming and gratifying somehow. But I was just a beginner. A newbie, if you will.

All that said, I can't help but wonder what kind of person I might have become or what kind of photographs I might have produced had I been on the earth just a bit longer. I mean, look at Mark Rothko. He didn't do his multiform paintings—his big, beautiful, shadowy blocks of color with oceanic depth and richness, his signature work, his breakthrough paintings—until he was in his forties. They are kind of magical. I understand that viewers are transported by them. He'd been painting for like twenty years before he did those paintings. Really. Who knows what kind of work I might have done? Or what I might have seen or learned if I'd hung around a little longer?

Of course, that's hardly relevant. What I can say is this: If I were to give anybody advice, it would be to ignore all the noise around you. Find the calm center. And observe the world around you. I mean the physical world and the metaphysical world. Period.

CHAPTER 46

Lester Daniels is coming up on sixty. He has built a chain of successful paint stores in Wilmington and around New Castle County and lives now in the town of New Castle. His home is in the historic district, Old New Castle, with its brick sidewalks and village-green row houses dating from the eighteenth century, and elegant, imposing three-story homes overlooking the water. A port town where the merchant class was the ruling class, New Castle is set on the Delaware River, on the back side of Wilmington.

Lester's mother, Annie Daniels, worked for Emma's grandparents as a housekeeper for four decades. She did more than clean the house. She managed it. She also managed the medications that kept Emma's grandmother on the edge of sanity. And she played no small role in raising Emma. When Emma's grandfather died in 1968, he left Annie Daniels a substantial trust fund and an established relationship with a financial advisor to guide her. Consequently, she never touched the principal. She reinvested the dividends. She watched it carefully. And by the time she passed it on to her son, it was worth a small fortune.

Lester is comfortable. Emma has known him her entire life. She wants to steer clear of Rolley Smythe until this is resolved. She wants to sequester, to feel safe, and no one feels safer to her than Lester. Old New Castle is like a hideaway. Small, quiet, remote. She arrives early, at 8:00 a.m. "Stay as long as you want," he says. "The third floor is yours." He points to the dog. "And the backyard is his."

Once she settles in, Emma calls the bursar's office at Columbia, tells them she hasn't been able to make it down to the university. "Would you mind resending the documentation on Rolley Smythe somewhere else?" she asks. She spells it out again. Pronounces it Smythe, with a long *i*, so it sounds like white or fight. Smythe.

"We have no record of anyone by that name either attending Columbia or teaching here," the woman says.

"No graduate student at the Business School?"

"No graduate student at the Business School."

"No one co-teaching a class in economics?"

"No, ma'am. There is no documentation on anyone named Smythe." The woman puts a lot of emphasis on the long *i* in Smythe, sharpening her tone.

Dumbfounded, Emma calls the economics department at Columbia, to confirm. Asks all kinds of questions. The secretary doesn't know the name Rolley. Or recognize the description. That's when Emma calls

Brodsky and tells him everything—that she knows the man in the photos, that he may have been masquerading as a student a few years before, that he may be following her. *Don't assume anything,* she reminds herself. She identifies him as Rolley Smythe. "But that may not be his real name," she says. It's not a short conversation. She describes him in some detail and makes it clear that he was a graduate student who audited one of her classes. "I didn't know he knew Seal until I saw these photographs," she says. But she doesn't tell him where she is. She doesn't tell anyone except Bill Kidman. She leaves a message on his secure line. Then she goes for a long walk through the old town.

Old New Castle is set on a grid, with the Green, a vast lawn designed as a town square, at its center and the Delaware River at its edge. An odd little brick cottage, easily three hundred years old, with a tiny door and a steep, handcrafted roof overlooks the Green, where a graveyard dating back several centuries surrounds an old Episcopal church. When William Penn arrived in America, he was granted this acreage on the river as part of his territory, part of the swath of land that became Pennsylvania and Delaware. His statue stands nearby, which lends a sense of significance to the Green. But the town itself is remote, a well-kept secret.

Emma spends a good hour on the Green that first morning with Seamus, sitting on a bench, watching an abundance of birds pass through. They are migrating. The stillness, the constancy of the place preserved over hundreds of years is calming, life-affirming, settling. And this is where she spends her time in the days that follow. On her third day, she spots a bald eagle atop the steeple of the old church. She stands, unmoving, observing. She's beginning to slow down. Relishing the isolation, taking Seamus along the river on a path carved out of the woods, dining alone at an old tavern near the waterfront. No one knows she's here, except Bill Kidman—and Lester.

CHAPTER 47

"I haven't threatened anyone. I just wanted to talk to her." Rolley Smythe is sitting in an interrogation room at the central offices of the FBI in the nation's capital, responding to this question: "Were you stalking Professor Quinn?" The FBI picked him up, because there is a warrant out for him in New York and Connecticut for the theft in Greenwich, because he crossed state lines, because he seemed to be following Emma—and most of all because Detective Brodsky believes he may have killed Lucille Lawson. But it was Bill Kidman who made the call.

Rolley had been attending a conference at Georgetown on the European labor movement in the nineteenth century and was easily traced to a B and B near the university. He was registered—at the conference and the B and B—under the name Rolley Smythe. But, by now, they've seen his driver's license and the spelling of his name, which could potentially sound the same, but, in fact, it doesn't: Reynolds K. Smith, a.k.a. Rennie Smith. They've taken his fingerprints and passed them on to Tomas Brodsky, who has found a match. Rennie Smith's prints are on the back door at Anna Lorch's gallery. They're on the highball glasses in Seal's studio. "We've got him," Brodsky had said to the agent, who is grilling him now.

"They're my photographs," Rolley/Rennie is telling the agent. "I never hurt anyone. I just wanted my pictures back."

"Why didn't you just ask for them?"

"Look, a friend of mine took those photographs. When she died, I wanted to retrieve them. I had every right," he says.

"Why didn't you just ask the lady at the gallery for them then, instead of breaking in?"

"I can't afford to buy them. And why would I? They are pictures of me. They are mine. I never gave anyone permission to sell them. I didn't want people to see them. I felt exposed."

"I bet you did," the agent says, leafing through a few images that were recovered from Rolley's luggage, photographs where he appears half-naked in a variety of poses. "Don't worry," the agent adds, caustically. "They'll be safe here."

Then they lock him up for the night. They are holding him until Tomas Brodsky and Bill Kidman can make it to their offices. "I want to call my lawyer," he says as they shut the heavy metal door that guards his cell. They leave him agitated, walking in circles, full of sound and fury.

CHAPTER 48

Emma has a name now. Reynolds K. Smith. She knows she has to go to New York, has to talk to Merna, go through Seal's studio, find out more. She makes a reservation for the morning train and calls Merna's Place. Merna picks up at the register out front.

"I'm coming to Manhattan," Emma says. "I want to see you. They have someone in custody."

"Custody," Merna says, rattled. "Hold on. Hold on. I can't hear you," she says. "Don't hang up." She hands the phone off to a waitress, then grabs it in the back.

It is Sunday night. Merna slides through the front of the house and the clatter of a busy kitchen, past the steam rising from the dishwashing station, the plates stacked one upon another in gray rubber bins, the remains of a successful evening. She picks up the phone in a small hallway, standing near the time clock, the staff restroom, the back door that leads out to an alley full of more trash. It's beyond the fray, relatively quiet. A corkboard covers one wall with OSHA bulletins, handwashing reminders, work schedules and tomorrow's menu. There's a page cut out of *New York* magazine with a photo of Merna and Maggie under the headline, "What's Hot in Harlem" and a Polaroid of a young Lucille—

of Seal—stirring a pot of something.

"Who is it?" Merna says as she picks up the phone.

"It's me, Emma."

"I know. I know," Merna says. "Who's in custody?"

"A man named Reynolds Smith. Sometimes goes by Rolley Smythe."

"No. I don't think so. No," she's shaking her head, pacing, pulling the phone cord away from the wall, stretching it.

"You don't know him," Emma says, half statement, half question.

"Oh, I do. I do know him," Merna says. "If you mean the Rennie Smith who went to school with her at Walden. And at Sarah Lawrence. The one who wanted to be an actor and a model. The handsome one. *That* Reynolds Smith."

"He went to Walden? And Sarah Lawrence?"

"I don't believe for one minute that he would have hurt her," Merna says. "They've known each other forever."

Emma is flummoxed. *Known each other forever.* "Were they romantically involved?" she asks.

"Lord no," Merna says. "They were friends. No. Nothing like that."

"When do you think she last saw him?"

Merna ignores the question. "In custody for what? For what happened to Lucille? For hurting her? I don't think so. No."

"He's been arrested for stealing some photographs she took of him. He's a suspect. That's all I know. They're just questioning him."

"Good," Merna says. "Just come on then. I'll see you tomorrow."

***

When the Sunday rush ends and Merna gets upstairs, it's close to eleven. She rolls into bed, but can't seem to settle in, troubled by the idea that Rolley could have hurt Seal. There's been a mistake, she's certain of that, but doesn't have a clear idea of exactly what's going on. Stole some photographs? A suspect? She tries to imagine what she might say to Emma or what she can do to help Rolley, poking around among her memories, recalling his expulsion from Sarah Lawrence, his habits, his inconsistency. "When did I last see him?" she asks herself. It might have been more than ten years ago, she thinks, wondering in the darkness if he might have done this awful thing, her head filled with ideas that weave themselves into emotions—fear and anger and sadness and confusion. The blanket feels like a weight, the pillow, flat, hard, unworthy of its purpose. It's after four in the morning before Merna finds some peace. Even then, she tosses and turns.

Given that her workday ends late at night, Merna always sleeps in. But on this Monday morning, of all mornings, she's awakened by the buzz of the intercom. It's 9:00 a.m., long before she typically rises. The staff won't be on-site until ten. She's normally the last to arrive. By noon, if you're in the neighborhood, you begin to smell the barbecue smoking in the back alley and the collards up front. Merna lifts the black mask over her eyes that enables the luxury of a late rising, rolls over and looks at the clock. The buzzer rings again. "What fool is ringing my doorbell?" she says to herself. Rising, throwing on a robe and padding to the front window, she looks down to see a van parked out front. It reads, "United Pest Control." Below that, "Commercial & Industrial" and beneath that, in cursive, "We're looking for a few bad rats."

"Pest control," the voice says over the intercom when she greets him, dizzy, tired and exceedingly grumpy.

"You got the wrong day," she says. "It's Monday. We're closed Tuesday. That's tomorrow. So come back tomorrow. And go round back, for God's sake. We don't need that van like that, with that business about the rats parked out there."

"Sorry," he says. "First visit."

"Well, get it right if you want to be invited back."

"I'm sorry, ma'am," he says, and she detects the sound of home in his voice. Curious, she goes back to the window, watches him get back in the van, but she can't see his face, just his jumpsuit and his orange-and-blue hat. "Wonder who thought those colors would work?" she says to herself. She heads back in to slip between the sheets, but it's too late. Her mind won't allow it, so she rises again and puts on the coffee and starts her day two hours early with half a night's sleep. She doesn't give a second thought to the pest control company. Doesn't even think to ask the manager about it. Too much else on her mind.

CHAPTER 49

Brodsky's people are on it. Emma knows that, but she cannot wait. When she gets into the city, she goes first to Columbia and directly to the bursar's office, gives them the correct spelling of Rennie's name. His full name, she finds, is Reynolds Knox Smith. She learns that he finished his undergraduate degree in the General Studies program at Columbia in 1978 and that he went to the Business School from 1982 to 1984, which is when Emma knew him. They can find no record of his teaching or co-teaching any course at Columbia this year or any other.

In her office at the university, Emma pulls from the Federal Express envelope the least revealing photo of Rolley she can find. It's a straight-up shot of him in a black suit, a white shirt and a skinny black tie—likely taken shortly before he donned a lady's wig. He looks much like he does today, with his hair almost to his shoulders, his high cheekbones, his dark eyes. She shows it to the history department secretary. "You know this guy?"

She shakes her head. "No, but didn't he come to see you like last week or something?" Emma also runs it by the people in the economics department, one floor down. "Never seen him before" is the universal response. All of which tells her that, last week, he probably came strictly to connect with her, which she finds confusing.

To find out more about who he is, about his relationship with Seal, she contacts Walden and Sarah Lawrence College. The people at Walden are eager to help. She makes an appointment for later in the day. When she reaches the registrar at Sarah Lawrence, Emma tells the woman that she's interviewing Reynolds Smith for a teaching assistantship, and she is told to send a formal request and they will fax her his transcript. But, with a bit of wheedling, she finds out all she really needs to know—that his record was "mediocre at best" and that he only lasted three semesters at the college. She also learns that he was expelled for selling drugs on campus. *It couldn't have been uncommon to find drugs on campus back then*, she thinks. *He must have been extreme about it.*

At the main library, parked at a large, boxy computer, searching the database, she finds Reynold Smith's birth announcement, confirming that he was born in 1956, the same year as Seal. Based on his parents' wedding announcement in the *New York Times*, which she reads on microfilm, they were both artists—a painter and a sculptor—who lived in Greenwich Village. Apparently, in the midseventies, they bought a house in Croton-on-Hudson, probably when their son went off to college, although they kept their Greenwich Village address. It seems the two were married shortly before Rennie's birth. Rennie's father is still living, a practicing artist. There is a record of a divorce in the early eighties, and it appears that Rennie's mother—a Barbara Reynolds Smith—is no longer living in Manhattan, unless, of course, she remarried and changed her name. But Emma can find no record of such a union. She also learns that the Reynolds family—the mother's side of the family—is from Baltimore and that Rennie's grandfather, Howard K. Reynolds, is a financial advisor of some kind. Further research tells her that he is still alive and that Rennie—a.k.a. Rolley—is employed by his grandfather's firm, which has an office in northern New Jersey, in Short Hills, as well as an office outside Baltimore.

***

It's past one when she meets Merna for lunch at her Harlem restaurant. Emma is eager for information more than for a meal. But the plate of blackened catfish and collard greens, cole slaw and cornbread is flavorful and intense. She finds it hard to put down her fork. Merna is doing most of the talking.

"I remember when they changed their names," she tells Emma, speaking slowly, holding a mug of coffee with both hands, her elbows set on the table, ignoring her own plate. "It was right after they left Sarah Lawrence—before Maggie Grace got sick. Neither of them had a job. They'd both dropped out. They had no idea what they were doing, no goals. They had no sense, if y'ask me. Just drifting. Maggie Grace was worried."

"Was Seal living at home then, with her mother?" Emma asks.

"No. Maggie Grace was supporting her, but the child was living in her studio."

"The same studio as now, the one in Chelsea?"

Merna nods slowly. She seems groggy and distracted. "Do you need anything?" she asks, rising in the middle of the conversation and turning back toward the kitchen.

"No. Thanks," Emma says, calling out after her. "Was she doing photography back then?" But there is no answer. Merna lingers in the kitchen for a moment, drawing a glass of water from the tap, then stands unmoving, staring at the wall, her hips leaning into the counter, people working all around her. She's guessing she had three hours' sleep, maybe four. Her hand is trembling as she lifts the glass, the exhaustion dizzying. She takes her time.

When the glass is finally empty, she returns to the table out front, responding as if she'd never left the room. "No. She didn't start in on photography until later. She started taking pictures when Maggie Grace was sick. But she didn't get serious about it until she went to the New School. That was after Maggie Grace died. She kinda pulled herself together all of a sudden. Maggie used to say she was trying to find herself. Maybe it took her mother's death to make that happen. I don't know."

"So where does Rennie fit in?" Emma asks.

"Maybe a case of opportunism. He knew they had connections—Maggie Grace and Seal." She nods in Emma's direction as she says the word Seal. "I think Rennie—or Rolley, or whatever the damn thing you want to call him—was probably using her to meet people. I know he was modeling back then. No question he wanted to be part of the scene. Anyway, he wasn't around for long, far as I could tell. One thing though—Maggie Grace thought he was a bad influence."

"Anything specific?"

"He was wired all the time and a cocky little bastard. I'm betting that he was doing coke. Maggie Grace thought that." By now, Emma has nearly finished her meal. Merna gets up again, still a bit unsteady. "You sure you don't want some tea?"

"I'm fine," Emma says, shaking her head. "You okay?"

"Just didn't sleep last night. I'll make it," Merna says, sitting back down. She calls over to the waitress at a nearby table folding napkins. "Sweetie, bring me another coffee, will you, with a little cream and grab a slice of pecan pie for our guest."

Emma goes on. "So, was he living with his parents?"

"I think he was living in his parents' studio in the Village, and they were living in some little artsy town in the Hudson River valley some-where. Parents were drinkers and not terribly involved. Maggie Grace was a good mother. She kept a tight rein on Lucille. That wasn't so easy once she turned twenty-one."

"But Seal and Rolley weren't romantically involved."

"Honey, that child was a homosexual. I have nothing against the gays. And he may have been bisexual or whatever, which is none of my business. But I can assure you that they were not having a romance. Frankly, I think he used her to pick up men. You know what a beauty she was. Or maybe she was using him."

Emma looks up, surprised. "The woman I knew as Seal didn't have any problem going out on her own or attracting men."

"I'm not thinking about men," Merna says, wrinkling her brow and shaking her head. "I'm thinking about her interest in connecting to the art world. That was *his* world, his *parents'* world. And my guess is someone in that family had big money." But then she shrugs, dismissing the thought. "Either way, doesn't matter. In the end, Maggie Grace was right. She left them alone, and before long, our Seal figured things out for herself."

Emma's pie arrives, and she takes a moment to ooh and aah, and to savor the first few bites; Merna, sipping her coffee. Then, discreetly, after the waitress has cleared up the other dishes and stepped away, Emma lays out a few of the photographs Seal had taken of Rolley. "When do you think these would have been taken?" she asks.

"Well, there, you see." Merna points to one of the images where he's wearing a wig. "You knew all along, didn't you?"

"No. Not really. For all I know, they were just experimenting with gender in staged photos." Merna gives her a skeptical look. Emma switches gears. "Based on what you're telling me, I'm wondering if once Seal became a real photographer, once she was on her feet, he asked her to take some pictures. Like a favor for an old friend. Does that make sense?"

"Where did you find these?" Merna asks.

"They were undeveloped. In her studio."

"So, you're saying these photos were taken recently."

"Some time in the eighties. Maybe recently. Maybe for his portfolio, I'm thinking," Emma says.

Merna nods, as if that makes sense, but her face says she's not at all sure. She takes another look at the image—the one where Rolley is half-naked with a snake wrapped around his upper arms, then the one where he's dressed in a black suit, wearing a wig that obviously belongs on a woman. "I don't think so," she says. "I mean, what kind of modeling would this be?" She grimaces, looking at Emma intently. "Do you think all this had something to do with her death?"

"I don't know," Emma says.

Merna shakes her head as if to say *no, that's impossible, he never would have done such a thing.* But she doesn't speak. She lifts the photo where he's dressed like a woman. "I think this one's pretty damning," she says. "I doubt that he'd want it going around if he's got a job or anything. I don't know. If he were using, that might tip the scale." But she keeps shaking her head. "I can't tell you," she says finally, handing the whole lot of them back to Emma with a look of disdain on her face. "What a fool thing," she says, still shaking her head. "Pitiful, really."

But Emma has a different perspective. Knowing the art world where Seal had been circulating—and assuming that Rolley was part of that world—these photos seem almost tame. Nothing earth-shattering about them. And she's thinking that either Seal was doing Rennie/Rolley a favor, particularly now that she knows he was a model and that they were friends, old friends, friends long before Emma knew either of them.

Or maybe he was doing her a favor, by posing for her in ways that were provocative, attention-getting, timely.

Later, when Emma gets back to the university, she leaves a message for Tomas Brodsky, sharing her thoughts, mentioning the possibility of drug use. She knows Brodsky will have access to a criminal record if there is one. Then, driven more by curiosity than anything else, she heads to the Walden School.

CHAPTER 50

Since Saturday, Reynolds K. Smith, a.k.a. Rolley Smythe, has been stewing in a cell at FBI headquarters in the nation's capital, not some branch office or remote location, but the main facility. It is imposing. He looks terrified, ratty, unwashed sitting alone on the edge of the cot. There is a toilet in the room and a small sink. He has not slept for two days, and he's barely used the facilities. His lawyer—his grandfather's lawyer— will not arrive until late that afternoon, leaving him to languish there. Howard K. Reynolds, his grandfather on his mother's side, runs the wealth management firm in Baltimore. It is a substantial firm, Reynolds Capital, and this lawyer—tall, fit, gray-haired—is a man who clearly would feel comfortable throwing his weight around, which means he does not have to. He arrives late with a spring in his step and a cheery hello to everyone he encounters. Tomas Brodsky has been waiting for nearly two hours, having taken a morning train from Manhattan. Before Bill Kidman even arrives, the lawyer has questions about due process, about Rennie's rights, about what the hell is going on, which he asks in a friendly manner, a fatherly manner. "I'd like to meet privately with my client," he says.

It's late in the day when the three of them—Reynolds Smith and his attorney, and Tomas Brodsky, sit down at a conference table, facing one another. Brodsky outlines the charges—breaking and entering and theft, without mentioning Emma Quinn and whether he was following her. By now, he's gotten Emma's message, and he has more information that his own people provided. He's beginning to think this is a wild-goose chase. Rennie hardly seems concerned, as if he's taking part in an interview for a job he doesn't want.

Detective Brodsky flips on the tape recorder and begins the questioning with this: "So, what did you do with the rest of the stolen photographs?" He is sitting directly across the table from Rennie, who does not hesitate to look him in the eye when he responds. There is no indication of contrition in his attitude or his response.

"I burned them," he says. "I didn't want anyone to see them. They're pictures of me. They are mine. I have every right to do whatever I want with them." Although he speaks with certainty, beneath the table his right leg is balanced on his toes and it's bouncing up and down at a rate of about five jolts per second.

His attorney turns to him. "Did you sign a release form?" he asks, laying his hand on Rennie's knee to silence it.

"No. I did not."

"Is there some reason you're not using your real name?" Brodsky says, brow wrinkled, bending forward over the table.

"I prefer to be incognito in my private life. I use my name for work."

"And where do you work?"

"I mean when I'm modeling," Rennie says. And his attorney's face registers a mild dismay, although it's hardly noticeable.

"But you have other work," Brodsky says. At this point, without any kind of greeting or introduction, Bill Kidman enters the room and leans against the doorframe, opposite Brodsky, behind Rennie and his attorney, whose head whips around. But no one says a word, except Rennie.

"I work as an investment advisor," he says.

"There's no need to contact the employer. It is Mr. Smith's grandfather," the attorney says, glancing over his shoulder.

"I've done nothing wrong," Rennie says.

"Well, you broke into a commercial establishment. And you stole twelve thousand dollars' worth of art," Brodsky says.

"It's not a product. It's not a car or a washing machine," Rennie insists. "It's a photograph of a person. That art was worth nothing a week ago. And it was worth nothing without me."

"Well, according to Anna Lorch, it was worth twelve thousand dollars," Brodsky says, and the attorney jumps in.

"Let's be clear here," he says. "Anna Lorch did not own it. She did not buy it. It was part of Miss Lawson's estate. And my guess is, she would have been just as happy for Rennie to have had it, as anyone. In fact, those photographs were not sent to the gallery by Miss Lawson. They were arbitrarily included in a shipment from her executor. So, there are some questions here about who owns what. Does Rennie have rights related to those photographs? I believe he does."

Brodsky basically ignores the attorney. "Tell me, Rennie," he says, looking up at Kidman, who has just shrugged, "how long have you been looking for these photos?"

"Since I found out she was dead."

"And when exactly did you find out she was dead?"

"When I read the obituary in the newspaper, of course."

At this point, Brodsky and Kidman exchange glances. Then Brodsky proceeds. "So, you didn't kill her?" he says.

The attorney reaches his arm across Rennie's chest, as if to silence him. But Rennie is agitated now, indignant. "Of course I didn't kill her. That idea is grotesque. I loved Seal. She was like a . . ." And now the attorney presses his arm firmly against his client's chest to cut him off. "Do you have any evidence connecting Mr. Smith to the murder?" he asks, and when neither Brodsky nor Kidman respond, he goes on, "If not, I don't believe you have grounds to hold him."

"We have him on the interstate transportation of stolen property," says Brodsky.

"The photographer failed to get my client to sign a release form. So, technically, those photos were his property. Worst case: simple breaking and entering in Connecticut. That's a fine. Ten thousand max. You don't have much of a case."

"We'll see about that," Kidman says, stepping away from the doorframe as he speaks and taking a seat at the head of the table. He's bluffing. In fact, he is growing impatient. He doubts that this is the man responsible for Seal's death. And his mind is on other matters. "I have only one question for your client," he says, turning to Rennie. "Have you been following Professor Emma Quinn?"

"Why would you ask me that?"

"She saw you on Connecticut Avenue on Thursday evening."

"I went to see her," he says. "She wasn't home."

"And?"

"I waited for her. When she came back, she didn't look like, well, like she was in the mood for a visitor."

"In the mood?"

"Yes. She'd been drinking."

"And what's your relationship with Professor Quinn?"

"We are colleagues. I was a student of hers. And I had only just discovered that she and my friend Seal knew each other. I hoped we could maybe"—he hesitates for an instant— "comfort one another."

"Is that right? Comfort one another. But you saw that she'd been drinking, so you changed your mind."

"Correct."

"So, what did you do then?"

"I left the area."

"And how did you know where Ms. Quinn lived?"

"I asked at the university. At Georgetown. I was attending a conference there last week."

***

"Doesn't seem terribly intimidated, does he?" Kidman says, afterward, when he and Brodsky are alone in the outer hall.

"Why would he?" Brodsky says. "Rich grandfather, fancy lawyer." He hesitates for an instant. "Only thing I can imagine, given that this guy uses drugs, is that it could tie in somehow."

"With all due respect," Kidman says. "I don't think we have anything here."

"Look," Brodsky says. "Whoever did this was looking for something, something so important to them that they killed for it. So far, this is the only person who fits the bill."

"With a shoehorn maybe," Kidman says.

"We'll see, won't we?"

"Okay. Let's hold him for a few days," Kidman says. "See what we can find out. I'm okay with letting him squirm a little. And I don't like this lawyer much."

CHAPTER 51

Emma is baffled. It seems unlikely that Rolley would have hurt Seal to get hold of these photographs. Instead, she feels certain he was looking for the images because he knew Seal was gone. The obit came out on Tuesday, so that would make sense. But why did he pretend he didn't know Seal—or know about her death—when he encountered Emma on the train? And why had he shown up at Emma's office and her hotel and her apartment on Connecticut Avenue? She wants to dig deeper. She's not at all sure where to look at this point, but she's fairly certain she's not going to find what she needs at the Walden School.

The school's development officer greets her on arrival, a fortyish woman in a black cashmere turtleneck and black pants. Reed thin, everything about her says progressive, chic, Manhattan. She introduces herself as the director of development, and reports that she "knew Maggie Grace Lawson personally. She was a force of nature," the woman says. "Gracious and beautiful and soooo creative," she says, then continues, exuberant. "Maggie Grace spearheaded all kinds of arts festivals and trips to the theater and special events for the children. She was a real presence here at the school." Then, when asked more about Lucille, about Seal, the woman replies only that she didn't know her well. "My kids were a good three or four years younger than Maggie Grace's daughter. Lucille, you say?"

"Lucy. She may have gone by Lucy or Lucy-Anne."

"Oh yes. Lucy-Anne. Of course. I had the impression that she was shy, not . . ." she hesitates as if searching for the right words and finally settles on "not easily noticed," an awkward choice.

"Meaning?"

"Meaning there was nothing particularly special about her," she says, adding, "I wonder if she could have been a disappointment to her mother." Emma finds this characterization inconsistent with the woman she knew, the grown Lucille, the photographer who, albeit a bit of a loner, was strong-willed, outspoken, productive and hardly lacking in self-confidence.

"How old was Lucy-Anne when you knew her?" Emma asks.

"Oh, I would say eleven or twelve," the woman says. "My kids had just started here. So, again, I didn't know her well."

"Right," Emma says.

She reviews their school records at the office. Teachers describe Rolley as "inattentive" and "disruptive" in on-the-record notes, and she finds the words "a smart-ass" on a sloppily recorded handwritten note from a teacher, paper-clipped to the file. For Seal, they use another set of words—"distracted," "remote," "never speaks in class." She comes off as a shy flower, he as a prick. His grades are indeed mediocre, hers, sterling.

A young man named Hunter is instructed to take Emma to the

school library, where he pulls a half dozen yearbooks off the shelf—the years 1968 to 1974—windows into another time. In 1969, all the seniors are wearing armbands in the group photograph. Political, progressive. There are images that the students obviously took of one another on the National Mall during what must have been a march against Vietnam. Emma recognizes it, because she herself would have been there, driven down from Bryn Mawr. That would have been nearly twenty years ago, such a great distance that Emma can't remember how it felt or the details of the event itself. Seal would have been only twelve at the time.

Emma has to search the caption to find Lucy-Anne Lawson in the class picture from the sixth grade. She looks younger than the other students and a bit like the diminutive creature the woman in black described—slight, pale, dressed in some sort of a smock dress. Emma searches the caption for Rennie/Rolley, his hair in bangs that cover his eyebrows, looking gangly and preadolescent. He's wearing a T-shirt that reads "Arts in the Park" and seems to have dark circles under his eyes. He does not look like a happy child. But, of course, Emma thinks, it's just a class picture. Still, there are maybe fifteen children in the class and, of all of them, Seal and Rolley somehow look the most fragile, the least happy and, more than anything, the most out of place.

Emma leafs through the rest of the yearbooks, watching the two grow more angular, less innocent, more like the people she recognizes. She knows she is feeding her own curiosity more than anything else. That her familiarity with Seal and with Rolley is clouding her thinking.

That this is a waste of time. When she gets to their senior year, when each of the thirty or so seniors has a page of their own, she says out loud to herself, "This is silly." Their pages reveal so little about who they are, who they became as adults. All the photos were shot outdoors, in wooded settings, probably in Central Park. Rolley looks jaded, worn, restless. Seal looks wistful, even dreamy, sitting cross-legged on a park bench. Their individual pages are full of quotes and poems and the lyrics of popular songs. Seal chose the poem "why do the fingers" by E. E. Cummings, the one with the line "nobody beautiful ever hurries." A poem Emma has always appreciated, it brings on a smile and a sadness, and seems to speak to Seal's southern-ness. Rolley's page includes this lyric from Led Zeppelin: "Upon us all, a little rain must fall," which strikes Emma as sad. He is pictured with an electric guitar, his hair flowing down his back. His page tells her that he was a member of the drama club, something called the Social Awareness Committee and the squash team. Seal is a member of nothing, not even the photography club. She closes the book certain that it was their outsider natures, even in this unconventional school, that drew them to one another.

CHAPTER 52

SEAL

The Walden School. That was a big mistake. For me, anyway. My southern accent was a dead giveaway. I know exactly what they thought. This girl is behind academically (which I was, actually). This girl is a racist (why would they say such thing?). And, in so many words, this girl doesn't belong (I agreed). My name didn't help. Lucy Lawson, with the double *L*, was a total setup for disaster. Then we decided to go with Lucy-Anne, which was even worse, pegged me as an outsider. But we couldn't take it back.

These were sophisticated kids. I mean, they all grew up in Manhattan. And they pretty near all had money. My mother said it felt safe. But it didn't feel safe to me. The principal talked to me like I was just off the farm. I was only like eleven years old. I didn't really even know what a racist was at the time. When my mother explained it to me afterward, I felt ashamed, not just for myself, but for the little white girl who called me that, and for all white people.

Of course, the Walden mothers were all progressives. Certified members of the radical chic contingent. All-in on civil rights and integration, although I don't recall seeing a lot of Black students at the school. Of course, when they found out my mother was the co-owner of Merna's in Harlem, that changed everything. They were all over it. They rallied around her, although it didn't make much difference for me. In the end, I never did like Walden much, but my mother, she loved it.

CHAPTER 53

There's something about the man at Table 12. Not Merna's typical customer. Maybe it's the fact that he's dressed all in black, with a silver belt buckle the size of Missouri. Or that one of his teeth, on the upper left side, is missing. Otherwise, he's fairly nondescript. His reddish hair is cut close and turning gray. There are the sideburns. And his accent. It's distinctive, but not easily identified. He orders a barbecue plate and asks for Texas toast.

"I been missin' this food," he says when the waitress asks him what brought him here.

"I mean to New York," she says.

"Just business," he says. He's playing with a toothpick, one that he brought himself, dangling it on the edge of his lower lip.

"So, you from Texas?" the girl asks when she brings him his ribs. She's twenty-four, but she's happy to call herself a girl.

He shakes his head no, but doesn't volunteer any information.

"Tennessee maybe," she says, then, smiling. "You from Nashville?"

He just looks down at his plate. "This is perfect," he says.

"You're a musician, aren't you?" she says, smiling, coy. It tends to help with the tips. But he wants none of it.

"Go on now," he says, licking his thumb.

When she gets to the kitchen, the waitress mentions him to the busboy. "There's a guy out there, looks like he walked off the set of *Raising Arizona*." He is seeing her through a wave of steam, gripping a stack of dirty plates beside the washing station, half-puzzled, half-annoyed. "You haven't seen *Raising Arizona* yet, have you?" she says.

"What are you talkin' about?" he yells over the noise of the kitchen rush, setting the plates in a rubber bin, wiping his hands on a big, white apron.

"This guy out there's dressed like Johnny Cash, got a belt buckle that looks like something Elvis Presley would wear."

He smiles then, shaking his head. "Make up your mind. Elvis Presley or Johnny Cash?"

"I guess Elvis." She grins. "He's got sideburns. When was the last time you saw sideburns?"

The busboy shakes his head again. "Give the guy a break."

***

After he orders a second cup of coffee and pays his bill to the penny with cash, the man with the sideburns and the big belt buckle and the missing tooth waits in the restroom until the restaurant closes and the building is still. Closing time is nine-thirty on Mondays. By ten, the restaurant is usually empty. He's been monitoring the place. He knows that Merna generally leaves within an hour of closing, and everyone is gone within two hours. By eleven, the light in the room overlooking 125th Street is always off. He's made a note of all this, incorporated it into his plan.

The United Pest Control van is parked around the corner on 123rd Street. Earlier, when the place had just opened and the staff was setting up and Merna was upstairs talking to Emma Quinn, he'd stashed his gear in a duffel on top of a toilet in the men's room, locked it in stall number three and climbed out through stall number two. Now that he's paid his bill, he heads back to the restroom and waits in the stall until well after closing. At midnight, he pulls the duffel out and puts on his gear—gray, long-sleeved overalls that cover his entire body, the ones with the United insignia over his heart. He slips blue rubbers over his shoes and rubber gloves on both his hands. Then he straps what looks like a gas mask over his face and swings a cannister over his shoulder. Using the ray of light that shoots from the gas mask to make his way, he moves slowly, creeping along the edge of the hallway, with its photos of regulars and celebrities and politicians and Merna and Seal and her family. It takes a good fifteen minutes for him to ease his way from the men's room through the hall, past the elevator and up the back stairs to Merna's apartment. She's finally sleeping. Soundly. And she hears nothing when he enters her apartment.

CHAPTER 54

On Wednesday morning, after Merna fails to show up and the restaurant manager finds her unconscious and they rush her to Columbia Presbyterian. And after Tomas Brodsky and his people arrive and go through her apartment, which has been violently torn apart just as Seal's own apartment was torn apart—that's when the police ask: "What's missing?" And everyone who works for Merna knows full well what's missing: the Alexander Calder. The magnificent mobile that hangs in her living room. For Brodsky, that simple fact serves as confirmation that someone is after the art. And when they determine the general sequence of events, it seems to confirm that the thief is not Reynolds K. Smith, a.k.a. Rolley Smythe, who has been in custody since Saturday. "Unless he's got a partner," Brodsky says. "Or partners," Kidman says later.

By noon, Tomas Brodsky is interviewing the staff. "Anyone see anything? Anything unusual happen in recent weeks? Anything." They come up with a short list: an employee who'd been fired, a break-in around the corner, an argument between Merna and one of their suppliers. The waitress who covered table 12 mentions the man with the sideburns. "He was here on Monday night," she says, describing him in detail. "Not your average customer. Felt a little out of place. Definitely from below the Mason-Dixon Line." And this: On Monday night, Merna had told the restaurant manager to expect United Pest Control in the morning. "He'll be here at nine. And don't wake me up." She'd been adamant, the manager reports. "First of all, he never showed up," the manager tells Brodsky. "We're closed on Tuesdays. And I was there on Tuesday morning, waiting." She is bereft. "It never occurred to me to check on her," she says.

"For all we know, she was fine then," Brodsky says, trying to reassure her. After all, they hadn't found Merna until Wednesday, when she failed to show up for work.

"I don't know what I was thinking," the manager goes on. "We don't even use a company called United Pest Control. But I wrote it on my calendar anyway, assuming she'd hired someone new."

"Did she tell you she hired them?" Brodsky asked.

"No. She didn't tell me anything. And I didn't ask. We were busy. It was a busy night." The manager is inconsolable at this point, sitting at a table, bowed over, her head resting in her hands. Another waitress has pulled up a chair and wrapped her arm around the manager's shoulder. "It's okay," the waitress is whispering.

"It's not your fault," Brodsky tells the manager. "We have no way of knowing. And it might mean nothing." But he suspects otherwise.

CHAPTER 55

Seamus is out back, chewing on a gigantic bone that Lester picked up from the butcher at the Acme supermarket. The yard is narrow and deep and backs up to a wooded area that separates the village of Old New Castle from the less idyllic side of the city of New Castle, which consists of coming-up-on-run-down homes with asbestos siding and crumbling stucco, and chain-link fences and barking dogs and potholes. There are lots of fast-food establishments in New Castle proper and plenty of strip malls. The nearest one, with a small hardware store, a Mattress Warehouse, a Blockbuster and a Vietnamese restaurant, backs up to a 7-Eleven. The city of New Castle is a place where, after dark, you might encounter someone carrying a handgun. Old New Castle is the village at its edge, cut off from the twentieth century, where the only thing you might fear in the evenings are the bats that swarm at dusk.

Lester lives alone here. He has grown attached to Seamus or maybe just to the idea of a dog. "May I keep him?" he'd asked when Emma announced her plans.

Emma had smiled. "For a time, if you don't mind."

"No," Lester said. "I mean keep him."

"Of course not. He's my buddy," she said.

"Then you might want to slow down on the traveling." That was when Lester first voiced his concerns, his objections to the trip. Now, over breakfast with Emma and Bill Kidman, he's raised the issue again. "You don't know anything about these people," he says.

"It just makes sense," Emma is saying. "I've told them I'm coming for the service and bringing some of her things for the family. Her aunt was generous—although I wouldn't call her warm. There was an aloofness in her voice. But she invited me to stay at the house."

"I don't think it makes sense," says Lester. "Neither of you have any idea who killed your friend. Or who attacked this Merna."

But they've decided—Tomas Brodsky, Bill Kidman and Emma Quinn—that she needs to go down to Tennessee. The trust fund was set up there. Maggie Grace's will was drawn up there. Her family is there. And too many questions—and phone calls to Plantersville—remain unanswered. "We need to connect with the family in a nonthreatening way," Detective Brodsky had told her.

Now, there is a pile of bacon at the center of Lester Daniel's kitchen table, and Bill Kidman, Emma and Lester are savoring it along with generous helpings of scrambled eggs and toast and hash browns, while Seamus gnaws on a bone in the yard. This is more of a chat than a strategic meeting, although Lester has made his feelings clear. Bill Kidman is explaining that the case has become a matter for federal law enforcement. "There is no United Pest Control service in New York, or anywhere on the East Coast for that matter. It's based in St. Louis and primarily serves the Midwest and the Mid-South," Bill Kidman tells Emma.

"What the hell is the Mid-South?" Emma asks.

"It's a distribution region, includes parts of West Tennessee and Kentucky, northwest Alabama and Mississippi, and parts of Arkansas and Missouri. Radiates out from Memphis at its center. It's exactly where you need to be," he says. "We'll have someone right there, nearby."

"So, are you making any progress?" Lester asks. "Emma says you had the wrong guy."

"Wrong guy unless he was working with someone else," Kidman says.

"He was in custody when Merna was attacked," Emma tells Lester, who just shakes his head. "Poor woman," he says.

"Just plain stupid, all of us," Kidman says. "But now we know. And Brodsky's got his work cut out for him."

"I can't believe we never thought of it. Seems so obvious. Perfect way to sneak into a building carrying questionable substances."

"Nothing's obvious until it is," Kidman says. "And now we know they're still looking."

"It has to be the art," Emma says. "It's worth a fortune. That means Lynley, Anna Lorch, Harriet—they're all on the suspect list."

"Why on earth would any of those people want to steal the art?" Lester says. "They're rich people."

"In my experience, rich people are always trying to get richer," Kidman says.

"But they have so much to lose if they're discovered," Lester says.

"Well, they tend to be overconfident, to feel above the law, immune," Kidman says. "So, they make a lot of mistakes."

"I say, you should be looking for a poor person."

"Problem is, you can't sell art unless you have some sort of connection. That narrows it somewhat."

"But it could easily be a team of professionals who do this for a living," Emma says. She's shaking her head. "There are so many things we don't know about Lucille Lawson and her family. Where did her money come from, for one thing? Who the other half of her family is, for another. I'll go meet them. See who is at the service. Go to the courthouse and nose around."

"In a town that small," Lester says, "everyone will know everything. You just be careful."

"Lester's right. Be careful," Bill Kidman says. "Follow your own rule—don't assume anyone's innocent, and don't assume anything is safe."

CHAPTER 56

Rolley Smythe—a.k.a. Reynolds K. Smith—is standing on Pennsylvania Avenue, the main thoroughfare in downtown Washington DC that connects the White House and the US Capitol. He is staring up at the

J. Edgar Hoover Building, home of the Federal Bureau of Investigation. His grandfather's attorney, the man who engineered his release, has departed and failed to offer his client a lift, perhaps as a lesson. This is not Rolley's town. Still, he knows enough to make his way to Metro Center, a major connection point on the city's underground Metro system, where the Red Line and the Orange Line and the Yellow Line meet. He hasn't shaved in four days, smells like a man who's spent more than seventy-two hours in a cell and hasn't had a decent meal in as many hours, but he's desperate to talk to Emma. His mind has been spinning since his arrest. Once he arrives at the Metro station, there's a frantic energy to the way he slips his quarter into the pay phone and presses the buttons to dial her number, and waits, pacing, for someone to answer, listening for a beep when the answering machine picks up and he finally speaks. "Listen," he says. "It's Rolley. I need to see you. I'm headed to your apartment." He starts to hang up, then yanks the phone back up to his ear. "I didn't do it. You know that, don't you? I did not do it."

The DC Metro is a surprise to anyone who's spent their life riding the New York subway. It's a different animal. They started building it in the late sixties and haven't finished yet, so it's brand-new. It looks like something from the future, with its high, arched ceiling and the smooth, silent, graffiti-free trains gliding into the station, like something from a space station, another time, another planet. Rolley settles on the platform among the commuters and government workers and tourists trying to get to the museums on the National Mall and the Washington Monument and the Capitol itself. He checks the big, glowing plexiglass map for directions. He's going to take the Red Line to Woodley Park-Zoo, the Metro stop near Emma's apartment. He plans to wait there until she gets home, which, of course, is one of the things that got him in trouble in the first place.

Part Four

"That farm," Brodsky told Emma shortly before she made the final arrangements to go to Tennessee, "that farm where she grew up. It's not some little farm. It's a two-thousand-acre farm in the heart of cotton country. Part of what must have been a plantation at some point."

"So that's where her money comes from. Old money," she said.

"No, no, no. You misunderstand me. It wasn't her family's farm that her mother grew up on and that her aunt lives on now. It belongs to someone else. They were the caretakers. The Lawsons were caretakers. And Jennifer Henley and her husband are just caretakers."

Just caretakers. The sound of it registers with Emma.

"It's a two-thousand-acre farm," Brodsky said again. "That's a big farm."

"So, who owns it?"

"Family named Holder owns it. The Holders. From Memphis. Apparently, they go way back, and they're descended from the family that originally owned all the land around the town of Plantersville."

Emma is listening, and as she listens, her perspective is shifting. Her understanding of Seal is shifting. And of Maggie Grace. They were not wealthy people. "Anyway," he went on. "I talked to this Simon fellow..."

"Didn't you tell me she'd been getting calls from his office, from Salomon Brothers?"

"Yes, but they weren't from him. Apparently, they were just sales calls, Salomon salespeople looking for prospective investors, for new accounts. We checked out all the numbers. They weren't coming from Simon Golding's offices. Anyway, the guy did go to Plantersville with her and met her aunt. They went down there to arrange for the mother to live out her last days on that farm with her sister."

Emma interrupted then. "So, is he still a suspect?"

"Hold on," Brodsky said. "I'm trying to tell you something. His feeling is that there is some bad blood between the Holders and the Lawsons, something to that effect," Brodsky said. "I don't know. I just didn't want you walking into a situation unprepared."

"I need to talk to him," Emma insisted. "To Simon."

✳✳✳

It's amazing what you don't know if you don't ask, Emma is thinking as she recalls her meetings with the coexecutors and with Merna, and her friendship with Seal herself. She'd known there was a farm, and she'd assumed it was the Lawsons' farm. People assume. They always do. Now, she's talked with this Simon Golding and followed up with Harriet Freeman, and she's clear, or she thinks she's clear on the family's circumstances. She'd asked Simon about this so-called bad blood between Lucille's family and the Holders. "All I know is Aunt Jenny was not crazy about them. That's all. Some kind of tension."

"What's makes you say that?"

"Just an impression. When Luce and I went down to Plantersville, she went to Memphis one day to visit one of the Holders. Her aunt tried to talk her out of it. I think maybe she was just resentful."

"Just resentful?"

"Of her position in relation to them. Of their wealth. Their status. That's my guess. You know," he said, "her people—they're farm people, *country* people."

"Is that right?" Emma said and moved on. "Why did she go to see the Holders? What was that all about?"

"Tell you the truth, I have no idea. Curiosity, maybe. I think she saw them as part of her mother's life."

"Meaning?"

"Meaning she grew up on the farm that they owned. They played together as kids. Her mother had stories. Nothing more," Simon told her.

"How about her mother? Did Lucille and her mother get along?" At this point in the investigation, Emma has learned to use whatever name makes sense in the moment for her friend Seal.

"When we first met, she was angry at her mother about something. She wasn't speaking to her. Back then, I'd have said they didn't get along. But when she found out her mother was sick, she really stepped up. She took care of her, moved down there to Tennessee with her. That's when we split, right before she and her mother moved down to Plantersville."

"And why was that?"

"I don't know," he said. "Never have known for sure. You knew her. She was an enigma, that one. She told me . . . well, this is exactly what she said, she said we'd run out our clock."

"Interesting way to put it."

"Yeah. Not to me."

"Sorry," Emma said. "How long were you together?"

"Two years, almost to the day." Then there was a silence on the line, Emma waiting, leaving him uninterrupted, seeing what comes next. "She was a true free spirit. Only one I've ever known. And that one broke my heart."

After that, they chatted a little bit, as friends might. "She was a unique soul," Emma said. "That's for sure." And he'd said something about "Luce didn't get close to many people," and he'd called her "self-contained." That seemed to Emma to be a pretty fair description.

"One more thing," Emma said, and she asked him about the art collection.

"What art collection?" Simon said. "I don't know anything about an art collection."

"Had you ever been to her apartment?"

"I'd been to her studio. I don't think she had an apartment back then. But who knows?"

"And her mother's apartment? Did you ever go over there?"

"Of course not," he said. "I never even met her mother."

CHAPTER 58

SEAL

In a way, I think my mother was glad to be back in Plantersville. It was as if she had roots. Merna thought it would be a good idea. My Aunt Jennifer, who turned out to be naturally cranky, was okay with it. She knew what was happening. We all knew. By that time the cancer had moved to her brain. We suspended treatment. That's what they called it. Suspending. As if they would start up again at some point. She had been sick for maybe two years. I was taking her to chemo, living with her in our apartment on Seventy-Second Street, where I grew up. We were on the ground floor and there was parking out back, which was amazing. So, we bought a space, and we bought a car. And I'd drive her over to Sloan Kettering for treatments. I stayed with her, took care of her. It was no picnic, but I'm glad I did it.

She kept on a pretty even keel. But if I ever expressed any of kind of sorrow or worry or said something that suggested that I was sorry she had to go through it or said, "I know it's hard for you," or anything that felt somehow realistic or compassionate, or, I guess, negative, she'd flash. "I'm doing well, I think. Don't you?" she'd say. "I feel like we're making progress." She was always upbeat. Never wanted what she called pity. "It doesn't help," she'd say. "It weakens the spirit."

Those final months, she spent a lot of time talking about Plantersville. They were not always pretty stories, but she seemed to cherish them, hold on to them. It was a part of her, of who she was. She wanted me to know the history. One night, we were in her room, Aunt Jenny and my mother and me, and she started talking about when they first arrived in Plantersville, with Nanaw. "You were just a baby," she told Aunt Jenny. "I remember driving all day from Cleveland. You and me, we were in the back. I held you the whole time." Then Jenny reached out and held her hand, and she looked like she was going to crack. My mother, her eyes set off in the distance, would just talk and talk as if we needed to know everything, the whole story, all the facts, until her head would slump, and she'd fall off to sleep. She began talking about my grandmother, about Nanaw, and the situation she found herself in as the Second World War drew to a close.

MAGGIE GRACE

It was 1945, and Nanaw said that your grandfather would not be coming home from the war and that her job at the factory was about to end. She said the advantage of the move was that we wouldn't have to pay rent. She worked it out so we could live in this house in exchange for keeping it up and tending to the yard and the Little House. The Little House isn't here anymore. That was for the Holder family. It's where they used to stay when they came in from Memphis. But that's gone. Since they put in the highway, right, Jenny?

I was five when we moved here. The thing I remember most about that first summer was that there were cicadas all over the place, stuck in the screens and the monkey grass leading up to the house. You could hardly go out back without stepping on an old, dry cicada shell. I used to collect bunches of those shells and sit on the screen porch and make little cicada families and build little cicada houses out of leaves and twigs.

Funny thing, her southern accent seemed to come back when we were in Plantersville. Natural, I guess.

Seems like I played with those old shells every morning until it got so hot Mama had to turn on the fan. Then I'd have to gather them up, so they didn't blow away and put them in a shoebox for the next day. After that, I waited until she finished her chores so we could go over to Deaver's store across the highway and get a soda and sit at the counter under the air conditioner. Same thing every day. Your Nanaw would carry Aunt Jenny in a little papoose. That was our break, our treat. And at night, the sky was black, with darkness all around, as if no one lived anywhere near and we were all alone. Even the air was still, except for the sound of those cicadas.

We used to stand on the screen porch at night and listen to the sound of them whirring in the trees. It would come in waves and Mama would trace the sound of it with her finger on the screen. It would start off real soft and slow and then get louder and louder and louder. Then they would quiet down again. And Nanaw would move her finger up and down with the waves, up and down along the screen, tracing the sound with her finger. "Do you hear it, Maggie Grace?" Nanaw would say. "Do you hear it?" I guess you were in the bed by then, Sister. Anyway, I remember that as the safest, sweetest time in my life.

CHAPTER 59

Emma fears that Angus is gone. She is driving to Memphis. She keeps asking herself why she is driving, and she always has the same answer. *Because I need to. Need to clear my head. Need to grieve. Need space. Need time to think.* Bill Kidman has tried to convince her that everything will be all right. "You'll see," he said. But now, headed through Virginia toward Tennessee on Interstate 81, surrounded by Mack trucks, she doesn't believe him.

It's a sixteen-hour trip from DC to Memphis, and she has no plan to stop until she gets tired. Passing through the Shenandoah now, she's looking downward, out the side window, to her left, at the small farms spread out in the valley miles below—green fields, silos, old farmhouses with pitched roofs and cattle grazing here and there, like something a crow might have seen a hundred years before when there were no interstates, just a winding road between the mountains and the valleys. She tries to imagine what it would be like to live down there before the electric grid. The thought terrifies her. She does not like the country. It's just too dark, too quiet, each house planted too great a distance from another, a breeding ground for a variety of sins—murder, incest, child abuse. She'd read Truman Capote's *In Cold Blood* when it first came out. Everyone in her world had read *In Cold Blood*—about the brutal murder of an entire family in an old farmhouse, no one nearby. A true story. It left an impression.

And the South, the South is new to her. Until now, she's never been farther south than the suburbs of Washington DC, except on a single trip to Florida as a child and she'd been on a plane, bypassing what lay between. Now, looking at the road map, she's not surprised to see that Tennessee stretches all the way from the southwestern edge of Virginia to the Mississippi River. Fundamental geography. But the eight-hour drive from Bristol, Virginia, where she ultimately spends her first night on the road, to Memphis, where her journey ends, feels interminable. It begins south of the Shenandoah Valley with an eight-lane highway that rises up toward the city of Knoxville, a mountain town threaded by highways that split off in all directions, then spin into a spectacular pass through the Smoky Mountains, all loopy roads and cliff-hanging views. Afterward, the landscape goes flat. And it feels like everything changes.

When Emma stops at a gas station halfway across the state, she sees some sort of a Jeep with a wooden flatbed trailer behind it—an open pen surrounded by chicken wire that holds a pig the size of a cow, fatter and rounder and dirtier than anything she has ever seen close-up. As its owner fills his tank, the pig shuffles around, grunting and snorting. The people coming out of the Quik Mart look poor—underfed, unkempt, unshaven. "There's no place like home," Emma says out loud to no one, closing her eyes as she speaks.

Her plan is to go to Memphis first and stay a bit, then drive to Plantersville on the back roads heading eastward to meet Seal's family, attend the graveside service, nose around. To get to Memphis, she must pass through Nashville, which sits in the middle of the state. From there, it's a monotonous three-plus-hours southwest to Memphis on two lanes of a long, flat, divided four-lane highway surrounded by what appears to be uninhabited country. There's nothing scenic about it. It's tangled, grassy, brown. The highway itself is crowded with passenger trucks and long-haul trucks and tractor trailers, everyone driving too fast. It's late afternoon and Emma is fighting off sleep. She's heard more than enough country music on the radio, which hardly comes across at all between cities. So, she's engaging her mind by mulling over the events of the past month and mulling them over again. At some point between Nashville and Memphis, her mind settles on Angus, on what might have happened to him. Was he on the ferry? If not, why did he buy a ticket? Why has she not heard from him? And what was he doing? That's what haunts her—a sense that knowing the truth is the only sure way to let him go, which, of course, is the purest of pipe dreams.

As if it will solve the riddle of his most recent assignment, she runs through their last visit again. He seemed as if he might want to leave the clandestine service, as if he was frustrated with what he was doing. As far as she knew, that involved amassing information as part of an investigation into illegal arms sales by British companies to forbidden buyers in the Middle East. She recalls him wondering about whether the

British government itself was involved. Unfortunately, all that she knows she has learned from inference—based on their history, his itineraries and what he may have told her.

Combing through her memories as she makes her way toward Memphis, she recalls asides: "Something just isn't right," he'd said at one point. And: "It's worse than I thought." His manner suggested sadness as much as anything else. And a restlessness. And, of course, frustration. "Our countries, both our countries, are complicit," he'd said. "No one wants to hear my news." Emma's job wasn't to ask questions, it was to listen. That's how they operated. After all, his work was classified, top secret. So that leaves her with nothing substantive.

Within an hour of Memphis, she passes through Jackson, which is as close to a city as anything she's seen since Nashville. It's a bottleneck where the highway is lined with enticements to eat, sleep, shop, play—a Wendy's, a four-story Hampton, a Walmart, a Nautilus fitness club. "OPEN 24 HOURS," a sign screams. This strip is an obvious stopping point for those headed west, across the Mississippi River to Arkansas and beyond. The narrow highway flanked by attractions awakens her, and as the traffic picks up in the miles ahead, a road sign triggers a memory. "Moscow," it says, "30 miles."

"I've been in the Middle East too long," he'd told her. It was during their last visit to Saranac in December, when they were lying by the fire. She can picture his head on her lap, feel his presence. "Coming up on nine years," he went on. "It's just not safe for me anymore. You know full well undercover in Moscow was more my speed." Moscow, more my speed. And she'd made light of it, blamed herself. "I guess you can credit me for the switch," she said, because he was drawn into a case involving her family back in the late seventies—one that took him to the Middle East.

"I can't blame you," he said, shrugging the idea off with a half chuckle. "More likely our CIA friend. Mr. Kidman. He's the one who brought me in on it. But now . . . now I'm stuck in this quagmire." Then he sat up, as if he was ready to move on, drop the subject, and stood, adding this under his breath, with a note of anger in his voice: "Anyway, it's about time for him to step up." Emma had no idea what that meant and might have asked—although, again, not their way—but he left the room and disappeared for a while, stealing her opportunity.

CHAPTER 60

SEAL

One day, my mother and I were alone. Aunt Jenny and her husband had gone for the weekend to some lake over in Arkansas. I think they just needed a break, the two of them. Fair enough, I thought. Anyway, that left just the two of us on the screen porch, and she started talking about the Little House—the one that doesn't exist anymore, the one that fell apart when they moved this house, the house we were sitting in. On that day, she was in an old rocker drinking a glass of tea. She didn't have her wig on because there was no one around, so she was just sitting, rocking, bald-headed, in her pajamas in the middle of the day. She was beautiful, but thin and parched. The disease had dissipated her looks, but her spirit seemed intact. She was trying to show me where the Little House had been. But she grew frustrated because the resettlement of the big house had disoriented her. What had once faced south, now faced east. And the Little House, which had once stood to the west of the big house, was now gone. She threw out her left arm, casually, as if she was swinging at something. "The Little House was over there, not one hundred yards away. Stop me if I've told you this story," she said. But even if I'd heard it, I wouldn't have stopped her. Then she started talking as if she just had to tell it.

MAGGIE GRACE

When I got to be about twelve, it was my job to clean out the Little House. I didn't mind it. It was like my own private place. At first, when I'd open the padlock, the air inside smelled old and musty, like an attic or a basement. And you could smell the rat poison. We had to lay that down to keep the vermin out.

When the Holders were coming, I would go over and open all the windows and the doors to the sleeping porch and air the place out. I'd dust and sweep the straw rug and put out the flowers. I always worked fast to leave myself time. Like a ritual. Then, I went over to Deaver's and got milk and eggs and butter and a bag of ice. They didn't have a refrigerator. They had an icebox. Your Nanaw always said they liked to be old-fashioned.

She'd stop periodically to take a sip of the herbal tea I'd been making her. Or just to take a breath. But then she'd plow ahead.

I would get me a bag of peanuts and a Coca-Cola, then sit there on the sleeping porch reading the Holders' magazines, *Town & Country* and such, and drink that Coca-Cola real slow, pouring the peanuts into the bottle.

She put her head back and shut her eyes.

I would dream that the Little House was my house, and that it was my great-grandmother who lived in the big old plantation house that burned down on that farm. And that we were rich people like the Holders. When I think of it now, it makes me feel ashamed.

The Little House wasn't like anyplace else in the world. Everything was painted pale blue, and the rooms were full of flowered chairs and matching pillows and photographs, lots of them. Over the mantel in the front room, there was this big picture of Black people picking cotton with long white bags hanging over their shoulders and under that, all over the top of the mantel, were pictures of Memphis and people from the family in frames that looked like they were made of wallpaper or the fabric from some chair in an English country house. That's the look they were going for, I think. Maybe not consciously, but . . .

Then she stopped and shook her head, and the tone of her voice changed.

Also, there were these little Black dolls everywhere. I don't think they even make that kind of thing anymore. I hope not, anyway. The whisk broom was a doll made of cloth, with a little black face and her hair wrapped up in a teeny tiny kerchief and her apron pulled over the handle of the broom. That's something you would never see in Ohio, where we came from. Or in New York. Like the paper towel holder in the kitchen had a painting of Aunt Jemima on it, all smiling with her big hands coming out to hold the towels. Your Nanaw hated that. She always said, "Round here, you'd think there never was such a thing as the Civil War." She was a smart woman. A good woman. Righteous, your grandmother.

Another thing. They had this book in the Little House where they kept a record of everyone who came out there to visit. It was written in all different hands, going back like fifty years. They wrote about the crops and the condition of the farm and about their parties and hunting and family holidays. I read the book so many times I practically know it by heart. It sounded like this . . .

Then she mimicked an unrecognizable voice, a southern accent, with a lick of pretension:

January 1, 1922. Lydie and Bill Harris joined us this weekend for an unforgettable New Year's celebration. The Victrola whirled until dawn, and we drank too much champagne for our health. On New Year's Day, Bill and I bagged ten quail near the lower pond. Will Jr.

She snickered a bit at herself, shaking her head. Then she did it again, in a very exaggerated way:

April 4, 1936. Today I brought my new bride to the farm to watch the planting and pick the wild blackberries. Imagine a New Orleans girl out here in Plantersville, Tennessee. She's a real sport. We filled the basket and then rode all the way back to the pecan orchard. This year, we planted all 2,000 acres in cotton, the first time in twenty years. If the weather holds, it may be our best year ever. It's certainly mine. Mary Beauregard Simmons, welcome to Plantersville. William Carrollton Holder III.

She was silent for a moment. And she got tears in her eyes, and she said, "They were living in the past, all of them."

CHAPTER 61

Landing at the Peabody Hotel, in fact, turns out to be rather like coming to the end of the yellow brick road. For Emma, at least. A man dressed as if he might be the emcee at a circus meets her car at the back entrance. There is a red carpet. "Welcome, madam," he says grandly, taking her keys, unloading her luggage, sending her into the most elegant of lobbies. It's enormous. The prairie-style ceiling—a grid of carved mahogany inlaid with panels of stained glass—soars a good fifty feet above. The details are all brass and marble, fine Persian rugs and palm fronds. Its center-piece: a grand fountain topped by a Grecian urn filled with a massive arrangement of fresh flowers and surrounded by a pool with live ducks swimming in its waters. That, and café tables all around it and a bar and a grand piano and cushy seating for the drinkers and the travel weary.

Still, more than anything else, what captures Emma's attention, what fascinates her, is the mix of people—the staff, the guests milling about, the waiters, the shopkeepers. It's truly multiracial. They are all shades of black and brown and white. Dressed up and dressed down. Young and old. Hip and unhip. What seemed on her arrival like a postage stamp of a downtown feels like a true city when she's standing in the lobby of the Peabody. It feels international somehow or maybe otherworldly, which was not at all what she'd expected.

The first thing Emma does from her suite on the seventh floor is call Bill Kidman. "Glad you're safe," he tells her. "And glad you called. I have news from Brodsky that should be valuable for you tomorrow. The FBI has gone through the Uniform Commercial Code filings in Tennessee. It's taken them a while, but they've found records of the funds transfer on June 18, 1956, related to the establishment of a trust fund in Memphis."

"Seal's birthday was June 17, 1956."

"Okay. That's illuminating. Are you writing this down?"

"Yes."

"The fund was set up at First Tennessee Bank in the account of Nancy McCorry Lawson of Plantersville, Tennessee," Kidman says.

"Seal's grandmother," she says. "Got it."

"A transfer of $250,000. The law firm was Barclay, Simpson and Thomas. They're in Memphis."

"Yes. Wow. Okay. I'm headed over there in the morning."

"I guess that's no surprise, then, is it? So, we calculated it. Based on inflation alone, that would be worth over a million in 1987 dollars. If wisely invested over these past thirty years, it could easily be worth

$2.5 or 3 million. So, it's pretty definitely what we were looking for. This is Seal's trust fund."

"Makes sense. That's a comfortable amount of money."

"Now we just need to get a hold of the actual document to find out exactly who the parties were and what the stipulations were. You've got to find it in Memphis or in Plantersville. It's going to show up in either the county or state records. I can have my guys check Memphis. You're going to need to check Plantersville," he tells her, adding, "Do we know who stood to inherit Seal's money?"

"According to Harriet Freeman, the New School in New York gets her art and the proceeds from the sale of her studio and her apartment," Emma says. "I wonder if Aunt Jenny knows that. And where exactly the trust fund went when Seal died?"

"You'll need the actual document to find that out," Kidman says.

"Damn this confidentiality agreement. Can we not get some sort of legal order to get the information from Harriet Freeman?"

"Let's get this first," he says.

"Okay. Back in touch," she tells Kidman, and she can't resist bringing the matter of Angus into the conversation. "Listen, before I go," she says, "I remembered something when I was driving down here. The last time I saw him, he said it was time for you to step up." There's a silence on Kidman's end that lasts a good long minute.

"Who did?" he says.

"You know who."

"Understood," Kidman says firmly. "Take care of yourself." And he's gone.

CHAPTER 62

SEAL

There was this one story my mother used to tell about a dove hunt. She told it two or three different times when we were in Plantersville in the months before she died, and two or three different ways. But every time she told it, she started the same way. "Have I told you about the dove hunt?" she'd ask. Then she'd explain, as always, "I'm telling you this because it's part of our history. I want you to understand about the Holders. I want you to understand who we are and who they are. That's why I'm telling you this story." And then she'd begin one version or another.

MAGGIE GRACE

Every September, the Holders used to have a dove hunt, as far back as that book goes anyway. People would come from all over, Mississippi and Arkansas and Tennessee. They parked all over the yard between our house and the Little House. They'd set up long brown tables, like the kind at church, behind the sleeping porch under the trees, and cover them with cloths and pretty flowers in old, empty Coke bottles. Then they laid out barbecue and beans and slaw from town in big aluminum pans. One time, your Nanaw went to help Mrs. Holder get ready. But she never did again. I want you to know that story, my sweet girl.

As I remember it, the way Nanaw talked to Mrs. Holder that day wasn't like I ever heard her talk to anybody else, except when she was down at the church. "Everything looks just lovely," was what she said. And I remember how she said the words real slow and careful. Old Mrs. Holder talked on and on about how hard it was to have a dove hunt and how she didn't think she would be able to do it again the next year, chattering like a little bird.

"Lord have mercy," she would say.

And here my mother would exaggerate the southern accent, turning it into a gentrified drawl, mocking the woman.

"I can't tell you what I went through this week with trying to get everything ready. Those people at that Pike's Barbecue have run me crazy. Why, half the guests that are coming just about invited themselves. I have been on the phone every minute since last Monday, giving directions on how to find this place. I must have talked to all of Memphis." This chatter, chatter, chatter. All about how challenging her life was, which is a laugh.

She was a hard woman to forget, just padding around the kitchen in her silk stockings and her shiny green shoes, chirping and chattering. "I believe this is going to be the hottest September we ever have had. Why these people want to drive out to this god-forsaken place in this heat is beyond anything I've ever known," she said. And I remember Nanaw turned to me and winked, like to say, *This is the craziest woman, don't pay any attention to her.*

Mrs. Holder brought her own help from Memphis that day and right when all the guests started driving up, she sent your Nanaw home as if she didn't belong. Mama was stirring the barbecue sauce over the stove. "Now never mind about that," Mrs. Holder said, real sweet-like. And I saw her put money in Mama's hand and then she said, "No need for you to bother yourself."

Then Mama got this look on her face like someone had slapped her. She pulled herself up and looked right at Mrs. Holder and said carefully, "Thank you for your kindness, but I can't accept this." Then she laid that money down on the countertop. I could see that it was a one-dollar bill. And Mrs. Holder tried to give her some of the barbecue to take home, but Mama said no and went on over to the big house, our house. She didn't even say goodbye. Just walked out. Then Mrs. Holder turned to everyone and said, "Isn't that pitiful, and with a child to feed." She said it right in front of me, me being that child. A one-dollar bill.

CHAPTER 63

Once she was settled in at the Peabody, Emma wanted nothing more than to go on an explore, to discover this place, this Memphis. She started out on foot, heading west on Union Avenue toward Main Street, then Front Street, where she caught her first glimpse of it—the vast muddy, roiling river, a big, old, flat barge slogging by with a tugboat running out ahead. She was looking down on it, as if from the top of a hill—the infamous bluffs on which the city was built. And there was a railroad track and a four-lane road between her and the river, and she thought better of heading down to the waterfront, which appeared to be undeveloped. Then, serendipitously, she spotted a low-lying mod-ernist building, obviously constructed in the 1950s or '60s, not terribly compelling except for the sign: Memphis Public Library. Once inside, she found her way to the Memphis Room and the microfilm machine, where she could look up anything that was ever printed in Memphis's newspapers. Until 1983, there were two major dailies—a morning paper, the *Commercial Appeal*, and an evening paper, the *Press Scimitar*. With some eight hundred thousand people, it was not a small town.

Emma did a search for Holder and for the name Carrollton, which was often paired with it, and found an abundance of references to the

Carrollton branch of the family—on the society pages, in the business section, in stories on front pages stretching back to the 1920s and 1930s and beyond. Most recently an Abigail Carrollton speaking out against a development on the riverfront, a Hubert Carrollton sitting on the board of the Tennessee Valley Authority, and a Brit Carrollton dominating the residential real estate section. Holders were less apparent. She found Raine Holder's wedding announcement from the late seventies, and a photograph of one of his children—a boy name Wilmott Holder—on the front page dressed up as a bunch of grapes for Halloween. Also, a photo of one Martha Holder, who looked to be about eighteen, enjoying her reign as the queen of something called the Cotton Carnival, pictured on the arm of a much older man. Based on the crown on his head and scepter in his hand, he was apparently the king. Emma found the pairing a little creepy. Her search for Maggie Grace Lawson yielded a single result, but it was precisely what she was looking for, in a photo caption in the Living section of the *Commercial Appeal* dated May 31, 1979.

Restauranteur Donates Art to University of Mississippi Museum. Born and raised in Oxford, Mississippi, Maggie Grace Lawson moved to New York City in 1966 to found the popular Harlem restaurant Merna's Place with Mississippian Merna Jones. A collector of fine art, Ms. Lawson donated twenty major works of art to the University of Mississippi's gallery, including works by Willem de Kooning, Robert Rauschenberg, William Christenberry and Louise Nevelson. A ceremony was held yesterday at the university's Kate Skipwith Teaching Museum, where the collection will be on display this summer.

Now, reading it through three times, Emma makes a mental note of the fact that there is no mention of Plantersville or even Tennessee in the description of Maggie Grace's roots. She also wonders why the coexecutors who are handling Seal's estate knew nothing about this. They are members of the art community, she thinks. And Harriet Freeman has Memphis connections. Surely, one of them would have at least known something about a donation this substantial. Again, Emma looks at the date. It would have been just months before she died. Maggie Grace was living down here, Emma thinks, in Plantersville. Smiling then, she shakes her head. The image that pops into her mind is that of a *New Yorker* cover, the famous one, the Saul Steinberg drawing that shows the view from Manhattan across the Hudson River to the rest of the world—or what New Yorkers perceive to be the rest of the world—an undeveloped New Jersey, the Pacific Ocean and little else.

Before she leaves the library, Emma does another search for Maggie Grace Lawson and finds that there was no follow-up obituary in the Memphis news, although she died only two months later. And then Emma starts on the arithmetic. Twenty pieces donated to the University of Mississippi. That leaves eight unaccounted for. Minus Merna's Calder and the four pieces Lynley Wright had stored for Seal, that leaves three missing pieces. But she's not at all sure which they are.

Emma contacts the university and gets the full list of the works donated by Maggie Grace Lawson. She passes that information on to Detective Brodsky, who shares it with his department and with Bill Kidman. And by the time Emma arrives in Plantersville, Tennessee, twenty-four hours later, Brodsky has confirmed that Seal Lawson kept—and her executor Lynley Wright has stored—a Gerhard Richter (the painted photograph of Jackie Kennedy and Lyndon Johnson), a William Christenberry photograph, a Carroll Cloar and a Mark Rothko. At which point, they know exactly which pieces from Maggie Grace's art collection are unaccounted for: a Jasper Johns, the other Mark Rothko and the other Carroll Cloar.

So why did Lynley Wright not know about this donation? Or Harriet Freeman? That's where Saul Steinberg's map of the world popped into Emma's brain. If they didn't handle it, they wouldn't have known about it—because it was a world away. And no one was watching. *Who made these arrangements? Who handled it?* she wonders. *Why did she do it? And where are the missing pieces?*

CHAPTER 64

"People get confused about Memphis." Edwin Raine Holder, known as Raine, is talking about his hometown, his hometown going back many generations. Raine Holder's family owns the farm in Plantersville. "Either they think, 'Country music, wee haw'—but that's Nashville—or they get a picture of Appalachia in their heads. You know, *Deliverance*, the hill people. Knoxville. The Smoky Mountains." He leans back in his chair. "Memphis is a different animal."

"I had no idea it was this far west," Emma says. "I'm staying near the river—at the Peabody."

"You know what they say—the Mississippi Delta begins in the lobby of the Peabody Hotel and ends on Catfish Row in Vicksburg."

"Right," she says. "I walked down to the Mississippi last night. And over to Beale Street."

"All by yourself?"

She nods, shrugs her shoulders. "Surely, it can't be any more dangerous than New York."

He is seated at a conference table in the offices of Barclay, Simpson and Thomas, a white-shoe Memphis law firm that plays against type—progressive, active in the civil rights arena and protective of the environment. BST attorneys tend to be rangy, spectacle-wearing, ready-for-battle. Raine Holder is not thin. In fact, Emma will describe him later to Bill Kidman as red-faced and puffy, as someone who perhaps drank a little too much Jack Daniel's and had one too many barbecue sandwiches—an uncharacteristically mean-spirited description. There is just something about him that puts her off. Maybe, she thinks later, it's his sense of privilege, which, perhaps ironically, is something they both share.

From the beginning, once Emma had an understanding of who the Holders were, the challenge was how to best connect with them. It was Harriet Freeman who made the appointment, set up through the Holders' own attorney, one attorney to another. "It's about the farm in Plantersville," she'd explained. Now, Emma and Raine Holder are meeting at BST's downtown office overlooking the Mississippi River. The attorney is not present, but, as Raine Holder said when Emma arrived, "He's here in case we need him." Standing at a window on the tenth floor of the downtown high-rise, Emma is amazed by the view from Memphis across the river to Arkansas—farmland, undeveloped as far as the eye can see. No smokestacks. No skyscrapers, no sign of human activity. Trees and fields. Rice fields, she is told, reconfirming that she couldn't be farther from Manhattan.

Raine Holder makes his living as a commodity trader, the commodity being grain. It's Emma's understanding, from a long conversation with her own financial advisor, that he likely trades the physical product, which, in some cases, means barges full of grain literally floating down the Mississippi River. "I assume he uses commodity futures to hedge his cash position. Probably on the Chicago Mercantile Exchange. But that's not the same as speculating," her advisor had said. "I'm guessing he's just a businessman protecting himself."

"Protecting himself from what exactly," Emma had asked.

"From a dramatic change in the price or damage to the product in transit. Something like that. Look," he'd explained, "there's a big difference between trading in the commodity markets and trading the commodity itself."

The offices of Barclay, Simpson and Thomas are not far from Front Street, home to the Memphis Cotton Exchange, once the largest cash cotton market in the country. But by now, most of the big cotton merchants have left downtown and the exchange floor is virtually deserted. Commodities such as cotton, grain and just about anything else, are traded on the big exchanges in Chicago and New York. And Front Street, once a bustling commercial center lined with cotton offices and wagonloads of cotton bales, is all condominium conversions and random offices and specialty shops and restaurants.

"Of course, I remember Mrs. Lawson," Raine is saying. "Her daughter Jenny still tends to things in Plantersville. We have an agreement to that effect."

"What sort of agreement is that?"

"I had my attorney pull it up for you. Given her mother's lifetime of service to us, Jenny Lawson has the right to continue to live there until her death."

"Is that unusual?"

"Perhaps. But we appreciated their loyalty over the years. They're like family to us."

"Is that right?" Emma says. Deeply aware of his southernness, she sees him as a confederate, an accomplice. She realizes immediately that she is assuming duplicity, that she is judging him as a historian would—as the product of a family that would have been at once deeply religious and steeped in the original sin of slavery. Denial would be inherent to his culture. Denial of wrongdoing. And they would have been eternally buffered from consequences of any kind. What she doesn't know or understand is the degree of intimacy between the Holders and all the people who have worked for their family over the years. It is a system, a culture, imbedded, inbred.

"But she's not family, is she?" Emma says.

"As you can see, we pay her a monthly stipend to oversee the farm, and she lives there rent-free. It's a common and perfectly legal arrangement."

"Can you tell me about Maggie Grace Lawson?"

"Of course. What would you like to know?"

"That depends on how well you knew her," Emma says, and he seems barely to react.

"She was my age," he responds. "She and I played together growing up. I would say we were like soulmates." Emma is taken aback by the implied intimacy. He is a jocular sort. To all appearances, open, friendly.

"Soulmates?" she says.

"She was a good ole girl." He is leaning back, comfortably, swiveling in the leather conference chair. "Growing up," he says, "our family went out there on weekends. Mostly my father and brother and me. What could be better for a kid? We had the run of the place. Shame my boys didn't spend more time out there. But it's a long drive from Memphis."

"So, when was the last time you saw Maggie Grace?"

"You know, I don't quite recall," he says. "Probably not since, well, not since we were little. Maybe once or twice when she was older. I'm not real sure." He speaks slowly, languidly, a pace that makes Emma sit on the edge of her seat. "I went out there hunting occasionally when I was in college. But she was gone by then. It seems like she got out of there when she was very young."

"Did she graduate from high school?" Emma says.

"I don't know the answer to that, Miss Quinn," he says, and Emma wishes now she'd gone to Plantersville before visiting with Raine Holder. Cart before the horse, she thinks. Bill Kidman had done a workup on the family, but Seal's Aunt Jennifer would have known more about the Holders. She decides to visit the courthouse in Plantersville, to dig a little bit into the family's history.

"I went away to school," he says. "So, after about the age of twelve or thirteen, I didn't really see much of her. Although I have a mental image. Oddly enough, her daughter came by, maybe ten years ago. Said she lived in New York. She was the spitting image of Maggie Grace." The way the name Maggie Grace slips off his tongue, smooth and slow, makes her sound like a sinner or a whore. Maggie Grace.

"Had you known her before?"

"The daughter? No," he says flat, matter-of-fact, then leans back in his chair, rocking it again. "So, tell me more about your visit. What's on your mind? My attorney said it was about the farm." That's the word that really trips Emma up. The farm, pronounced fom, sounding like rom-com or prom, but longer, drawn out. Faaaahm. *Such a lazy way to talk*, she thinks.

"Did you know that Maggie Grace had a baby when she was about fifteen? She would have been living on the farm."

"Would that be the young woman I met?"

"Yes. Lucille. She was born in 1956."

He blanches slightly. "What exactly are you thinking, Miss Quinn?" he says.

"Well, Maggie Grace was actually quite wealthy. So much so that she amassed an impressive art collection. Her daughter died recently."

"Oh dear," he says, not showing anything other than what seems to Emma to be polite acknowledgment of her death.

"And apparently, there was a trust fund set up with Nancy Lawson, Maggie Grace's mother, the day after Lucille was born. Do you know anything about that?"

"I have no idea what you're talking about. Are you suggesting . . ."

"Would you mind explaining what you meant by soulmates? You said you were soulmates."

"Well, this is just plain silly," he says. Sitting with his legs crossed at the knee, he rearranges himself, switching legs and leaning forward slightly. His face is flushed. "No, no, no," he says. "You misunderstand my meaning. I'm happy to explain. I have a clear recollection of her lying in the fields behind the house one night, just looking up at the stars."

"Sounds romantic."

"No. It was not romantic. We were children. We were maybe eight or nine years old at the time." He's adopted a patronizing tone, as if he's being forced to explain something to an uninformed person, an uneducated person, a child. "We got ourselves all stirred up, talking about life on other planets. About life. About God. I think we all got kind of spooked. It was hard to forget. One of those things children do when they're children, things that maybe scare us and excite us. We explore our world, imagine what lies beyond, predict the future. Isn't that what we all care about, really? The mysteries of life." He is staring directly at her, into her eyes, so steadily that it makes her uncomfortable. "Can I get you anything else?" he asks as he turns away. He is clearly in control.

Parsing his words, she settles on this response: "We . . . Who is we?"

"We?"

"You said we all got spooked."

"Oh. Maggie Grace and I, I would think, more than the others. But my brother was there, my older brother, with his friends. They were being teenagers. She and I were both younger. My brother, older."

"Your brother?" she says. "How much older?"

"Four years older.

"And where is he?"

"Right now?"

"Where does he live?"

"He lives in New Jersey," he says, lost in thought for a moment. "In a little town in northern New Jersey. I guess you'd call it the suburbs of New York. I'm afraid I don't see much of Fourth anymore," he adds.

"Fourth?"

"Well, that's just what we call him," he chuckles under his breath. "She came up with it, actually. Maggie Grace did. And it just stuck. William Carrollton Holder the Fourth." He shakes his head. "We were friends, all of us." He seems to have calmed down. "And who established this trust fund?" he asks.

"Your law firm set it up," Emma says, alert, watching him closely.

"Well, good God," he says. "That means nothing. That could have been anyone in this town, in this state, for that matter."

CHAPTER 65

Back in Arlington, Virginia, in a simple brick foursquare on a quiet street, not too far from CIA headquarters in Langley, Bill Kidman's wife is in the kitchen, still in her pajamas, puttering around in practical wool slippers. Kidman himself is reading in one of a pair of overstuffed chairs just beyond the kitchen counter in an alcove that looks out on the front yard.

"Get this," he says. "They've got a story in the *Times* about Reagan's staff training him before a press conference about the Iran-Contra situation. It says he did so well that the mood at the White House is 'upbeat and self-congratulatory.'"

"What?" his wife says.

"I assume because he didn't flub the thing. Sounds like they set the bar pretty low. When asked how Reagan did, Alan Simpson said something about the president doing 'little damage.'"

"Stellar," his wife says, laughing.

"Apparently, he did a good bit of tiptoeing around anything substantive. And I quote," Kidman says, reading from the *New York Times*, "Mr. Reagan did not make new disclosures about the Iran arms case." Then, paraphrasing, Kidman adds: "But apparently, he did acknowledge that it led to trading weapons for American hostages held in Lebanon by pro-Iranian Shiite militias."

"Bravo," his wife says. "Negotiating with terrorists."

"I suspect at some point it will become obvious that only one hostage has ever been released."

"So, what do you think? Do you think he knew about the deal?" his wife is saying while he's rolling his eyes and shaking his head.

"Now you're trying to get me in trouble?" he says.

"Oh stop," she says in a very loud voice, looking up at the ceiling.

He sticks his tongue out at her, plugs his thumbs in his ears and waves his hands at her like an obstreperous child. They've been sharing this kind of back-and-forth—about his work, about whether or not the house is bugged, about how much they can safely discuss—for more than thirty years. And, in truth, as he approaches retirement, Bill Kidman has become more risk-averse and finds it less amusing.

He rises from the sofa, approaching the kitchen counter where she's steeping a tea bag, dangling it by a thread over her mug. Coming toward her from behind, he wraps his arms around her waist and rubs his ear against her cheek.

"Hmm," she says happily.

"Truth?" he whispers.

"Truth," she replies.

"I don't think our president is all there anymore."

She pulls back, surprised, looks him in the eye. "Really?"

"Really," he says most quietly. "So, if he says he doesn't recall knowing anything about the mission, it's because he really doesn't recall, well . . . anything."

"Ah," she says, wriggling free of him. Through the front window, she can see a van pulling up the driveway, a man getting out. "Did you call Arlington Power?"

"Oh shit," he says, looking out. He recognizes Angus McLearan immediately by his size and his walk, although he's wearing an outfit that comes with the van. "You'd better go upstairs."

"Do I have to?" she pleads, teasing him, and Kidman heads outside.

The surprise is visible on his face as Kidman makes his way down the front walk toward the van. "We thought you went down with the ferryboat," he says softly, reaching out his hand.

"Good," Angus says, doing the same, their grips tightening. "That was my intention."

"I don't want to be around when you explain that to Emma. Does she know you're back?"

"No," Angus says, opening the van's rear door. "I haven't even tried to reach her. Wanted to connect with you first. Can you tell me where she is?" Kidman is giving him a fatherly look of reproach. Standing behind the truck now, Angus puts his hands together as if in prayer. "So, I don't have to leave messages all over kingdom come," he says.

"She's on her way to Tennessee. Actually, she may be there already."

"Tennessee? Perfect."

"Perfect. Really?" Kidman squints his eyes and shakes his head, his face beginning to redden slightly, a flush of anger. "You plan on surprising her, don't you?"

Angus breaks into a shit-eating grin.

"That's just plain evil," Kidman says. "Do you realize what you've put her through? Well, I can tell you. Hell. First, her friend. Then you. The last thing that woman needs is a surprise." He turns his back to Angus, begins to move toward the house. "She's going to be angry," he says.

"Well," Angus says, following with a bag full of tools. "That's not my intention."

"And what is your intention today?" Kidman asks, feeling less than generous. They are both standing still now, shifting gears, talking business.

"I think you need to be involved in this."

"I've told you." Kidman is dead serious. "Keep me out of it."

"Look," Angus says, starting to reach for Kidman's arm, but wary of his surroundings, of onlookers. "It's not what you think." And as they enter the house, all conversation ceases.

CHAPTER 66

SEAL

Finally, one day, just weeks before my mother died, she brought up the legendary dove hunt again. But this time, she told me more, maybe more than I wanted to know. About her dreams and wishes. And about the Holders. She started with the same old question: "I told you about the dove hunt, didn't I?" Then she took it in a different direction. She was a little groggy that day. Lying on her side in the bed, her breathing heavy. Not feeling so good. But she had this determination about her. "I told you about the way Mrs. Holder made Nanaw feel so bad. You remember?" she said.

And when I answered, "Of course I remember," she went on.

MAGGIE GRACE

You know, I've always regretted that I stayed on that day after Mama left, playing with the other kids—including those two Holder boys. I thought they were my friends. We used to play together on the weekends when they came out with their daddy. Before they were old enough to go hunting with the men, they used to get left with us. They were about my age. Raine and Will Jr. That's what they call him anyway. One time he told me he was really William Carrollton Holder the Fourth. So, I got to calling him Fourth. His brother thought that was funny.

Anyway, they came out later that day with the men and the guns. And after your Nanaw went home, I didn't see her for a long time. She stayed in the house like she was hiding. Later, I heard Mrs. Holder telling the other women about it, how Mama wouldn't take any money for helping and calling her insolent. One of the Memphis women said it was always better to get Negroes—only she pronounced it Negras.

She shook her head then, rolled over in the bed to face the wall and lay there in silence for a time. After a few minutes, she turned back and started talking again. I was lying on the floor, propped up on a pillow, my elbow resting on the floor. I'm sure I was tired too. By then, she'd been sick a long time. Aunt Jenny was probably downstairs cleaning up the kitchen, and it was maybe six or seven in the evening. I remember she was talking softly, and I had to nudge closer to hear her.

That day, the day of the dove hunt, the Holders didn't close up the house until well after dark. I just stayed and stayed, because your Nanaw never did come and call me in. After we ate our barbecue, me and the boys went out to the pasture behind the blackberry hedge. We went so far we could hardly see the lights they'd set up around the barbecue tables. I kept thinking Mama was going to come out to find me, but she never did.

Then she squinted her eyes as if she was trying to see something or remember something, and spoke again.

We lay down on our backsides in the grass and watched the stars. Fourth and his friends started smoking cigarettes. And Fourth said to me, "Now, no one needs to know about this, Maggie Grace." About the smoking. That was his way.

I'll never forget that night. Raine and Fourth and two other boys from Memphis were talking about things I never heard of before.

Then she made a noise, a puff of air, like an exhale, like a laugh.

I remember Raine showing me the Big Dipper, putting his hand right up next to mine and tracing out the shape of it so our fingers touched.

Fourth said, "I think other people live on those planets," pointing at the stars. Then they talked about God. Fourth was the oldest, and he announced that he didn't believe in God. He said he thought God was something man invented. Even then, it seemed to me he had it backward, but I didn't enter into it. And Raine—he was such a sweet boy—he asked me if I believed in ESP. He was about twelve at the time, same as me. I didn't even know what he was talking about, but I said yes.

Then she did that soft, hidden laugh again, and she was half smiling as she talked. Her voice was so soft, and her words were coming out so slowly that I had to move up against the bed to hear. "I'll never forget it," she said, going on, smiling and chuckling every now and then, her eyes all innocent like those of a young girl.

He got all excited, and he had me guessing the numbers he was thinking of. I remember we played that game for a while. And every time I guessed a number, that old Fourth would give the score, like, "That's two out of eight." After a while, I stopped guessing and he stopped counting, so we all just lay there real quiet, Raine's shoulder right up against mine.

At this point, she stopped for a minute. And when she started up again, she was staring up at the ceiling all dreamy-eyed, speaking into the air.

That was a special night. I felt like I was part of something that went way beyond McNeely County, beyond Memphis even. I felt, for just a little while, like I was part of the Holder family and imagined that they would roll me up and take me home with them. To Memphis.

Then I thought she was finished, but she wasn't. She took a deep breath and said in a dark voice, "Then, something awful happened." And she just kept on like she was seeing a picture in her mind.

As we were making our way back on the dirt road that runs back from the fields, I was looking at my mother through the kitchen window, and my foot hooked up under something and I fell at the edge of the road. Fourth and his friends were laughing even before I hit the ground. I could hear it. I had to fight to make myself not cry. Then I realized my right hand landed on something sharp lying by the side of the road, sharp and bloody. Even in the darkness, I could see the blood on my hand. But what was worse,

I could feel it. Those stiff little bodies lying in a pile on the ground, dead birds, a stack of them, left to rot and me with my hand in the middle of them. It made me puke right there in front of those boys. I was so ashamed. Raine helped me up, but I was a mess.

When I got home, even though she cleaned me up, your Nanaw was angry at me. "They're not our people," she said. Her voice was harsh. "They never will be our people, and don't you forget it," she said. When I told her the Holder boys invited me, she made a kind of humph noise, and when she left the room, she said, "One of these days you're going to get yourself in trouble, Maggie Grace Larson." And everything she said that night was right and true, but I was too young and too stupid to know it.

She hesitated for a minute, propped herself up on her elbows to get my attention, and said: "You know, the very next day, I went over to the Little House and looked in that god-awful book where they recorded everything that ever happened on that farm. I was twelve, so it would have been 1952," she said. And, again, she contrived this exaggerated upper class southern drawl and turned toward me when she spoke:

September 4, 1952. The dove hunt to end all dove hunts. Seeded twenty acres west of the lower pond. Got over a hundred doves. Old Homer Wentworth almost brought in a bag of sparrows. Did we laugh! An unforgettable day for McNeely County. William Holder III.

"And," she said in her natural voice, but with a kind of regal tone to it. "There began a list of everyone who came that day. Each one signed on a single line and put down the name of their hometown. Even Raine and William the Fourth signed the book. I didn't sign it, though."

CHAPTER 67

Angus has the gear—backpack, compass, canteen, hiking shoes, all with the patina of age and repeated use. Arriving at Great Falls early, he parks in a lot the size of a football stadium and pulls out a map. He's unfamiliar with this spot in Northern Virginia and the spectacular terrain that lies ahead, but he doesn't plan on much sightseeing. He just wants to keep moving. *As long as I haven't been followed*, he thinks, *I'll be okay.*

After a little more than an hour, he arrives at the Belmont Shelter, a stopping point on the trail. Bill Kidman is sitting on a log at the edge of a clearing that spans out from an old wooden shed. He's wearing a black sweatshirt with the hood pulled over this head, like a teenager headed for some trouble. "What took you so long?" he says, looking up at Angus, smiling.

"I think my hike was a bit longer than yours," Angus says, and the two embrace. Three trails fan out from the clearing. One has a sign that says "CLOSED." That's where they head. It's obviously not maintained, a place where the uninitiated could get lost. A good fifteen minutes in, Kidman stops, looks around, opens up, "So, what's so important that I had to come out here?"

"That was your call, I believe," Angus says.

"Can't be too careful." The sun is peeking through the canopy of trees, still leafless, many of them. Black branches against the blue sky. It's a weekday. There's no one around, probably within miles.

"I stumbled into something unexpected over there," Angus says.

"So, it's not what I think it is?"

Angus nods. "Affirmative."

"Okay, okay. What?"

"I have proof that an American company is working with a guy in the Netherlands. They're shipping chemical agents through Jordan that are going to Iraq."

"We already know they're using chemicals."

"This is proof that some of it's coming right out of New York. They bought the stuff from that company in Maryland."

"You have physical proof?"

"Right here," Angus pats his backpack. "Photographs. Shipping certificates. Everything you need."

"We already have them on the shipments to Iran."

"This gives you the New York firm. And the contact in Europe. Enough to shut it down," Angus says, handing Kidman the backpack.

"I can't do anything with this right now," Kidman says, setting the backpack on the ground. There's a flock of birds coming through with a clatter, heading north for the spring. They settle in the surrounding trees, cawing and cackling.

Angus shoots him a puzzled look. "We both know you're shipping hardware that's moving through Europe. Going directly to Iraq. I've got proof of that too. That's yours. I know it is. I've been tracking it. But this is different. This is for chemical weapons. That's against all the rules."

"You don't know the half of it," Kidman says.

"What are you talking about? What's going on with you?"

"I can't take this paperwork. I can't touch it. Look. We're compromised in every direction. This business with the Contras and the deal with Iran, that was one thing. But now we're leaning heavily toward Iraq, the administration, the organization."

"What can't you tell me?" Angus says, raising his eyebrows.

"I can tell you that I'm getting ready to retire," Kidman says. "What I can't tell you is that it goes all the way to the top. POTUS says Iran can't win it. And there's no moral to this story."

"So, you can't do anything about chemical shipments."

"Nope," Kidman says. "That should tell you all you need to know.

But hold on to it. For future reference."

"You're kidding me, aren't you? Do you know what they do? Mustard gas—your skin blisters and gets infected. It burns your windpipes, your lungs. Causes blindness. And nerve agents like sarin and tabun. They cause seizures, paralysis, unconsciousness. The Iraqis are putting these things inside artillery. They could easily strike civilians. And contaminate entire communities."

"You don't think Iran is using them?" Kidman says, unyielding.

"But the US isn't working with Iran, is it?" Angus says, adding cynically, "Except on top secret deals that aren't so top secret anymore."

Kidman just shakes his head. "I'm telling you. I can't help you with this."

"It's not only against the Geneva Conventions. It's morally wrong to look the other way on this."

"Don't imagine we don't know what's going on over there," Kidman says as he reaches down and returns the backpack to Angus. "You made copies of this paperwork?" he asks.

"What? You think I'm not going to make it out of this jungle?"

"Crazy world we live in," Kidman says. The two men stand facing one another head-on for a few solid minutes, knowing there's nothing more to be said. Kidman moves toward Angus, as if for an embrace. But Angus turns away and starts walking.

"What about Emma?" Kidman says, calling after him.

"I'll handle that myself," McLearan says. Then he stops, turning back toward his old friend. "You know, I've about had it with all of this."

"Copy that," Kidman says and they part, each making his way back to civilization on a different route.

CHAPTER 68

When Emma arrives in Plantersville, her first impression is not unlike Seal's own almost a decade earlier. She had imagined something like a farm in Upstate New York—rolling hills and verdant pastures, cattle grazing, lush stands of trees—or South Jersey with its sprawling fields of corn and beans and melons, and acres of old-growth pines. Either way, lots of green. Not so, this farm. With spring arriving, the color is beginning to come back, but there's a flatness to the land and a dryness, as if all the twigs might snap and the fields might wither. The palette, all browns and grays and yellows. Of course, Emma knows nothing about the repositioning of the place, so she pictured a big, old white house maybe with ionic columns and a grand entrance. Instead, she follows a dusty road between two unplanted fields to a modest farmhouse clad in blue siding, the yard sprinkled with a few old tires and garden tools, a wheelbarrow and some sort of four-wheeler. The driveway itself leads not to a front door but to a screen porch, which serves as the main entrance. A dead vine dangles from a broken trellis running up its back side. Oddly, she notices later, the original front door faces a field behind the house.

The welcome itself is awkward. Three dogs meet her at the screen door, two of them barking furiously, teeth bared, as Seal's aunt, Jennifer Henley, emerges from a kitchen filled with pies and cakes, wiping her hands on her apron, screaming, "Now hush up. Now hush up, you two. Randolph. Pettypie. Both of you. Hush."

Finally, after the dogs settle down and the door opens and all the animals buzz past her, Emma puts her hand out to say hello, but they can't quite pull it off, Jennifer Henley still engaging with the apron as if it is a towel. "Come on in," she says, welcoming enough but without the warmth one might expect in this situation, escorting Emma directly up the stairs to her bedroom, introducing her to the bathroom across the hall—"You have your own," she says—and turning immediately to head back down. But Emma stops her.

"Mrs. Henley," she calls out. "This . . . this painting"—and Jenny's face falls as she turns back. "It's beautiful," Emma adds.

"Yes. Isn't it?" Aunt Jenny says, slipping back to Emma's side. They stand together for a time, silent, unmoving before the painting. It is a large piece dominated by flagrant dots of color—the brightest of oranges, reds and yellows—that form the leaves on a tree that dominates the canvas. A young woman dressed in pearls and her Sunday best is standing among them, big and bold, perched there on a branch.

"Maggie Grace called it magical realism," Jenny says. She has a slight southern accent, barely noticeable, and she speaks softly, thoughtfully.

"The artist spent some time in Mexico as a young man."

Emma takes a step back. The woman in the painting looks stiff and formal, in her simple pinkish dress and white stockings, standing in the tree as if suspended in midair, flat against the bright burst of leaves that surround her. There is definitely something magical—and surreal—about the piece, Emma thinks, and she wants to know more, asks about the artist.

"He lives in Memphis. A man named Carroll Cloar," Aunt Jenny says. "It's called *Girl in a Tree*. He painted it in 1972. It was given to me by my sister—when she was sick, to thank me for taking them in. I said, 'But of course I took you in.' But she said it was her way of thanking us."

As Emma responds, she watches for a reaction. "I understand she gave the rest of her collection to the University of Mississippi."

"She did. We went to the ceremony." Jenny's eyes are still fixed on the painting, her expression unchanged. "I mean, I went with Maggie Grace and Lucille. Roy was traveling."

"So, why is something so beautiful hiding up here?"

"It's not hiding," Jenny says lightly. "We just don't want any sunlight on it."

"Carroll Cloar," Emma says. "I've never seen his work before."

"Why would you?" Jenny shrugs. "He paints the South. The Delta. But don't be fooled. He may be a *regional* artist, but he's not a regional *artist*. He's very widely known. His work is in major collections—the Museum of Modern Art, the Metropolitan Museum of Art, the Whitney."

"I wasn't suggesting . . ." Emma begins, but Jenny cuts her off and keeps talking, speaking slowly, as they both stand transfixed before *Girl in a Tree*. "He's from the Delta, of course. Born and raised in Earle, Arkansas, on a farm with seven brothers and sisters, no less. But he left home to go to college in Memphis. At Southwestern. They call it Rhodes now. It's a good college. I don't know if you've ever heard of it." She glances at Emma. "I know you're a college professor."

"I have," Emma tells her, and she seems to light up.

"Anyway, eventually, he studied at the Art Academy in Memphis and at the Art Students League in New York. He survived the war and won some fellowships, and he traveled around Europe and Latin America." She stops for a moment, as if for effect. "Then, in 1955, he came back. He must have been about forty years old. He settled in Memphis and started making these wondrous paintings of the Delta—this place fed by the Mississippi River that is like no place else in the world. Right?"

Emma is impressed by this woman in her soiled apron, living in this run-down farmhouse with three scruffy dogs on what she perceives to be the edge of nowhere, and her encyclopedic knowledge of this artist and his work. She stands in silence for another few moments, not realizing that her mouth is agape.

"What?" Jenny says, reading her mind. "You thought maybe we didn't know anything about art down here?" She smiles. "I went to a retrospective on Mr. Cloar recently. In Memphis. At the Brooks Museum. It was so beautiful. There was a painting of a flock of butterflies chasing girls in summer dresses. It was just lovely, truly magical. He called it *Hostile Butterflies*." She lets out a chirp of a laugh. "And there were a few paintings that made it clear how uncomfortable he was growing up like he did. One was a family portrait painted in a field, where he is a young person divided from all the others by a deep ravine. That reminded me of my sister. She never quite fit in. He also did a portrait of his father, where the man is as big as a giant. He has on a humongous black suit and a big black hat. And he towers over a minuscule child that is riding some sort of little motorcar beside him—obviously the artist." Then she turns to Emma and says simply, "I never knew my father."

This, Emma realizes then, is a complex lady and not a very happy one. "Tell me something," she says, deftly shifting gears. "When your sister gave away the collection, did it feel like a loss for the family?"

Jenny Henley hardly gives the question any thought before answering. "Not really. I mean, it wasn't my collection. And, actually, I didn't like most of the paintings. I'm just not terribly fond of abstract art or photography, for that matter. No, this is the one I chose. Well, actually, it wasn't my first choice. Seal took my first choice. Something by the same artist called *Blacktop Road*. It was a wonderful painting too." Then she adds, almost as an afterthought, "Although it's funny you should ask. At first, Seal was very angry about the donation. She loved their art so much."

"So, you each got a painting?"

"I got one painting. I don't know how many paintings my niece got. That was between the two of them. I know she was allowed to go first, to choose before me. That's how she got the other Carroll Cloar." Emma cocks her head slightly, and Jenny goes on. "I see no harm in that. Lucille was her girl. And, at the time, she wasn't terribly happy that her mother was giving away all their art."

"And you?"

"I couldn't have been happier," Seal's aunt says. "I love this picture." But Emma gets the impression that this woman is not being totally honest, that she's full of resentments.

Then, for the first time, Emma offers a condolence of sorts that she'd neglected on the front end. "Your niece was such an amazing person, so full of life," she says.

"Just like her mother," Jenny answers flatly, still looking at the Cloar. They are quiet again for a time and, finally, Jenny speaks. "Roy wants me to sell the painting. It's worth some money, you know. We had someone appraise it a few years ago when we were having a bad year. But I couldn't do it, couldn't let it go. I love this picture. It's the nicest thing I own."

***

After a brief interlude in the kitchen—Jenny puttering around, moving and removing dishes, organizing the refrigerator, checking the turkey roasting in the oven, Emma offering to help, with hardly a word passing between the two—Emma left for the courthouse. Now she is waiting for a public information request for documentation of a trust fund that was initially set up in Memphis through the offices of Barclay, Simpson and Thomas and registered in McNeely County.

She knows that the trust was officially established on June 18, 1956, the day after Seal was born and that the confidentiality agreement was signed by Raine Holder's law firm. She's also requested documents regarding the ownership of the farm. So far, she's waited for an hour. Not at all sure what is making her most anxious—the wait itself, finding out the truth or the prospect of spending a night with the Henleys—she wanders around the center of Plantersville, wishing she still smoked cigarettes. Maybe it's the belief that all the scary things happen in the country—the *In Cold Blood* syndrome—or that the lack of a good education is the root of all evil. Of course, quite a few people who live in the country see things from the opposite perspective.

Either way, this town looks mighty tame. The courthouse, with ionic columns of its own and a cut-stone façade to match, overlooks a classic town square with all the requisite storefronts—seed shop, hardware store, bakery, barber shop, a restaurant called the Blue Plate and a barbecue shop on the adjacent corner. And there's nothing contrived about this picture. This is no revitalized town square like one might find on the East Coast. This is the real thing, the original, the authentic center of a town established one hundred years ago, with all its nicks and scratches.

It feels small and remote, but it is the county seat, and all the relevant paperwork will be on record here. When Emma returns to the courthouse, everything she requested has been set aside for her. The documents related to the farm are stacked in a six-inch pile next to a copy of a single twelve-page document establishing the trusteeship. That's where she begins.

CHAPTER 69

SEAL

We had this running joke, me and my mother. When Aunt Jenny married Roy Henley, we started calling her Mrs. Henny Penny, after the old children's story. You know, Henny Penny gets hit by an acorn and decides the sky is falling. And runs around like a chicken with her . . . well, you know how it goes. We only said it because Aunt Jenny became Jenny Henley, which seemed worse even than Lucy Lawson. It just made us laugh. When we were together those last few weeks at the farm, anytime Aunt Jenny got weird, which she did all the time, we'd roll our eyes and mouth the words *Henny Penny* and then we'd laugh. It was good for her, for my mother. That laughter. I never did figure the two of them out and how they got on.

Aunt Jenny is not as pretty as my mother. She's five years younger, which may account for the difference. I don't know. It's as if you took my mother and made her coloring just slightly darker, her features just slightly more exaggerated, and you've got an entirely different look. Similar, but not the same. Also, she had an ornerier nature. Seems like maybe she came at a bad time. Nanaw called my aunt her "home-on-leave baby," because her husband was on leave from basic training when the child was conceived. Creepy. Not the conception, the moniker.

The story they told about how they got to Plantersville may well have been a bit of a fairy tale. Nanaw told everyone that her husband wasn't coming home from the war, so they had to leave Cleveland. But, according to my mother, who was about six years old at the time, Nanaw told her that it looked like the war was going to end soon and they needed to find a nice safe place to live, which, of course, scared the shit out of my mother. "I thought the Nazis were coming or something," she told me. "The lady next door said Hitler was the devil come to life, and I thought he was going to be our new president." Anyway, according to my mother, they just packed up and quietly left their home in Ohio. "I have no idea what happened to our furniture and everything," she told me once. And when I asked about her father—my grandfather—she said she never really knew him anyway. As I got older, I figured that when the man came back from the war, if he came back, he arrived to a house full of things and empty of people. But then, maybe he never even went off to war. Once, my mother intimated that he was a wife-beater, abusive, not a good guy. But I don't know the truth, and I have no way of knowing it.

So, anyway, Aunt Jenny was just a baby when they arrived in

Plantersville. It's the only place she's ever lived in her whole life. Not just the town, but that house. She was thirty when she got married and Roy moved in with her. Of course, I didn't know him growing up, so I was never comfortable calling him Uncle. He said to just call him Roy. But, if I ever mentioned him to Mom, I always called him Mr. Henny Penny.

Mr. and Mrs. Henny Penny. I laugh every time I think of how hard my mother laughed at that name. She just lost it. She had tears in her eyes, all bent over, couldn't stop. Such a joy to see that. I'll never forget it.

CHAPTER 70

It's almost five when Emma finishes reviewing the trust agreement. She does little more than glance at the deed to the farm and the various documents transferring property from the Holders to various other families. It seems their ancestors owned all the land around Plantersville and gradually sold it off over the years, keeping just these two thousand acres. Apparently, an old plantation house burned down in the 1920s. The map puts the plantation house somewhere east of Jenny Henley's place. The trust agreement tells Emma just about everything she needs to know about where Seal came from. It was signed by William Carrollton Holder III, Raine's father, in 1956.

"Here are the possibilities," Emma tells Detective Brodsky, standing at a pay phone outside Miller's Seed Store. "Based on this agreement, Seal's father has to be either Raine Holder, who lives in Memphis, or his older brother, William, who lives in North Jersey, or their father—which seems unlikely but is certainly possible. How that happened, who knows? But I can't imagine any other reason William Carrollton Holder III would have set up a trust fund for Seal the day after she was born."

"Well, that's an ugly proposition," Brodsky says. "And the trust itself."

"The trust was passed to Maggie Grace from her own mother when she turned twenty-five. And it was to go from Maggie Grace to Seal when she turned twenty-five, or in the event of Maggie Grace's death."

"I'm not sure that changes anything," he says. "Although it tells us that Maggie Grace would have to rely on her own money once Seal turned twenty-five. Which makes the value of the art collection particularly meaningful. I'm assuming it was her nest egg."

"And when she knew she was going to die, she donated it," Emma says, cradling the phone against her shoulder.

"Smart woman," Brodsky replies.

"Good woman," Emma says. "And another thing. According to the agreement, when Seal dies, if she has no heirs, no children, the trust fund reverts back to the Holder family. So, for sure, Jennifer Henley wouldn't have anything to gain from Seal's death. And the Holders might."

"Okay. But wait a sec. Jennifer Henley may not have known the terms of the trust fund," he says, adding, "Tell me about this Fourth."

"His name is William Carrollton Holder the Fourth. They call him simply Fourth. Apparently, he works for Citibank. In New York. Lives in North Jersey."

"Citibank. Okay," Brodsky says, and Emma can hear lift in his voice. "I'll follow up on it. Good work. Anything else?"

"One of those paintings. Her Aunt Jenny has it. The other Carroll Cloar—it's hanging in her upstairs hall."

"Got it. And, based on Maggie Grace's files, we think the Calder mobile in Merna's apartment was the real thing," he says, slowing down, drawing the next word out, "But . . . according to an expert, when it comes to Calder mobiles, the real things were reproduced in limited quantities. So, in fact, Merna was right. Valuable, but not extremely. Not like some of this other stuff."

"So that leaves two missing pieces, both paintings, both very valuable," Emma says firmly, as if they've solved some grand riddle.

"Right," he says, leafing through the paperwork before he speaks. "A Mark Rothko and a Jasper Johns." At that point, they're interrupted by a prerecorded message that begs for more quarters, so Brodsky speeds up. "I'm waiting for word on United Pest. Should hear any minute. They're looking for people at the company—and who left the company. People in New York and Tennessee. Call me in an hour."

"If I can," she says, blurting out the Henleys' phone number before the line goes dead.

CHAPTER 71

SEAL

By the middle of July, Mama was too weak. She'd pretty much stopped telling stories. Although she had these flashes of memories. She'd say, "Remember when we drove up to New York and you were playing that silly Mad Libs game," and she'd just start chuckling. "When was that, 1980? 1981?" Or "How about that time I took you to that exhibit at MoMA and you met Robert De Niro?" The hospice lady started coming at that point, and my mother was on some sort of drugs. She gave Aunt Jennifer a letter to mail to Merna in New York. It turned out it was for me. After she was gone, I kept it in the dresser in my front hall. She was saying goodbye with the letter. Just like by telling me all these stories about growing up on the farm, she was sharing our family's history. The farm is part of who I am. And I've always thought that makes the Holder family part of who I am too.

When Simon and I came down together, I went to Memphis to meet the Holders. Aunt Jenny knew it at the time. But I never mentioned it to my mother. Seemed like it might upset her.

Nothing much came of it, of course. I left Simon at the farm by the telephone and drove into Memphis myself. It was a Friday afternoon, and I put the radio on loud and made a road trip of it. Memphis was more than an hour's drive from Plantersville on Highway 64. I found the Holders' house in the old part of the city, a historic district, not far from downtown with tree-lined streets, magnolias everywhere and everything spruced up nice. I didn't call ahead or anything. I just went to the address that Aunt Jenny gave me. That's when I met Raine Holder. He was living in the family house where he'd been raised, he said. And he told me that he was a friend of my mother's when they were growing up. He asked after her. She had already been diagnosed, but I didn't tell him that. I just smiled and was courteous and friendly. I'd bought a special dress to wear to their house. It was a Diane von Furstenberg. A wrap dress that kind of wound around your body and tied in the front. They were popular back then, even though I thought they were ugly as shit. I wore it with black tights and cowboy boots, just to be true to myself. Other than that, I thought it would be perfect for Memphis.

Mr. Holder was home by himself. He came to the door carrying a *Wall Street Journal* in one hand. There were portraits of their ancestors around the house and antiques—not the kind we had, but the elaborate European kind, very formal. And they had a little rat of a dog that yapped when I came in and nipped at my ankles. Mr. Holder offered me an iced tea and ushered me out to their backyard, which was enclosed by a high fence and lavishly landscaped. It was late morning and there was a slight chill in the air, but the sun was so bright I had to shield my eyes. They still owned the farm. I knew that. And he asked after Aunt Jenny. I told him I lived in New York and that my mother had opened a restaurant up there. In Harlem. He raised his eyebrows at that, and I knew just what he was thinking. "So, are you planning to go into the restaurant business?" he asked. There was a fountain in the garden. The sound of the falling water ran through the conversation. "I don't think so. I'm planning to go back to school," I told him.

At one point, his wife suddenly appeared, and he rose from his chair as she emerged from the house. "We have a visitor, dear," he said. "It's Jenny Lawson's niece." His wife clearly had no idea who Jenny Lawson was. "This is, uh, Miss Lawson. She's been staying with her aunt at the farm."

"Seal," I said.

"Oh, of course," she replied. "Such a pleasure to meet you."

She was wearing the same dress as mine, but in a slightly different pattern. That was embarrassing. She had paired it with stockings and heels. I stood when he introduced me, then announced that I'd better be going, that I was glad to meet them both, and that I had an appointment in town. I shook both their hands. I remember her palms were sweaty.

"Give our best to your Aunt Jenny," he said as he escorted me to the door.

I was glad I went that day, but I was happy to leave. I thought he might be my father or know who my father was. But I realized on the drive back to Plantersville that it was a ridiculous idea. I didn't tell Simon that. Or Aunt Jenny. I just let it go.

I thought about it all those years later, about how Aunt Jenny felt about the Holders. And my mother's strange youthful infatuation with them and their wealth and their old ways. A few weeks before she died, I had to go into Memphis to pick up some meds that the New York doctor had prescribed, meds that he said would serve her during what he called her hospice phase. I remember that word *phase* striking me as so odd. As if she were going through adolescence or postpartum depression or something. When I got home, I heard a ruckus upstairs, which was frightening. My mother was very weak at the time, and, at that point, most complacent. I couldn't imagine what was going on. I thought maybe she'd fallen or something. When I got to the foot of the stairs, I could hear Aunt Jennifer screaming at my mother. "You left me here all by myself," she said. I could tell that she was crying. "You had no business." She was frightfully angry. As I started up the stairs, I heard her say, "You are a selfish, selfish woman, Maggie. And I hope you burn . . ." She froze when she saw me at the top of the stairs, her face flushed, her eyes filled with tears. I could see that mother's lunch tray had fallen. The last of the chicken soup was splattered across the floor. Dishes were broken. A glass of milk, a handful of crackers, all spread across the floor. "You'd better take care of this," Aunt Jenny whispered as she swept past me.

CHAPTER 72

Merna Jones has yet to awaken. She's been at Columbia Presbyterian Hospital for three days now. The doctors have told Detective Brodsky that they just don't know. "We just have to wait," they've said. "These things can take time." They now believe Merna's attacker came for the Calder—and whatever pieces from the collection they didn't find in Seal's apartment. "They may not have known exactly what they were looking for. But it's quite possible they found nothing, then went to her studio and then to Merna's apartment," Brodsky had told his people. "That would explain the anger, the drilling, the torn-up flooring," one of his people had said. But Brodsky's still not sure what's going on.

He's standing over Merna's bed when the call comes in, listening to the relentless sound of the bedside monitor and observing the stillness of her entire self. She looks as if death has already taken her, as if she's fallen into a deep, irrevocable sleep. It's seven in the evening, well past dinnertime at the Brodsky house. That's what he's thinking of when the nurse on duty comes into the room, about his family—two boys and a girl who fill their small apartment with energy, and his wife, the curls in her hair, her smile, coming up on forty, the four of them sitting around the kitchen table without him. Feeling a mix of gratitude and regret, and a feeling of detachment, of remove, from this woman, this Merna, for whom he is not responsible. This is about work, he tells himself, observing his own lack of emotion, justifying it to himself. "You have a call, Detective," the nurse says.

Brodsky has been waiting for this call for three days. He'd contacted United Pest Control headquarters in St. Louis immediately after they discovered Merna's body. But it wasn't until he called Bill Kidman, asked him to intervene, to get the FBI involved again, that they'd responded. Now, standing at the nurse's station, he jots the information down and immediately calls Bill Kidman. The first words he says are, "Thank you."

"Watcha got?" Kidman says.

"We got a guy who left United two years ago. Has a record, of sorts. State police are getting a warrant."

"What's that mean? A record of sorts?"

"Never been arrested. He was questioned."

"Tell me more."

"He was fired a few years ago. Had an argument with a customer. She complained that he was spraying that boric acid indiscriminately all over her windows. He got angry and sprayed it in her face."

"Nasty."

"Also, he was questioned in an armed robbery incident last year, but there was insufficient evidence. Prints are on file. We're checking them against everything we have. But get this—he lives out there, near Plantersville, Tennessee."

"Oh shit," Bill Kidman says. "And Emma's there."

"I know. I spoke to her a little while ago. She's confirmed that the Holders, the people who own the Henley farm, set up that trust for Seal. Although maybe that's not so relevant anymore."

"I'll try to call her," Kidman says.

"If I can push this thing through, we'll get the local police to pick him up tonight," Brodsky says. "His name's Melton. Herbert Melton."

"You know what this means, don't you?"

"I do. It means he could have been working with someone else from Plantersville. Like the Henleys."

CHAPTER 73

Seal's Aunt Jenny is fussing about in the kitchen, stirring the black-eyed peas and checking the potatoes that are boiling on the stove. She's making a vegetable plate, her specialty, and they are drinking Budweisers from the can, the three of them—Emma, Aunt Jenny and her husband, Roy. Jenny has set out a tin of peanuts on the tin-top table. "Enjoy," she says. She's been lighthearted, and downright chatty since Emma arrived home from the courthouse to find the two of them relaxing in the kitchen. It's either her husband's presence or the beer, or both, Emma thinks. But she's not at all the same woman who walked her through

Carroll Cloar's life and work at the top of the stairs earlier in the day.

"So how was your trip downtown?" she'd asked when Emma arrived. "Oh my goodness. You were gone longer than I expected. We thought you might have been lost, but then Roy here thought you might be doing a little shopping or something."

Roy had stood when she entered, shaken her hand as an adolescent might, with a sense that he would rather not, but had been instructed in advance. He has the bearing of a construction worker, someone who uses his body in his work, and of someone who perhaps lacks a sense of humor. He hadn't smiled when he said hello. Jenny had smiled for him.

She'd wiped her hands on her apron, which appears now to be a sort of compulsive habit, and taken a sip of beer. "We'll have a nice old-fashioned vegetable plate tonight. You don't serve those up north, do you?" she said.

"Not so much," Emma said. "But they serve them at Merna's Place."

"Beer?" Jenny replied, eagerly, as if to say, *We want you to like us, we want to make you feel at home, we want you to feel comfortable.* But it had the opposite effect. Emma was standing just inside the doorway. She'd yet to remove her jacket or put up her things, and she was carrying a briefcase, which would have made it obvious that she was doing more than shopping. "Let me just freshen up a little bit," she said. "I'll only be a minute."

Now, Emma is on her second beer. And they have talked about the weather and the farm operations—"It's rented to a fellow who plants soybeans," Jenny explained—and Emma's job teaching history. "I was doing some research at your courthouse about the town's history," she had said, "curious about the plantations around here and landowners." That had led to a brief discussion about the Holders.

"They go back generations," Jenny had said. "I believe they owned everything all around Plantersville at the time of the Civil War. Then they sold off parcels over the years, probably to stay afloat. I would guess most of it was sold by the end of the Great Depression. That was long before I got here," she said.

"Honey, tell her about your family," Roy said then. "Jenny's family has been on this land since the 1940s. Her mother came down here from Ohio after the war. Jenny has roots here."

Jenny had shot him a look and a mild shake of the head, but Emma hadn't seen that. Her eyes were on her plate at the time. "She'll never leave here," Roy said.

After that, there was a bout of silence, and Emma had asked for that second beer, and now she's turned her attention to Roy. "I understand you travel quite a bit," she says. "What kind of work do you do?" Jenny's made fried green tomatoes. They are a regional delicacy, and Emma is savoring the last few bites. "Raised them in my greenhouse," she'd explained earlier. And Roy had pointed his own thumb her way, as if he were hitchhiking, bragging on his wife, "This one has a green thumb," he'd said.

"Wildlife management," he says now.

"Is that like conservation?" Emma asks, her mouth still half-full.

Roy, who is finished now and on his fourth beer, leans back in his chair. "Not exactly conservation. More like pest removal. If someone has a raccoon in their attic or a herd of 'em on their land making a mess, we take care of it. Move them to another location out in the woods. We work all over the Mid-South. I was in Missouri last week," he says. "Spent the afternoon today in Selmer. Some lady scared of a damn opossum," he says. "Silly woman. They're harmless things. And they eat other pests."

"They're specialists," Jenny says. And at first Emma thinks she's talking about possums, but she's talking about Roy and his partner. "Very good at what they do. Roy works with the Memphis Zoo and some of the big companies around here."

"So, you have your own business," Emma says.

"I do," he says. He's cleaned up for the evening and for the service tomorrow, shaved his sideburns and gotten a close haircut. He's wearing an Oxford cloth shirt that Jenny pressed earlier in the day and khaki pants, what he calls his come-to-Jesus clothes. No big belts, no cowboy hat. But he's missing a tooth, which gives him a distinctly unpolished look.

"H and M Wildlife and Pest Control," Jenny says proudly.

Emma has made the connection. She coughs into her hand to conceal her facial expression. Takes a sip of beer. "Sorry," she says softly, as Jenny goes on: "Henley and Melton."

"Excellent," Emma says. "So how long have you been in business?"

"A good few years," he says. "We just keep getting busier and busier."

Jenny stands, kissing her husband on the forehead, and Emma pops up as well with an overly enthusiastic "Great dinner!" and "Let me help." Her mind is moving way too fast. She'd never considered Jenny and her husband as suspects. Although, early on, the possibility of Seal's nearest relative wanting access to her funds had come up. But this feels like something else. It feels as if Roy is involved, but maybe not his wife. Jenny is humming around like a happy bee. Roy has repaired to the living room with his beer, where he's turned on the television. Emma's not at all sure what she should do. And Jenny is still drinking.

***

When Emma finishes up the last plate and sets down the dish towel, Jenny comes in closer, as the sound of canned laughter from some sort of sitcom drifts into the kitchen.

"She jumped out the window, didn't she?" Jenny whispers with a look of anguish on her face. "Why would she do that?"

"I don't know," Emma says, not wanting to engage or reveal her involvement, conscious of the company. "She didn't seem unhappy to me," she says, and when Jenny's eyes meet hers, she adds, "It may well have been a fall, an accident."

Jenny pulls out her seat and seems to be pondering that, in a muddled sort of way. After a few too many beers, she's slurring her words.

"I thought Lucy had a hard time of it. Not knowing who her father was. Raised by a woman with a broken heart. Shipped off to Mississippi, then to New York," Aunt Jenny says. "You know, she came down here once with her boyfriend before she and her mother moved in. She had a tattoo. And he was Jewish—I'm certain of it. And there was nothing whatsoever Christian about her," she says, waiting for a reaction from Emma. When it fails to arise, Jenny goes on. "One day, she left that boy here and ran off to Memphis. She was obsessed with meeting the Holders, as if they were so important." Then her countenance changes. "Do you think someone killed her? That someone killed Lucy?" she says, gripping Emma's arm.

"I don't know what happened. All I know is I lost a friend," Emma says, stepping back, then resting her hand on Jenny's shoulder. "We have a big day tomorrow. I'd probably better head up."

But Jenny isn't ready. "When they called me, the police, they told me she was dead. That she'd fallen from a window. But I suspect that she jumped. She was an unhappy girl." She takes another sip of her beer. "Selfish people, the two of them. They had everything. But still she jumped out a window."

Then Emma can't resist. Foolishly, carelessly, she says, "May I ask you a question?"

Jenny takes a last sip of her beer and tosses it across the room into the trash bin. The dogs, all three of them, come running when the can bangs against the side of the bin, as if it must be their dinnertime again.

"Of course. You can ask me any damn thing you like," she says.

"Do you know about the trust fund?"

"Do I know about the trust fund?" Jenny says, her voice full of scorn and rising steadily. "Did I know about the trust fund? Get the hell out of my kitchen." And Emma feels as if Jenny would have scratched her eyes out if she'd been any closer.

The can toss, the dog traffic, the tone of Jenny's voice, all conspire to awaken Roy, who had fallen into a comfortable half sleep in the living room. When the phone rings, bringing mayhem to the mounting madness, Jenny nearly trips over herself to get to it, speaking as clearly as she possibly can to whoever is on the other end of the line. "She can't come to the phone right now," she says. And Roy, emerging from his BarcaLounger in the living room, says lightly, "What's goin' on in here, darlin'?" To Emma's good fortune, she realizes that he is a happy drunk and his wife is the opposite. Nonetheless, she's trying to imagine in an instant who is calling her, why she can't come to the phone and how the hell to get *out of there*. Where are my car keys? she is thinking. My purse? And where is my jacket, she thinks, as her eyes land on the brown leather jacket hanging over the back of the fourth kitchen chair, the one that sat empty during dinner. Still, she doesn't move.

"Well, Emma had a few questions about the trust fund," Jenny tells her husband. "Wanted to know if I'd known about it."

"So, that's fine," he says. "Don't get all worked up. Just answer the woman's question."

"I did. I said I knew about it. That's all."

"Do you have all the information you need, Miss Quinn?"

"I'm fine. I just . . ." Emma feels a fool.

"You're just . . ."

"I was just curious," Emma says. "Seal told me there was a trust fund. That's all. Just curious."

"Morbid curiosity, I'd say." Roy follows this comment with a laugh, then adopts a tone of contrived politeness. "Well, you'll just have to wait until tomorrow morning when we all have a little less beer in us. And I'm sure my wife would be happy to answer any questions you might have about the trust fund." He grabs Jenny somewhat forcibly by the arm and moves her through the living room and toward the stairs, Emma watching from the kitchen doorway. "But right now, we need a little rest. Don't we, darlin'? You have a funeral in the morning."

CHAPTER 74

SEAL

Roy's an ass. But the truth is, we didn't make his life any easier. They'd only been married a few years when Mama got sick, and we moved in and took over their lives for almost a year. I'd only met him once before. They visited us in New York after they first got married. That's when the Henny Penny thing really got going. They called the trip their honeymoon, but they really came up to see the World Series at Yankee Stadium. Roy was a big baseball fan. The two of them stayed in my old room, the so-called Marilyn room, in Mom's apartment on Seventy-Second Street, during this so-called honeymoon. At the time, I was living in my studio, so I didn't see much of them. But we all met for dinner the night after the last series game.

Rolley got them the tix, and Roy was forever grateful, blah, blah, blah and took us all out to dinner. But the Yankees had lost, and Roy was pretty glum about it, disappointed. Seems it was the fourth game in the series, and it was the first time any team had lost four in a row, or the first time the Yankees lost a series in straight games or something like that, which made it a bona fide tragedy. "That's not the kind of record you want to break," he said at dinner, after he explained it to us. He drank a lot that night. I assumed we'd be going to Merna's Place, but we met them at Mama Mia's Spaghetti Emporium near Forty-Second Street. Their call. I guess it was a tourist attraction or something. It was horrible Italian American food. He ate an enormous volume of spaghetti *alla Bolognese*, along with his whisky sours. Mom said he spent his entire last night in the john throwing up. Poor Mr. Henny Penny, we said. The sky is falling.

As I remember it, Aunt Jenny was all dressed up, wearing blue eye shadow and sparkling pink lipstick. She looked very pretty. They had gone to see the sights—the Empire State Building and the Staten Island Ferry and the Museum of Natural History—before the World Series got here. Her eyes lit up when she talked about all of that. And during dinner, she kept putting her hand over his at the table, trying to console him about the unfortunate Yankees loss. I remember she looked at him as if he were the handsomest man in the world—although the only way I can describe him would be average. Plus, he wore the most ridiculous clothes, looked like he was planning to perform in a rodeo. I thought Rolley was going to make fun of them, but he didn't. Said he liked them.

Just last year, they were going to come back, said they wanted to come see me, come for a "little visit," they said. Emma had already gotten her place in Washington, and the Loves weren't coming for at a least a month. So, there was this little window when they could have come up and stayed in her place. Right next door to me, I told them. They were planning on it, wanted to catch up with me and Rolley, they said, but something interfered. I don't recall. Maybe his work. They canceled. I had the feeling they really wanted to go to a baseball game with Rolley, who I was pretty much out of touch with at the time. Anyway, they never made the trip.

CHAPTER 75

"We can't put you in her room, sir," the man at the check-in desk had told him when he arrived at the Peabody late in the evening. The hotelier's body language and the look on his face said something more like, *You gotta be kidding me.* "Not without her permission," he said.

"Can you call her?" Angus McLearan had said, and the hotelier had checked his records. "We don't have a number for her, sir. But she's slated to return tomorrow afternoon."

Angus had called Bill Kidman as soon as he got to his room. "We have a lead on this murder, her friend's murder," Kidman had reported. "It's a guy in Plantersville. That's where she is. Plantersville. I'm going to try to reach her there."

"Fill me in," Angus had said.

"Name's Melton. Seems he and the victim's uncle are in business together. Company called H and M Wildlife and Pest Control. Long story. I'll fax you everything you need. And remember, there's a funeral there in the morning."

"Where?"

"No idea."

"I'll find it."

CHAPTER 76

"Why would he want to hurt me?" Emma is lying in bed, asking herself that question. He has no reason to hurt me, she tells herself. He can't possibly know that I suspect anything.

Believing that the man who killed Seal Larson will be sleeping in the room across the hall, she finds herself in an untenable situation. In order to prepare for bed, she must exit the safety of her bedroom and visit the bathroom. Never has a visit to the bathroom seemed so unwise. She's locked the bedroom door, but it's a flimsy thing. Her only hope is that she hasn't revealed her suspicion, that he has no way of knowing that she's working with the police department, that he has no reason whatsoever to harm her. One thing is certain: she doesn't expect to get any sleep.

Of course, Emma has the option of slipping away. She knows that. She's thinking that she could find an excuse to go down to the car and drive off, into town, to police headquarters, and it would be over. She also knows that someone called her. Aunt Jenny had specifically said that she could not come to the phone. So, someone is trying to reach her. And Emma knows there's a chance that whoever it is—Tomas Brodsky? Bill Kidman?—would have suspected something, would have sensed the danger. Whoever called may be on their way, may have sent someone, she thinks. She can hear murmuring through the walls of the farm-house, hear Roy talking to Jenny, perhaps getting her to bed. Emma does not think she's given herself away. And as she lies in bed, still as a stone, she imagines that she'll be perfectly safe. That no harm will come to her. That the danger lies in making a move. And so, trusting her instincts, she doesn't.

***

"She's awake," the nurse is coming out of Merna Jones's room. "She's awake and she's talking crazy. She keeps saying 'Is Andy Warhol dead?' over and over."

In New York City, Merna has awakened. She is pressing the buzzer by her bed. At the nurses' station, the sound is unrelenting. There is a policewoman outside her door. Standard practice, although they doubt that Merna is still at risk. "Your lady. She's awake," the night nurse tells the cop, who peers into the room.

"What happened?" Merna looks frightened. Her speech is slurry, but her mind seems sharp enough. "Why am I here?" Once they've explained, she lies awake for a good hour before she buzzes again. "Did they take the Calder? The mobile?" The policewoman knows nothing about the case. She's just a guardian, there as a precautionary measure. "I need to speak to someone," Merna says firmly. "It's important."

"She's awake and she's talking crazy," the guard tells Tomas Brodsky.

"How crazy?" he says.

"She wants to know if Andy Warhol is dead."

"I'll be there as soon as I can," he says. It's 3:00 a.m. on the East Coast.

***

Although Emma may have slept without even realizing it, she has, for all practical purposes, been lying on top of her bed all night awake, unmoving. She has asked herself why he would have done it—why he would have killed Seal, and her night mind has generated all kinds of possibilities. She assumes he knew they wouldn't inherit her money, so he—or they—went after her art. Those two pieces—a Rothko and a Jasper Johns, or whatever he thought Seal had in her possession. Emma is certain that Roy is in possession of the Calder mobile, which, although probably real, is also probably worth relatively little in the grand scheme of things. Her mind wandering, she considers the fact that whoever did this failed to recognize the value of the Toulouse-Lautrec—an original signed, limited edition—that hangs in her apartment or the African masks in Merna's place, all of which are surely worth quite a bit. It makes sense, she thinks. Whoever it was knew nothing about art or its value. The thief had a shopping list. She wonders whether Aunt Jenny was, in fact, involved. And how Roy could have pulled it off. Surely Seal would have recognized him if he came to her apartment, Emma reasons. And in her anxious bout of a half sleep, she thinks there was an accomplice, perhaps his partner. Or maybe he told his partner—this pest control partner—about the paintings, and he killed Seal, without Roy Henley's knowledge. Like in jail, she thinks, when a convict spills the beans to their cellmate. Like something in the movies. Like *In Cold Blood*. She hopes that's what has happened, and that Roy doesn't even know. She thinks that makes more sense than a man killing his own niece for some paintings. And that's what she's settling on as she witnesses the sunrise through the east-facing window at dawn. After a time, she hears someone moving about across the hall and the dogs rummaging around below, scratching at the kitchen door. She checks her watch. It's 6:00 a.m. central time. She is still wearing her street clothes from the day before. And the service is at nine.

***

Across town, Herbert Melton is wearing handcuffs. The local sheriff is holding up the Alex Calder mobile. It's suspended from his right hand, and he's examining it, musing: "Is this what he stole? This here thing?" he says. "Looks like a damn toy." Undoubtedly, the description would have made Alexander Calder smile. After all, *Calder's Circus* is one of the most playful works of art ever created. Born in 1898 to a sculptor and a painter, Calder went on to study engineering and become one of the most popular artists who has ever lived. He entertained generations of children and adults with his *Circus*, a mechanical circus with a full array of animals and acrobats, giants and clowns and everything else imaginable, crafted of wire and cloth and metal and yarn and paper and bottle caps and corks and other household materials. Early on, he carried his *Circus*—which is now in the Whitney's collection—around the world in five suitcases, and he himself manipulated it to the delight of all in what was one of the earliest forms of performance art. Then there were his mobiles, large and small, and massive public sculptures at places like the Empire State Building and Rockefeller Center, his drawings and his paintings. This particular piece will go back to Merna Jones, and Herbert Melton will go to prison.

***

It's past seven. Emma has yet to emerge from her room. She hears footsteps on the staircase, heavy steps, Roy's steps, the sound of the back door opening for the dogs and kibble falling into their metal bowls, then the smell of coffee rising up through the house. Finally, there is the distinct sound of high heels on the floorboards, of Jenny rising. Once Emma's sure they are both downstairs, she slips into the bathroom, splashes her face. Her mouth feels dry, and she has a mild headache. She examines her face, close-up against the mirror, the dark circles under her eyes, the puffiness, the sallow look of her skin. "Shit," she says out loud to herself. The service begins in a few hours.

Back in her room, she can't quite muster the energy to dress. Sitting on the edge of the bed, she stares at a room that feels empty, unclaimed. There is no sign that anyone ever felt at home there. The decor is from another era: pale blue walls, an old rocking chair painted yellow, a rag rug woven in pastel colors—pinks and blues and lime greens. The bedspread is a chirpy yellow gingham, the window shades, white vinyl. There are no curtains on the windows and there is nothing on the walls. Emma is trying to imagine Seal in this room, her mother growing up here, life in Plantersville and the immensity of the distance between this place and West Seventy-Second Street. Emma rises, and as she slips on her black dress and begins to gather up her things, she hears the two of them—Jennifer and Roy down below. They are going in and out of the back porch—or front porch, as the case may be— filling the old Chevy wagon with casseroles and salads and desserts from the old fridge. From above, she can tell that they are bickering, and she watches as Seal's Aunt Jenny slams the car door and drives off in a kind of huff, kicking up the dusty driveway, the dogs chasing after her. As Emma hears the slam of the screen and his footsteps on the stairs, she flips the lock again, knowing it probably won't keep him out, hoping it might slow him down. Roy Henley's not hiding his destination.

"Open up," he's saying. "Sounds like you have some questions. Come on. Open up." He's not yelling, just speaking with a firm, authoritative voice. "I want to talk to you."

"I'm dressing," she calls. "Just a minute," she says, trying to keep the fear out of her voice. Emma doesn't have a weapon, just her own strength and her presence of mind. She can hear him in the next room, knocking things about. Probably getting a weapon, she thinks. And she's remembering why she hates the country. And that there is no one within a mile of the house.

***

"Hurry it up. I got to get to the church," was the last thing Roy had said before a stillness took hold. She's not at all sure what he's up to, but it's quiet now. She's weighing the options—wait for him to make a move, arm herself with something, anything and confront him in the hallway or try to climb out the window and down to the car and make a run for it. He knocks again. Brisk, loud, angry knocks. "Hold on, Roy," she calls. "I have a run in my stocking. Just give me a minute." She can't imagine why he's not just barging in. She hears him making his way down the hall, down the stairs. That's when she hears the dogs going bonkers and someone banging on the porch door, and through the window of her room, she watches Roy running through what used to be Seal's grandmother's front door and sneaking around the back of the house and into his van, the United Pest van, and speeding out the dusty drive, the local sheriff giving chase.

***

In Manhattan, when Detective Brodsky arrives in Merna Jones's room, she is fully awake, lucid, cogent, and has had a meal. "I know what they were looking for," she says. "And I know why."

"Good. Good," he says heartily. "Glad to see you waking up. How are you feeling?"

"Got this god-awful taste in my mouth," she says. "But the doctor says I'll live."

"I have some good news," he says. "We got them this morning. Down in Plantersville. You know Roy Henley? Lucille Lawson's uncle?"

"Never met him. But I know who he is."

"They had your Calder."

"Did they now?" she says, looking up at him, grinning. "Well, they got the booby prize." He stares at her, waiting, while she takes a sip of water through a plastic straw that's attached to a hospital-grade plastic cup, which she then holds in the air, declaring: "I figured it out."

"What's that?" He cocks his head slightly.

"They were looking for Marilyn."

"Marilyn. Okay," he says skeptically.

"Marilyn Monroe. Maggie Grace had a Marilyn Monroe painting from Andy Warhol. A gift."

"No kidding. And she didn't give it away with her art collection?"

"Nope. It's in the bank. Apple Bank. I got it. I'm in charge of it."

"Is that right?"

"I didn't know anybody knew about it but me and Miss Lucy. I guess

Maggie Grace told her sister."

"Hard to know. That would be more valuable than the Calder, I assume. Especially now that Andy Warhol's dead."

"He just died, didn't he?"

"Now you're beginning to make sense," he says, leaning over her, smiling. "So, does it belong to you?"

"Nope."

He gives her a quizzical look, pushing his glasses up along the bridge of his nose.

"Belonged to whoever needs it," she says. "I'm just watching over it."

"So, you're suggesting that they killed Lucille Lawson and very nearly killed you, and they didn't even get what they wanted."

"They must be pretty angry, don't you think?"

"And pretty stupid."

CHAPTER 77

SEAL

For years, I was angry at my mother. I was probably the angriest teenager you ever met. She knew full well why I was angry. Because, for as long as she lived, she couldn't tell me who my father was, and I had no idea why. I thought maybe she was ashamed. Or that I was the product of an assault or something. Turned out, she was forbidden to tell me. How can that even be legal? It pissed me off. And I got angry at her again before she died, when she decided to give away her collection. Our collection. Then she told her sister that we were keeping the Marilyn painting as an insurance policy for all of us. By then, she'd given away most of the paintings, which I finally began to appreciate only because, really, what was I going to do with all that extraordinary art? Besides, if you think about it, it's not at all fair for one person to get all that joy out of all that beauty. She convinced me of that. She made her will when we were down there in Plantersville. I went with her. She gave Aunt Jenny her money—not Roy Henley, but Aunt Jenny. That is, anything that wasn't in the trust fund. But she had this Marilyn that Andy Warhol had given her way back in the early days. One of his Marilyn paintings. It was as if he was using it to draw her to him. I don't think she realized at the time how valuable it was—or would become. She didn't tell anyone about it except, at some point, she told Merna, of course. Before she died, she put Merna in charge of it. So, if anything catastrophic happened—with the trust or with the restaurant or with Aunt Jenny, like maybe a tornado hits the farm or terrorists blow up Merna's Place or the stock market crashes, we had the Marilyn. At that point, she knew that it would be worth a lot of money some day and she just put it aside. She kept kinda quiet about it. I knew about it, of course, because I was there when he gave it to her. He gave it to her offhandedly. Like he was giving her one of his piss paintings, or the way he gave me those photographs when I asked for a copy of our film. Like it was nothing. At first it was in a closet in our apartment, rolled up in a tube. And nobody knew about it, except me and her. Then, when I moved out, it was in my old bedroom, because nobody ever slept in there. Except, of course, the Henny Pennies, that one time.

I admit, when I was a kid, I told Rennie about it. Told him it was our secret. And he promised never to tell anyone. I don't think he ever did, in fact. And he's probably forgotten by now. But when Mama was about to die and she gave away all her art, she told her sister about Marilyn and the insurance policy part. I didn't know whether that was smart or not. I mean, what if Merna had needed that money? Or me? Aunt Jenny might not be too happy about that. I just didn't know whether we could trust Aunt Jenny. My mother said, "I wanted her to know that I would protect her. That if there was ever a disaster, all she had to do was contact Merna. I made her promise not to tell Roy." We didn't like Roy. And she didn't trust him. She called him a ruffian. And not too smart. That's what my mother said anyway. "Dumb as a snake," she called him. I think she regretted it afterward—not the thing about Roy, but about telling Jenny. But, with the Marilyn, she and Merna had it all arranged. She knew she could count on Merna if anyone ever needed the Marilyn money.

My mother felt guilty because, no matter what, the trust would never go to her sister. That part was cast in stone. And Aunt Jenny had resented it all those years. So, my mother not only left her own money to Aunt

Jennifer, but she just couldn't resist telling her about the Marilyn. And when Andy Warhol died, I guess Aunt Jenny knew the Marilyn would be worth a fortune and she couldn't resist telling Roy. So, in the end, it seems, I was right. We could always trust Merna. We really couldn't trust Jenny. And Roy was a ruffian.

As for the thing about my father, she set that straight too. Not long before she died, she sent that letter to Merna, the letter for me, that explained everything. And Merna brought it to me after my mother's funeral. "No more secrets," she said when she gave it to me. She hadn't even opened the envelope, but I suspect she knew exactly what it was. I saved it in my dresser drawer, and, every now and then, I used to take it out and read it. Because it was such a gift to know the truth.

CHAPTER 78

Angus McLearan pulled up to the Henley's screen porch at around 8:00 a.m., like a ghost out of nowhere, to find Emma dressed in black, drinking a cup of coffee she'd assembled in this stranger's kitchen. When she heard the car, she'd assumed it would be someone from the sheriff's office. Now she is trembling. And he is holding her tight. They're standing next to his rental car, a little white Taurus with Michigan plates resting in the patchy grass beside the Henleys' porch. The dogs are barking.

There is no one else there.

Emma has tears in her eyes. Angus's eyes are closed.

"I have to go to the service soon," she whispers. But still they don't move. They have been standing like this for a good ten minutes. "I thought I lost you," she says.

"I know. I'm so sorry. I didn't have any choice," he says, tightening his grip around her.

"You didn't have any choice?" she says, throwing her head back. Her voice rising ever so slightly. "You didn't have any choice?"

"It was too risky."

"Who? Why? What?"

"You know I can't tell you." He's shaking his head, and he's still holding her, firmly. "Too much going on. On all sides."

She holds his face in her hands. "I thought I lost you. I thought you were on that ferry."

"I know. I know. I made it look that way. I had to."

"You had to."

"No one wanted me to know what I knew. I can explain. I promise. But not now."

"Is this safe?" she turns, sweeps her arm across the landscape.

"Right now? I think we're okay here in Plantersville, Tennessee."

She is still shaking, and he is kissing her neck and holding her with a steadiness that is keeping her on her feet. "It'll be okay," he says.

"I want you to take me back to the Peabody," she says.

"I can do that," he says, smiling.

"After the service," she says.

***

Heading into town on Highway 64, Angus signals toward the glove compartment. "You have ten messages on your machine at home, and I found a note on the floor. Must be important. Apparently, someone slipped it under your door," he says. "It's in there."

She ignores the note. "You went to my apartment. In DC?" she says.

"I thought you would be there. I wanted to surprise you."

"And it wasn't safe to call me and tell me you were okay."

"I snuck in."

"I thought I lost you," she says again.

"I know. I know." He puts his hand on her shoulder.

"I'll let it go," she says. "Someday, maybe." He's not surprised when she gives him a little smack on the arm. She's not smiling. He looks sheepish, like someone who forgot to pick up the dry cleaning or make a dinner reservation—not like someone who neglected to tell a woman he loves that he is still alive.

"It's not funny," she says. "You couldn't call me, but you could sneak into my apartment. You couldn't send word via Bill Kidman. You couldn't send me a gift with a secret note in it. Or a letter."

"What? Or a coded message? Via satellite?"

"Okay. Okay," she says, but she knows the conversation is not over.

***

It's a small Methodist church on the outskirts of town, simple, with an arched door and a white clapboard façade. No stained glass. Barely a footpath leading to the door. When he comes around the car to open her door, his eyebrows are furrowed, but he also has a smile on his face, which gives him the irresistible look of a puppy that's torn up someone's room and is about to be punished but won't be. "I couldn't. I couldn't do anything to try to reach you until I was sure that I was in the clear. I'll explain it all later. We'll take a hike."

"You can take a hike," she says, getting out of the car and pushing him away. Then immediately pulling him back to her, she points a finger at him, up close, so that it touches his nose. "If you ever, ever do anything like that again. I'll . . ."

Then they melt into one another, until finally she has to pull away. "It's already started," she says, looking at her watch.

"I'll go in with you."

"You can come with me?"

"I can come. We'll go."

"Okay," she says, walking toward the entrance. "And afterward, we're leaving."

"Yes. Afterward, we're going back to the Peabody Hotel."

"Yes."

As they enter the sanctuary, Angus McLearan's hand is her anchor. She cannot hold it any tighter. "I was mourning you," she whispers as they sit.

"Well, I hope so," he says, grinning. And then the singing begins, the entire congregation joining in, a rapturous swell of a sound that brings the tears to Emma's eyes, Angus solemnly passing her his handkerchief. It's a traditional hymn for southern funerals, most often sung at the end of the service. But Emma has never heard it before.

Tempted and tried we're oft made to wonder why it should be thus all
    the day long
While there are others living about us, never molested, though in the wrong
When death has come and taken our loved ones, it leaves our home so
    lonely and dreary
Then do we wonder why others prosper living so wicked year after year
Farther along we'll know all about it; farther along we'll understand why
Cheer up, my brother; live in the sunshine, we'll understand it all by and by
Faithful till death said our loving master; a few more days to labor and wait
Toils of the road will then seem as nothing as we sweep through the
    beautiful gates
Farther along we'll know all about it. We'll understand it all by and by.

There are maybe a hundred people in this small Methodist church set on the edge of Plantersville's town square, friends and neighbors of Jenny and Roy Henley. Emma imagines very few of them knew Seal, although some of them may well have known her mother growing up and pondered her fate. There is a graciousness to the fact that, although the local sheriff has arrested Herbert Melton, and Melton has already identified Roy Henley as an accomplice, they let Roy accompany his wife to the service and stand by her at her niece's funeral. "I didn't mean for her to die," Roy had told the sheriff. "That wasn't what we planned." There are police at every exit, and of course, Herbert Melton is in custody. As far as they know, there are still two paintings missing—a Rothko and a Jasper Johns. But there is no sign of them, not yet anyway.

CHAPTER 79

Emma is trying to reason with herself—or maybe she's just tormenting herself. It is Tuesday morning. The sweetness of Angus's return is easing. On Monday, they spent a full day in his suite at the Peabody Hotel, entwined with one another. They'd dined on lobster and caviar at Chez Philippe and languished in the lobby drinking whisky, laughing, talking politics a bit, even addressing serious matters. Still, Emma has yet to confront him with what she considers a great betrayal—his disappearance after the accident at Zeebrugge and failure to get any kind of message to her. And it's turning into anger.

She keeps rolling it around in her mind. *Did he not know I would be bereft? Did he even try to reach me? Does he feel no remorse?* Worse still, she knows now that he saw Bill Kidman and still no one reached out to her—which deepens the betrayal somehow. She decides that the experience is a metaphor for their entire relationship—the secrets, the dangers, the distance between them. Now, she at once dreads his departure and welcomes it. Suddenly, everything about the way they live seems too great a burden. Too risky. And she doesn't know quite how to broach the subject with Angus.

They'd ordered some coffee and croissants. Emma is standing at the window, cup in hand, dressed in one of the hotel's robes, crisp and white and too big, looking out the window at nothing in particular, mulling. She knows he'll be leaving, if not this morning, sometime in the next twenty-four hours. She hasn't raised the issue, perhaps for fear of tarnishing the moment. But it's time and Emma knows it.

"How about a walk on the river?" she says. He looks up from a newspaper. "Let me shower first," he says. And minutes later, she joins him, their intensity and passion, her anger and confusion, their shared knowledge that they will soon have to part—all of it coming to a head in the colossal glass-enclosed shower. The act itself is loud, too loud, almost violent. Afterward, she will dress quickly, quietly. "I'll meet you in the lobby," she'll say.

***

It's balmy out and sunny, a beautiful day for a walk. They make their way toward the river without speaking. He's wondering what she wants to explore that might be confidential. Maybe this Iran-Contra business, he thinks; but then again, he feels as if they've covered it. She's silently running through exactly what she should say and how to say it, as if she needs a script or it will come out all wrong—desperate and needy and selfish, although her rational self knows her demands are reasonable enough.

The walk feels interminably long through the center of Memphis's downtown. It's early, nowhere near lunchtime, and the crowd is thin. They cross what was once a bustling Main Street, but the street itself was bricked over in the midseventies and made into a kind of promenade with a trolley line running through it, a trend that was popular back then and hasn't really worked. There are signs of a resurgence—a coffee shop, a funky clothing store, a sidewalk café—but some of the old storefronts are boarded up. And most of the people walking around seem more like panhandlers than working people.

A few blocks to the west, they finally reach the river. To get to an open green space with pathways to the riverfront, they must cross a four-lane freeway. But once they arrive, they have an unfettered view in all directions—of the vast, muddy river, the Arkansas shoreline and a cloudless open sky, endlessly blue. Close-up, the water is choppy and it's obvious that the undercurrent is strong. "Keep Out," a small sign at the edge of the park tells them.

"Soooo," Angus says, once they are situated on a bench. "What are we doing here?" He still assumes it's something about his work, some theory Emma wants to share or a question she wants to ask. As she turns toward him, her knee settling against Angus's thigh, it reminds him of a time after they'd first met, how she'd turned to him in the car and her knee had grazed his leg, how he'd felt that first time they touched.

"I don't think I can go through it again," she says, beginning it. He looks at her confused, and she explains. "Your death. I don't think I can go through that again. The grief." He understands instantly and his face seems to sag. He looks ten years older. "Not anytime soon anyway," she says.

"Oh God. I didn't think," he says, running one hand through her hair. "I just didn't think."

"I know. That's what upsets me. And if I can't trust you to give me a signal that you're okay . . ."

"This was unu—" he says, but Emma cuts him off.

"Don't even say it." Her voice is firm. "This is the work you do."

"But the circumstances, they were just different."

"So, explain it to me. Explain it now. This is as safe a place as we'll find," she says looking around. "Don't you think?" He can hear the controlled anger in her voice.

"Listen. Just listen to me. Please," he's speaking slowly. "This has been an unusual assignment. Neither my government nor yours, or for that matter, Iran or Iraq or Russia or Israel or most of the other countries involved," he pauses, "nobody," he says emphatically, "wants to be held accountable for what's going on in the field over there. I can't give you the details, but these are activities that are widely recognized as criminal and against international law. So, a lot of people don't want this information to get out."

"Understood," she says, nodding. "But—"

He holds his forefinger up to her lips. "Someone I don't trust knows more than I want them to know. Someone I work with. So, when I found out about the ferry, I decided to put myself on it—just to give myself some time. So, I could disappear, safely."

"But that doesn't explain why you couldn't get a message to me."

"As I said, it's an unusual situation," he says. "This person knows who you are. They know about our involvement. I didn't want to put you at risk. It's always best that you know nothing. And let's not forget, someone had just been killed in your apartment."

Emma sits very still, and it begins to make sense. Except this idea that it's someone who knows Emma. Someone she knows, she assumes. "It's not Bill . . ."

"Kidman? Oh God no. We may not always agree, but no." He is emphatic.

"So, who on earth?"

"You don't need to know right now."

She grows more concerned then. "You're still not safe, are you?" she asks, silencing herself as a woman pushing a baby stroller approaches.

Once the stroller is well past them, Angus speaks first. "What I'm trying to do at the moment is keep you safe."

"But listen," she says, more slowly, more softly, moving in closer to him and putting one hand on his cheek for a moment. "From here on, if we don't have a way to communicate, I'll feel like the proverbial sailor's wife—that woman waiting at the edge of the sea, with no way of knowing whether he's been hurt, whether he'll return, whether he's safe. I can't do that. I can't live like that now that I know what it feels like to lose you."

He's quiet for a long time, looking out at the water, his arm across her shoulder. "Okay," he says matter-of-factly. "Then we have to decide."

"Decide?"

"Whether it's time for me to give up my career or time for us to give up this." He waves his hand back and forth in the air between them. "You know. Us," he says.

The conversation is not going as Emma had imagined. She tries to backtrack. "But what if we were just to have a signal . . ." she says, trailing off, waiting for him to come up with an idea. But he looks at her hopelessly.

"Only in the movies," he says, gently. "If I'm in a difficult situation, I can't be—"

"Of course," she says suddenly, holding up her hand, interrupting him.

"It's not that I don't love you," he says then. "I do. But, apparently, now, these two things are not compatible."

She's not understanding, and he can see it in the expression on her face. And then she begins to digest what he is saying. *Time for me to give up my career. It's not that I don't love you. These two things are not compatible.* And she's recalling how tentative he's been about his work this last year.

"It may be time for me to settle down," he says. "But that would change everything, you know."

Now they are both sitting, staring out at the river, holding hands, their grips tightening as the idea begins to sound real, as they each begin to imagine what life would be like if they combined their lives into one. Is that something to celebrate? Or to fear? They both know it's something they've never considered. Before they leave the banks of the Mississippi, they have agreed, however awkwardly, to give it some thought.

***

Later, after Angus received some sort of cryptic telex that arrived at the Peabody front desk and the two of them are parting ways at Memphis International Airport, each flying to different destinations, again, they agree they'll think about it. And, at the very last moment, he whispers in her ear. "By the way, we're safe now," adding, "Your tenants—the Loves—they won't be coming back." She freezes, knowing full well that he's deliberately left no time for questions, then steps back. "You rascal," she says, realizing what has occurred, shaking her head. Grinning like a Cheshire, he kisses her on the cheek and, as he turns to go, walking backward, he half whispers the words: "We're going to be okay."

CHAPTER 80

"I saw her, you know." William Carrollton Holder the Fourth is sitting on a divan in his living room in Englewood, New Jersey. It is a contemporary house, doubtless designed by a prominent midcentury modern architect. It feels woodsy, in a Wrightian sort of way, and is set in the woods or, rather, designed to feel as if it is set in the woods. The living room looks out through a wall of windows onto a yard that's bounded by trees and has a swimming pool at its center. The pool closely resembles a natural pond. It reminds Emma of something that might belong somewhere else, somewhere that is not northern Jersey.

His wife is not at home.

"It was around Christmastime. Maybe 1985 or 1986," he says. "A retrospective of Andy Warhol's short films. We're involved in the arts, so we had a nice box. By that I mean a nice view of the screen. And the audience." He has a pronounced southern accent, distinctive in its smoothness. And he speaks like a man who sees no need to hurry.

Emma is prone to impatience. She makes a conscious effort to slow down, to listen, to overlook nothing. His pace gives her time to peruse the room—a Jasper Johns over the fireplace, one of his signature flag paintings, doubtless worth a fortune. And there is a Rothko on a dividing wall between the living room and dining room. This one's stunning—red, yellow and orange—translucent in the daylight, almost gauzy where the colors meet, and huge. Brodsky had assured her that the two paintings would be there.

"Tell me more about your involvement with art," she says.

"I started out as a commodities trader. It's in my blood, really. My father was a cotton broker. That's the middleman between the cotton farmer and the mill," he says. "He used cotton futures as a hedge. I approached it a little bit differently. I used it as an investment vehicle, a way to make money. I started trading commodity futures—grain, cotton, corn—on the Chicago Exchange. Then, in the seventies, I went to work for Salomon Brothers. I made a little money, and we moved to the New York office. It got a bit wild there in the early eighties, and I wasn't at all comfortable with the attitude. So, I went to work for Citibank. My wife was involved in the arts, and I got drawn into that. Now, it's my business, really," he says. "Are you familiar with the name Jeffrey Deitch? No? Well, he founded the first advisory service for art investing at Citibank in 1979, and I joined that division. It was the first of its kind—anywhere. Very exciting. We finance art acquisitions, and we help our clients determine the value of what they're buying, make recommendations and so forth. It's been groundbreaking, really."

He hops up then. "Come," he says. "Let me show you my collection." He had skipped easily from her introduction—that she had a few questions about Lucille Lawson and the Lawson family—to himself.

"So, you met Seal Larson at Lincoln Center," Emma says as they walk through the house.

"I did. At the reception after the film. She was lovely. Looked just like her mother. We spoke briefly. That would be it, really. But I do remember it, because, of course, I knew Maggie Grace growing up. She lived on our farm in Tennessee." Fourth doesn't look the least bit like his brother, Raine. He's smoother, fitter, blonder. He could easily be one of the boys she knew growing up, one of the ones who went away to school, the dashing ones who had everything and were just a tad too cocky for her tastes.

"Right," she says. "Did you ever see Maggie in New York?"

"How is that relevant? As I said, I only met her daughter that once."

"It's not a trick question."

"The answer is yes. We ran into each other at an opening at Leo Castelli's gallery years ago. She was quite locked into the art scene for a while. I saw her often at events." He seems at ease then, not the least bit uncomfortable with the subject, as if he were talking about a business deal or a distant relative, someone of little consequence. "I helped her with some acquisitions," he says.

"Art acquisitions?"

"Of course."

They are moving from the Mark Rothko to the Jasper Johns. "After she became ill, I helped her with the logistics of a donation to the University of Mississippi," he says. "She asked me to handle it. I ended up buying these two paintings from her through the advisory team at the bank. It was all perfectly legitimate. She wanted her sister to have more funds. And, as I said, I'd helped her with acquisitions in the past. We weren't strangers."

They have arrived at the master bedroom where a massive Jackson Pollock, with all its reckless energy and splattered paint, and drips and drops of red and yellow and black, hangs over the king-size bed. Emma keeps her eyes on the Pollock as she speaks. "And she had never told you she had a daughter?"

"No," he says casually. "As I said earlier, I had no idea until I met the girl at Lincoln Center." Then, after hesitating for a moment, he asks, "What difference does it make?"

"You haven't talked to your brother, have you? About the trust fund?"

"Excuse me?" he says, making it obvious that he has no idea what Emma is talking about. His voice, his eyes, his entire demeanor sharpens, as if he is going on alert. Then he turns and escorts her through a long hall, past a series of photographs, back toward the living space. She recognizes a Cindy Sherman among them, the photographer looking shifty-eyed in an outfit that would have been comfortable in the forties or fifties for a day at the office in Manhattan, skyscrapers looming above her. Fourth stops for an instant. "One of her film stills," he says, motioning for Emma to go ahead, stepping up his pace.

"Would you like a drink?" he asks when they arrive at the kitchen.

Emma checks her watch, declines. "A bit early for me," she says.

"You don't seem like a typical New Yorker," he says, filling a glass with ice from an ice maker that's somewhere beneath the kitchen island, which is massive and marble and divides the living space from the kitchen space. "So, where are you from?"

"Delaware. Wilmington."

"And what kind of place is that?"

"I don't know what you mean."

"I'm trying to understand what gives you the authority to come into my house and ask me all kinds of personal questions. Detective Brodsky said you were a friend of the family?"

"I was a friend of your daughter's. That's what gives me the authority. I represent her. And I represent her spirit. So . . . what about the trust fund?"

"Daughter? Trust fund?" he says, indignant at first, then a stillness settles in, his face reddening, the realization of it dawning on him. "No," he says skeptically, softly, looking at his half-constructed scotch on the rocks. "That can't be," he says, shaking his head. Then, head bowed, his hands resting on the marble countertop, the weight of his body against the stone, he emits an almost plaintive "Oh my Lord."

"Didn't you set up the trust fund to support her?"

"No," he says flatly. He has lost his composure. He takes a sip of the scotch.

"Your father signed the documents."

"Then he must have known, but he never told me." There is anger in his voice. "It never would have occurred to me."

"But you and Maggie Grace Lawson did . . ."

"Yes, we did. We certainly did."

There is a moment of awkwardness then, but as he turns to lead Emma toward the door, Fourth recovers easily. Guiding her by the elbow and chatting away, he tells her that Maggie Grace found a home in the world of collectors. "People found her incredibly charming. Well, she *was* charming. But what they didn't get was that she was so smart. She hid that behind her southern accent. You know, Yankees make all kinds of assumptions about us southerners," he shakes his head. "But she was embraced, included in everything. And she wasn't a flipper, so she had access to some of the best work."

"A flipper?"

"She cared about her art. If she wanted to add a piece to her collection, it was because she wanted to appreciate it, enjoy it. She wasn't about to turn around and sell it for a profit," he says. "That would make her a flipper."

"Ah. I see," Emma nods.

And as she prepares to go, he holds out her coat so she can slip her arms through the sleeves and she says, speaking into the air, "And she never told you?"

Fourth doesn't answer, but as he opens the front door to let her go, he looks at her straight-on and says simply, "Well, I guess my father did the honorable thing, didn't he?" and closes the door behind her.

CHAPTER 81

Ten days later, they meet at a coffee shop on the waterfront, Rolley and Emma. She'd insisted. "I got all your messages," she said.

"I'm afraid I'm in Baltimore," he said.

"Perfect. I'll meet you there." It's been more than a month since Seal died. She and Angus have been holed up in her apartment in Washington for a week, and she hasn't seen Rolley Smythe—or Knox Smith as he's now calling himself—since he followed her that night on Connecticut Avenue, the night she drank too much. She hasn't wanted to see him. But she'd arranged it, nonetheless.

"What were you thinking, breaking into her studio?" she says to him, after a low-key greeting. The place has the feel of a sidewalk café, overlooking the city's Inner Harbor, which is undergoing a transformation into a major attraction for tourists and the rising class of young urban professionals. It's midmorning, and the café is very nearly empty. She's ordered a glass of water. He's ordered a black coffee. "Have you any cinnamon buns or something sweet, a donut or something?" he asked the waitress before responding to Emma. "I wanted my photographs back," he says.

"Do you have them now?" Emma says, and he nods. "Well then," she says.

He looks exactly the same as he's always looked. Like a model, a very tall, substantial one. Almost too perfect—the pure olive skin, the white teeth, the dark, noticeably shiny hair. You don't see many people who look flawless close-up, except the very young. He must be thirty years old by now, Emma thinks. She notices that there's something just slightly off-center about his face, which is what makes him so beautiful.

"So, were you looking for anything else when you broke into Seal's studio?"

"No, of course not. Just the photographs."

"You know that she hadn't even developed most of them, don't you? That the police had to do it. You'd have been wise to have looked for the film cannisters," she adds.

"Did you see them? The photographs?" he asks, sweat forming on his upper lip.

"I did." He's silent, still, waiting for her appraisal. "Look, they surprised me," she says. "But there was nothing profoundly disturbing about them. You—dressing up. You—undressing a little. You—looking like a woman. Nothing more than a bit of drama. All done for effect, I thought."

"Well, had they gone public, I would have felt compromised. My family would have disowned me."

"They didn't disown you for being apprehended by the FBI, did they?"

"Well, no," he says. And he can't quite look her in the eye.

"There's nothing to be ashamed of," she says.

"I'm not ashamed. I'm just embarrassed. Some things are better left private."

"Yes. So maybe stay out of photography studios?"

He smiles then. At this point, he's barely touched his coffee and his donut sits half-eaten. He is obviously uncomfortable. When he begins to stand, she puts out her hand. "Wait, I have so many questions," she says then, her expression a kind of plea. "Can you tell me about Maggie Grace? About her art collection? And what she was like?"

Then he seems to relax, looking into thin air as if he's searching for his memory there and his composure. "She was positively lovely," he says, looking back at Emma then. "No pretense. Completely herself. A very ethereal sort of person, but practical at the same time. And positive. She had this optimistic grace. I remember one year she came back from the Venice Biennale. You know, it's a huge event. And only the best people are invited to the opening parties. Well, she was invited. And she'd worn this stunning dress—she showed it to us, modeled it. I guess it was around 1970 or the late sixties. We were just teenagers, if that. Everyone was wearing sequins and metallics and maybe a little Pop Art back then. And she put on this elegant, understated, long black dress that hugged her body. She was wearing her hair short in those days. Looked a lot like Jean Seberg, if you know who I mean. Just stunning. And she came back and told this story about how she was at an exhibit inside a Venetian palace, and she was wandering around from room to room and found herself in a bedroom. She thought it was a museum, but it was someone's home and a woman appeared at the door and said, 'What are you doing in my bedroom?'" He laughs out loud then, recalling it.

"It was classic," he says. "Seal would have done something like that too. So, anyway, she explained that it was a mistake, and the two of them became fast friends. And the woman took her out to dinner or something." He shakes his head, smiling, as if the recollection itself has brought him joy. "The thing is, she had this innocence about her. In New York, people were fooled by that and the southern accent. But she was smart as a whip, so she would confound them, win them over. She charmed everyone."

"And her collection?"

"The art was beautiful. All of it. Some of it was valuable. She had a bit of a thing for Gerhard Richter early on, as I recall. And she had a photograph of his going way back. Those are worth something for sure. Gerhard Richter's work wasn't even showing in this country back then. She was ahead of her time. And she had an amazing eye." He hesitated a moment, as if for effect. "And good connections." He wrinkles his nose, grinning.

"She gave most of her collection away, you know. To the University of Mississippi."

"No kidding. I like that," he says, nodding his head. "Yeah. That works."

"It seems she was troubled by the fact that the price of art was becoming so outrageous, it was falling out of the reach of most museums. So that ordinary people would never get to see it. And the people least likely to see it might be in that part of the country, the Deep South, far from the center of the art world."

"Noble," he says. And Emma can't tell if he's being serious or sarcastic, in his postmodern sort of way. He has finished his donut and throws down the last drop of coffee, as if that's the end of it. But she's not stopping.

"So, you must have a lot of connections in the art world," she says, with a kind of determination. And he shrugs.

"Not really," he says and changes the subject. "So, they got the guys that did that to her?" He can't bring himself to say a word that rings with death—that killed her, murdered her. "And stole some of her paintings, right?"

"Not paintings. Just a Calder mobile," she says. And he nods, although a glint of surprise registers on his face. "It was her uncle, Roy Henley," Emma says. "Did you know him?"

"Don't think so," he says, his brow registering a look of confusion.

"Actually, ironically—and sadly," Emma tells him, "when she died, Maggie Grace left all her money and assets to her sister—Roy Henley's wife. Seal's aunt just never told her husband. In the end, I don't think she cared for him very much."

"So, if he'd known, Seal would still be alive, wouldn't she?"

"I didn't think of it that way," Emma says, knowing that it's untrue and knowing that he knows it's untrue. He mistakes her dismay for sadness and reaches out his hands then, holding both of hers, which feels terribly awkward to Emma. And she gradually pulls her hands away.

When she finally asks him whether he'd known that she and Seal were neighbors, he chuckles softly to himself, shaking his head. "No," he says. "No idea."

"So why were you looking for me?"

"What?"

"Why were you looking for me in my office? And calling me and leaving me almost a dozen messages? And appearing on Connecticut Avenue at my apartment building?"

"Because I wanted to see you. You know, I didn't realize that you knew Seal until I ran into you on the train. So weird. I mean how likely was that?" He sounds younger, seems younger as he says it. "Then I really wanted to see you, so we could talk about it, so we could commiserate."

"But your voice messages were quite urgent. And your note. I got your note. You said it was something important. You said, I quote, 'I think I know what they were looking for.'"

"Oh, that. Yeah. Doesn't matter now, I guess. I mean, they got the guys, right?"

"The guys. Yeah," she says. "So maybe you wanted to tell me that Seal had one of Andy Warhol's paintings of Marilyn Monroe. That maybe the murderer—or *the guys*, as you call them—might have been after it?"

She's caught him completely by surprise. His face flushes, and his tongue is tied. When he finally speaks, he betrays himself. "Did they find it?" he asks.

"Did you?" she says, raising one eyebrow, freezing him in place. She calls for the check, and the Baltimore police emerge from the back of the house.

"They talked, didn't they?" Rolley says.

"Of course they talked," she says.

"You can't hold me. I didn't touch her. I never would have hurt her," he tells the man who's slipping a pair of handcuffs around his slender wrists. "I want to call my lawyer."

"But you lured them into it, didn't you? With the promise of a fortune, of a Warhol, hoping they might find it. And if they didn't, you might find it in the studio and have it all to yourself. Am I right?" she says, standing then, approaching him. "You bastard. You as good as killed her."

CHAPTER 82

When Emma finally clears out Seal's apartment so that the estate can proceed with the sale, she finds—in the drawer of a small pine table in the front hall—a white letter-size envelope, wrapped in a shiny, red satin ribbon, with the name Lucille Anne Lawson written in script on the front. No address. Just her name, the names her mother and grandmother had chosen for her. Sitting on the edge of Seal's mattress, Emma unties the ribbon and opens it up. The letter is dated July 7, 1979.

My dearest Seal,

I am so grateful for you and so grateful that we have had this time together in Plantersville, so you could reconnect with your roots, and I could reconnect with mine.

I want you to know where you came from and who you are. I've told you about life on the farm and about the Holder boys— Raine and Fourth. That Raine was a sweet boy and Fourth, maybe not so much. They're a part of our story.

After I turned thirteen, we didn't see much of the boys. They came out at Thanksgiving or Christmas to hunt. And when I asked after them, Mr. Holder always said they were away at school. Then, one fall afternoon when I was fifteen years old, Fourth came by himself. It was in September. And we thought the whole family would be coming, because it was the beginning of dove season. So, I went over to clean out the Little House one afternoon.

I'm going to tell you this because you're old enough to know, and I hope you'll understand. I was still there, in the Little House, when Fourth came in out of nowhere and surprised me. I was done cleaning and I'd been to Deaver's, and I'd had my Coca-Cola and all. But I wasn't on the sleeping porch. I was in that little bedroom, lying right in the bed with one of their magazines. I was in my own little world when I heard somebody coming in and I hardly had time to gather myself up. He said, "Well, Maggie Grace. What are you up to back here?" And he was smiling. He got down on the bed and kept smiling and got real close and told me how much he always liked me. I was hardly a woman, and by the time we got right up next to each other, it seemed to me that we were falling in love, and I was smiling too. If you're reading this, I know that you're old enough to imagine the rest. Afterward, he said, real serious, "Now nobody needs to hear about this." And I agreed, because it was private, and it felt like it was the beginning of something important. I invested it with meaning and had no idea of the possible consequence.

I didn't see him again until after Christmas. I had carried our secret around with me all that time. My dear Seal, I was so young and naïve. On New Year's Day, the two of them, Raine and Fourth, rolled up to our front door carrying a basket of fruit and a turkey and some presents for me and Nanaw. And they brought a couple of girls with them, Memphis girls, wearing hunting jackets and blue jeans and boots with high heels on them, all fancy. I was crushed.

When they left, I went over to the Little House and looked it up in that god-awful guest book I told you about. It said something like this: *January 1, 1956. Raine and I brought the dogs out today. Shot nine quail, west of the pecan orchard, enough for a small feast. With us are Sissy Owens and Peggy Tabor, both of Memphis. The score: Sissy 0, Peggy 2, Raine 4, Fourth 3. William Carrollton Holder IV.*

I'll never forget it. I was so hurt and angry. I went back home and said something to Nanaw, something spiteful and small-minded like, "Those girls weren't even pretty." I can still hear myself. I had a bad case of a broken heart. Nanaw gave me this look like I was crazy. She said, "Maggie Grace. You get that idea right outta your head." And then she said these exact words, "They're not even thinking about you." *They're not even thinking about you.* And, of course, she was right. But I was so young and enamored with the idea of the Holders, the romance of it. I was fifteen years old, and I had no idea what the boundaries were. I told her that she was wrong, and then I told her what had happened.

She laid into me. She said I shouldn't have been in that bedroom in the first place, and that I couldn't go back there ever again. And, as you can probably imagine, she had a whole lot to say about what kind of girl I was and how she was ashamed of me and what was I thinking. I ran upstairs and shut my door and lay down in bed for a long time.

Then, after it got dark, she came up to my room. I was being such an ass. I wouldn't even speak to her. I may have pretended to be asleep. But she sat down on the edge of my bed and grabbed hold of my hand. She was so gentle with me. And, of course, she asked me the obvious question. And, together, we counted backward. I had no idea. She told me she thought there was a baby coming. She held my hand real tight, and I remember her words exactly: "Sweet mother of God." Then she got real quiet and put her arms around me, and we lay there together for the longest time. And that was you coming. I didn't know it then, but that was the greatest gift of my life.

Sometime in the night, when I was in that half sleep, that twilight sleep when you're going back and forth between being asleep and being awake, I was picturing me and Fourth in the Little House, him with his arms wrapped around me, and I was dreaming that we were lying there in bed together waiting for our baby. Waiting for you. Mama must have read my mind because she lifted her head. Then real softly, she asks me if I'm awake. "Twilight," I said. And she told me not to worry, that she was going to ride into Memphis the next day to have a good long talk with Mr. Holder. She was stroking my hair, and I was still dreaming about me and Fourth. I remember thanking her and feeling better, because I was certain that when they told Fourth about me and about you, everything was going to be different.

But that's not at all what happened, my sweet. I went down to a place near Oxford, Mississippi and you were born, and I never saw young William Holder IV again. It was my secret and Nanaw's. But she made sure the Holders took care of us. In return, I promised that, as long as I lived, I would not reveal your father's name. I hope you'll forgive me for that. But, thanks to Nanaw and the Holders, we were able to get out of that godforsaken place. We paid a price. You paid a price. If you're reading this, it means I'm gone, and you are free to do whatever you choose with this information. But know this: I have no regrets, and I love you more than anything in the world. Always have, my sweet girl.

The letter is signed *Your Loving Mother* and written in Maggie Grace Lawson's hand.

When she finishes, Emma falls back on the mattress, staring at the ceiling. *What is the measure of this tragedy*, she asks herself. Since before she even met Emma, Seal had known full well who her father was and had apparently done nothing about it. She thinks of Fourth, his complacency, his ignorance. His father and brother, who kept it a secret from him. And surely Jennifer Henley was complicit. And she thinks of Maggie Grace, whose own mother made it impossible for her to tell her own daughter who her father was—although she knew the man.

And of a young, beautiful Maggie Grace, crushed at the age of fifteen. What was her revenge exactly, Emma wonders.

Looking around, she sees a place that is stark, empty, and as she repairs to the master bath to blow her nose and splash her face, she notices a photograph that had inadvertently been left in place. At least she thinks it's a photograph, a black-and-white image of a space where a wall meets the floor, a wall that's just a few feet deep, like a divider wall, jutting out into space. It is a near-perfect drawing of the shadow cast by an insignificant little wall. But it is precise, beautiful in its simplicity, with a graininess to it made up of almost imperceptible dots that define the wall, the edge, the shadows. The image is clean, modern, elegant, and, in truth, impossible to capture with words. It must be seen to be appreciated. For it is nothing more than a wall where two rooms meet. The drawing is signed, but even now, Emma can't make out the signature. It looks like Clement Lhet or Clemet Hept, but she can't find an artist by either name. The name is hopelessly hidden by the artistry of the signature itself. When she'd first removed the drawing from the bathroom wall, she found the name of a gallery on the back. "West Gallery," it said. And an address in SoHo. But the gallery had disappeared. Although, she'll probably never know the name of the artist, she treasures it, nonetheless. In the end, it is the only piece of art—in fact, the only item from Seal's studio or apartment, aside from that gorilla mask—that Emma chose to keep for herself. When the Loves had moved out and Emma had moved back into her home at 370 Riverside, she hung the drawing of the divider wall and the floor and the shadows in her front hall at eye level, right beside her front door, so that, now, every time she leaves or anyone else arrives, Emma is reminded of Seal and her gifts.

POSTSCRIPT

To give the reader a sense of the ballooning value of major works of art over the past half century, in 1967 a Rothko sold for $22,000. In 2003, a Rothko sold for $7 million. And, in 2012, a Rothko sold at auction at Christie's for $87 million. Given his socialist leanings, it has been said that doubtless he would have found this profoundly disturbing.

As for the value of Andy Warhol's Marilyn paintings: on May 9, 2022, Warhol's *Shot Sage Blue Marilyn*, a 40x40-inch silk screen of Marilyn Monroe's face painted in 1964, sold for $195 million dollars at a Christie's charity auction, setting a record for a piece of American art sold at auction.

NOTES

The following stories and cover illustration are quoted or referenced in the text. They are listed in order of appearance.

William Tuohy, "51 Bodies Recovered from Ferry: 84 Still Missing, Believed Dead; Search Halted," *Los Angeles Times*, (March 9, 1987).

"Speedy Rescue Effort Saved Many Aboard Capsized Ferry," *New York Times*, (March 9, 1987): A3.

Saul Steinberg, "View of the World from 9th Avenue," cover illustration, *New Yorker*, (March 29, 1976).

Steven V. Roberts, "Reagan Moves to Shift Public Attention from Iran," *New York Times*, (March 21, 1987): 1, 8.

In addition, the description of Gerhard Richter's *Candle* and *Skull* paintings that appears in Chapter 27— "hover brilliantly between the precise and the vague"—is from a Lot Essay on the Christie's website at www.christies.com/en/lot/lot-5371715. And in Chapter 36, the quote regarding Jim Goldberg — his "in-depth collaborations investigate the nature of American myths about class, power and happiness"— is from Goldberg's biography on the Magnum Photos website (magnumphotos.com).

ACKNOWLEDGEMENTS

I want to thank the following people—

Illustrator Alejandro Milà and the talented Taylor Martin for another great cover design, Stewart Williams for impeccable work on the interior design and proofreaders Louise Stahl and Jennie Cohen, for their professionalism and thoroughness.

The loyal readers who reviewed my early draft—Anne Brand, Kelly Brother, Margaret Craddock, Kathy Doelling, Emily Keplinger, Helen Lance Robinson, Pam Walker and Emily Wyonzek.

The book clubs that have invited me to their meetings, and all the members of the Downtown Bookies for their insights and good humor—Terri Alford, Cam Armstrong, Brooke Ballenger, Kathy Doelling, Juli Eck, Shelley Fragale, Priscilla Hernandez, Debbie Keller, Sandra Livesay, Sara Waterbury, Molly Willmott and Emily Wyonzek.

Carol Buchman, Paula Kovarik, Anne Edgar, Pam Hamilton, Catherine Cotter and Beatrice Tier, who have helped me in immeasurable ways.

My extended family for their support— including Meg, Jay, Karen and Greer. And Theresa out in Phoenix.

My brother, Brud, who is always there when I need him, and all the Bacons up in Delaware—Liz, Eliza, Kane and Julia—for all they do.

And, of course, for their love and support, their contributions to this book and all else: Max and Michelle, Evie and Owen, and Mindy and Alex—my anchors.

One final note: I live in Memphis, Tennessee. It's a town full of interesting and creative people who make it a vibrant, supportive, inspiring place to live and work. And for that, I am most grateful.

I'd like to thank four people here in Memphis who helped me with the research for this novel: Artist Roy Tamboli for his recollections of life on Manhattan's Lower East Side; long-time collector James Patterson for sharing his knowledge and his wonderful stories; gallerist David Lusk, who represents the Carroll Cloar estate, for his input on the artist; and, finally, my friend Amery Staub, for his thoughts on subjects that shall remain undisclosed for now, because I'm saving them for the sequel to *The Art Collector.*

FROM THE AUTHOR

Thank you for reading *The Art Collector*. I hope you enjoyed it. If so, I always appreciate a nice review on Amazon and/or Goodreads. And I thank you for spreading the word among your friends.

For book clubs, you'll find reader's guide questions for both *The History Teacher* and *The Art Collector* on my website at www.susanbacon.com. I'm always happy to join in a book club discussion via Zoom or Facetime. In fact, it's one of my favorite things. You'll find contact information on my website.

I look forward to hearing from you. As always, thank you for your interest and support.